Visit Frances Brody online:

ww.frances-brody.com
vw facebook.com/FrancesBrody
twitter.com/@FrancesBrody
.instagram.com/@francesbrody

Praise for Frances Brody:

ces Brody has made it to the top rank of crime writers'

Daily Mail

y's writing is like her central character Kate Shackleton:
acerbic and very, very perceptive'

Ann Cleeves

tful'

People's Friend

ing and under-used period for new crime fiction . . .
leton is a splendid heroine'

Ann Granger

A MANSION FOR MURDER

FRANCES BRODY

PIATKUS

PIATKUS

First published in Great Britain in 2022 by Piatkus

1 3 5 7 9 10 8 6 4 2

Copyright © Frances McNeil 2022

The moral right of the author has been asserted.

*All characters and events in this publication, other than those
clearly in the public domain, are fictitious and any resemblance
to real persons, living or dead, is purely coincidental.*

A CIP catalogue record for this book
is available from the British Library.

ISBN 978-0-349-43197-0

Typeset in Perpetua by M Rules
Printed and bound in Great Britain by
Clays Ltd, Elcograf S.p.A.

Papers used by Piatkus are from well-managed forests
and other responsible sources.

To Jake and Lindsay Attree

AUTHOR'S NOTE

On a visit to Saltaire village and Salts Mill, I walked with a friend through Roberts Park and along a pathway through woodland to the site of the nineteenth-century grand mansion Milner Field. Trees grow where this fine house once stood. There are traces of the conservatory's mosaic floor, a fraction of wall, a glimpse into a cellar, blocks of stone, a few well-made bricks, and weeds growing amidst the rubble. An Elizabethan manor house was demolished to make way for the new Milner Field, and of that manor house there is no trace.

Milner Field mansion was the dream house of Titus Salt Junior, fifth and youngest son of Sir Titus Salt, wealthy textile manufacturer, who opened his new mill by the banks of the River Aire in 1853. Sir Titus commissioned a village to house his workers, also providing for their social, educational and health needs, naming the place Saltaire, after himself and the river.

What remains of Milner Field mansion are the stories of a house with a reputation as unlucky, a risky place to set down roots. Those stories and the scant remains of former grandeur inspired this thirteenth story of Kate Shackleton's investigations, a work of fiction.

For the facts, I highly recommend *Milner Field: The Lost Country House of Titus Salt Jnr* by Richard Lee-Van den Daele and R. David Beale.

In December 2001, UNESCO designated Saltaire a World Heritage Site.

LONG AGO

Long ago, Nick lived with his grandmother in a hut on the land called Milner Field. On Sundays, his grandmother washed his face at the well that belonged to the old manor house nearby. She put her shawl over her head and shoulders and her empty basket over her arm. They would walk along the towpath to Shipley, to the Chapel of Golden Light. They sat on chairs that hurt your bottom, listened to Bible stories, and sang hymns. When he could write his name, Nick joined the Band of Hope and signed the pledge. Never a drop of alcohol would pass his lips as long as he should live. On the day he signed the pledge, a Golden Light lady gave Nick a pair of clogs.

After repeating words called declarations, they drank warm sweet tea, ate a slice of bread and butter sprinkled with sugar, and left with their basket half full of food and their souls saved. Walking back along the canal, cheerful, relieved to be out of it, the pair of them sang, 'For the Love of Barbara Allen', 'Ten Green Bottles' and 'A-hunting We Will Go'. Nick had all the actions off pat, made up by himself. His grandmother copied him as best she could.

*

One day, when he was squidging and squelching along the muddy path, carrying their bucket to fetch water from the manor house well, he stepped in a puddle. One of his clogs came off. He set down his bucket, giving him two free hands to rescue his clog, making a watching frog jump. You can have too much rain.

At the well, he turned the handle, lowered the big bucket, and then slowly raised it. When he took water for his own bucket, he saw a bone that had come from the well to present itself to him.

His grandmother had eyes in the back of her head. She found his bone. 'This is no good for soup,' said she. She was pretending, thinking that he did not know the bone once belonged to a live person.

Nick held the bone next to his arm. 'It matches me. It belonged to a child.'

'From long ago. Only dry old bones float. Times past, that well ran dry. Bury the bone near to where it came from, to be close on Judgement Day.'

On the day he buried the bone, his grandmother told him that the old manor house had stood for over three centuries and that the well was much older than the house. One day, she would tell him a story from the mists of time, the story of a young shepherdess whose life came to an end at the bottom of that well.

The ground by the well was too muddy for digging. Nick found a better place to bury the bone. Two builders were removing the gates from the old manor house. These gates were to be kept for one of the entrances to the new mansion. Another entrance would be a fine arch, called Gothic.

When the men had gone, Nick dug a hole by the new gate-post. The ground was easy to shovel out. He buried the bone, and said the prayer he knew from the Chapel of Golden Light.

4

ONE

My name is Kate Shackleton. On that Saturday afternoon in August, 1930, I boarded a train from Leeds to Saltaire, looking out at smoke-blackened factories and rows of red-brick houses. The landscape gave way to trees, mill chimneys and stone-built cottages. Nettles, nightshade and buttercups brightened the railway embankment.

Investigating as a profession crept up on me unawares, almost a decade ago, just as I was wondering what to do with the rest of my life. After the Great War there was much upheaval. My husband was one of the many who did not return from the battlefields.

Across the world, so many lives would never be the same again. During that aftermath of war, I discovered my knack for investigating. I engaged a housekeeper, Mrs Sugden, and recruited a former police officer assistant, Jim Sykes. In the summer of 1930, hard times and warm days swallowed requests for our services. Mrs Sugden planned to fill the quiet time by doing some decorating.

The arrival of a letter on the last Monday of July broke a

spell of inertia. The envelope was neatly written in black ink, by someone who had practised his penmanship. There was just one tiny blot where the writer had pressed too hard on a comma. The envelope was formally addressed to Mrs Gerald Shackleton, so from someone who knew my husband's name. Bank letters and business letters address me that way. My mother and aunt have now replaced Gerald with Catherine. For cousins and friends, I am Mrs Kate Shackleton. Did the 'Mrs Gerald Shackleton' mean I ought to brace myself for some old comrade's story about Gerald?

I sat at the kitchen table to read this letter from a stranger.

> South Lodge,
> Milner Field,
> Saltaire
> 26th July, 1930

Dear Madam,

Please excuse a stranger writing to you. I found out your address through a pal. I am twenty-two years old and live with my parents, who take care of a mansion you may have heard of – Milner Field. The mansion is up for sale. The Lodge, where we live, is part of the sale so I may not live here much longer. My mother is housekeeper at Milner Field. My father is head gardener. The possibility of moving away made me write to you today.

I work for Salts Mill in the maintenance department and am shortly to take on bigger responsibilities. I tell you this so that you know I am not someone out of *the blue with a bee in his bonnet, but a man who is building his reputation and wants to do things right.*

Here is the matter in a nutshell. I have something to tell you, a story about the past that I know will be of interest to you. Please trust that I cannot say more at present.

If it is convenient, please come to the Milner Field South Lodge a little after 6 p.m. next Saturday. There is a good reason why I ask you to come here rather than me come to you. I would meet you at Saltaire railway station but people are nosy. If you arrive in Saltaire early, in time to hear the mill hooter, press your back against the wall to avoid the stampede as two thousand workers leave the premises.

Yours faithfully,
Ronald Creswell (Ronnie)

My correspondent included a map and directions from Saltaire railway station. I reached for the magnifying glass. His sketch fitted neatly on to the reverse of his writing paper. He had drawn railway station, mill, streets, arrows, canal, wood, river, farm and a cross with the caption, 'Entrance Milner Field. Go to South Lodge'.

This was a man who might reproduce the *Mona Lisa* on the back of a postage stamp.

Mrs Sugden came in from the garden, wearing her hessian apron over the print frock she'd made from a pattern that came free with the local paper. I told her about the letter as she stood at the kitchen sink washing her hands.

'He could be a madman,' she said, picking up the worn

striped towel, 'or a prankster sending you on a wild goose chase.'

'Is it the season for a goose chase? Anyway, I've never been to Saltaire, and by all accounts Milner Field mansion is remarkable.'

Mrs Sugden was not convinced. She reached for the letter and turned it over to see the map. 'I don't like the sound of a mansion named after a field. Where's the grandeur in that? And why doesn't this Creswell chap offer to meet you on the station platform as any polite person would? I don't hold with him sending you through hill and dale.'

I found myself playing defence barrister. 'He guesses I prefer to find my own way, or he has an awkwardness about making polite conversation and wants to come straight to the point when on home ground.' I looked at the letter again. 'He's twenty-two.'

Mrs Sugden turned on the tap and began to fill the kettle. 'That's what he tells you. He could be any age, waiting in the woods, wielding an axe.'

'I'll tread carefully.'

She dipped into the coal scuttle, picked up a big cob of coal and rinsed it under the tap. 'Put this in your bag. Any trouble, whack him one.'

'No! I've no intention of being charged with assault. It would be an inconvenience.'

This would be my first visit to Saltaire. It was home to a gigantic mill, I knew that much, and that the visionary founder of Salts Mill had a village built to house his workforce. Of Milner Field mansion, I knew nothing. The quickest way to find out about something is to ask a person who knows. For me that person is usually elderly Mr Duffield – librarian, archivist and walking encyclopaedia when it comes to local matters.

I found Mr and Mrs Duffield sitting in their back garden under the supervision of a tiger-striped cat with prominent cheekbones and a sprinkling of white hairs who took pride of place on the table.

There was tea in the pot, tonic wine in a decanter and biscuits on a decorative plate. I told the Duffields about the mysterious letter from Ronald Creswell and asked what they could tell me about Milner Field and Saltaire.

Mr Duffield proved willing to give his wife and me a history lesson. He cleared his throat and took a sip of tonic wine. The cat closed its eyes as Mr Duffield began.

'Sir Titus built the largest mill in the world and a village to go with it. It's my opinion that his youngest and cleverest son, Titus Junior, saw himself as having something to live up to. Titus Junior inherited his father's business acumen and his grand ambition. He reached for the stars, never put a foot wrong, married well and wanted a life that matched his place in the world. Sir Titus had been content to rent a house. Titus Junior wanted a mansion where he could entertain, and land to go with it. He and his wife had expensive tastes. Titus Junior bought the Milner Field estate, with farmland and Elizabethan manor house. He promptly demolished the manor house and engaged an architect to build a mansion fit for a millionaire. Milner Field became a social hub, Titus Junior and Catherine even played host to the Prince and Princess of Wales. His Highness planted a tree to commemorate his visit.'

'And did the tree thrive?' Mrs Duffield asked.

'I expect so.' Mr Duffield took another sip of tonic wine.

He shook his head, announcing mournfully, 'But at age forty-four, Titus Junior died suddenly in the billiard room.'

Mrs Duffield had just picked up a copy of *County Lady*. She put it down. 'Oh dear, how sad.'

'Quite.' Mr Duffield refilled our glasses. 'I can think of men who would have done the world a good turn by dying at the age of forty-four, or even thirty-three, but he was not one of them. In no time at all, the company went into liquidation and the house and estate were mortgaged. The company was bought by four Bradford men. The leading figure among those men, James Roberts, bought out the rest. Sir James moved with his family into Milner Field.'

The name James Roberts brought me up short. This was the generous man who grew up in modest circumstances in Haworth, bought Haworth Parsonage from the Church of England and presented it to the Brontë Society for the benefit of the nation, just one of his many philanthropic acts.

I felt suddenly lacking in knowledge to have been unaware that Sir James once lived at Milner Field and was pre-eminent in Salts. I had been volunteering as a nurse while much of this making-a-fortune-from-textiles was taking place. 'I hope no great misfortune befell Sir James.'

Mr Duffield gave a heavy sigh. 'Three of his four sons died young. His remaining son, Harry Roberts, brilliant and resourceful, his father's right-hand man, was so badly wounded at the Front in France that he remained an invalid. Sir James lost heart. He moved away. Milner Field was put up for sale in nineteen twenty-two.'

'Don't tell me more,' I said. 'I can't bear to think of Sir James and Lady Roberts suffering such a loss.'

The cat stood, glared, flicked its tail and walked away.

'Milner Field remained on the market. Its grisly reputation counted against a house that had become slightly shabby and in need of attention. It remained unoccupied until a syndicate purchased Salts Mill and the property. The managing director and his wife moved in. That move did not end well for them, nor for their successors in the business and in residence at Milner Field. Pneumonia is easily caught in a damp house. I will refrain from names and details because the most recent funeral was in August last year. It would be indelicate to linger on subsequent calamities, of which there were many.'

Mr Duffield could not pinpoint the precise date when Milner Field mansion became known as an accursed place. The belief grew gradually, as one set of diminished families left and another set took over, only to be wearing mourning and attending funerals sooner than may have been expected. As far as Mr Duffield knew, the former mansion, dating from Elizabethan times, had attracted no strange and disturbing tales, but then Elizabethans and their descendants were used to plagues, wars civil and foreign, disasters, early deaths and sinister doings. However, Mr Duffield had heard folk tales of the area dating long before the manorial lands of that place came to an uneasy truce with fate's sharp edges. He heard tell of marauding bandits, parties of hunters laying claim to lands and livestock, of times when families hid their daughters.

'The house is up for sale again,' I said.

'So I heard. Whether anyone believes in it or not, the curse – or the suspicions of a curse – permeates the place like a thick fog. To be on the safe side, do not let anyone for whom you have the slightest regard consider putting in a bid for it.' Mr Duffield gave me a frank look, as if I must be warned against recommending the place.

'I don't know anyone who is looking for a mansion. An outsider with sufficient money for a country house in the North would want to be by Lake Windermere, not the Leeds–Liverpool Canal.'

'Of course there's no such thing as a curse,' said Mr Duffield, somewhat undermining his own accounts of ill-fortune across generations. 'People look for explanations, and a curse fits the bill. But it will be an enormous pity if the mill goes to the wall due to lack of cash reserves. What with the Wall Street Crash, the strikes, reduced orders, it would be useful for Salts to have money from the sale of the mansion. With things as they are, the whole village might join the ranks of the unemployed.'

Mr Duffield poured more tonic wine all round. Mrs Duffield perked up as her husband took a deep breath and prepared to continue his story.

'I recollect a tale told to me by a young reporter trying to make his mark. It's historical, perhaps Middle Ages. It tells of a wronged young shepherdess, just a child, and her cruel murderous death. There's also an account within living memory, around eighteen seventy, of a tragic accident to a little lad who was trespassing during the building work and toppled to his death. Some say it was no accident, it was murder.'

Mrs Duffield sighed heavily. 'Heartbreaking! This shines a light on how the curse came to be. The mothers of the shepherdess and the little lad cursed the place. They were hundreds of years apart in time, but close in grief and sorrow. Such agonies leave a memory on the land and the mansion that was built on it. I read something similar in *Reader's Digest*.'

TWO

I set off for Saltaire and Milner Field no wiser about Ronnie Creswell's mysterious letter. How had he come to pick on me? I wondered. I did have a connection with a mill from several years ago, but twenty-two-year-old Ronnie would have been too young to have heard anything about that.

The train's engine seemed to sound out the name of the house: *Milner Field, Milner Field, Milner Field*. I wanted to see this mansion. Yes, we were in hard times, but there are always people with money to spare, ready to snap up grandeur and bask in delight.

I was the only passenger to leave the train at Saltaire.

Being in good time, I took a brief look about. The first thing that struck me was the neatness of the place: row upon row of stone houses. Their red-brick city counterparts frequently gave me a feeling of being shut in. These dwellings gave no sense of being closed in from the sky and the world. I allowed myself a little diversion along Albert Terrace, passing George Street and Ada Street. I should have liked to explore, but thought it better to follow Mr Creswell's directions.

His map led me to a neatly kept park where a board of instructions spelled out the hours during which residents might make use of the amenity and listed the activities that would draw a frown. I spotted the cricket pavilion that he had dotted in as a landmark.

From the park, my way led to a wood where the ground dipped and rose so that I needed to keep my eyes down for a long stretch. The overgrown path and spreading roots of trees gave the hint that I had deviated from the popular way through the wood. Coming into the country, I ought to have known better than to wear silk stockings, the favourite bait of brambles. I picked my way carefully.

Just as I was beginning to feel the letter writer possessed a warped sense of humour, the path broadened. The land to the left sloped up towards an old well and then rose to form the perch for a farmhouse and outbuildings. Bilberries were ripening. A woman with a basket picked busily. There is always someone who beelines bilberries first. She paused to give a glaring assessment of me. Rival picker? No, not dressed for it.

I wished her good evening.

'Is thah lost?' she asked.

'I don't think so. I'm on my way to Milner Field.'

'Then keep going, if thah must.'

At that moment two shots rang out in quick succession, followed by the frantic craw of crows as they flew from the gunshots.

Eventually, a broad driveway curved, cutting through the land from a road up the hill on my left. I heard the distant clip-clop of a horse and cart.

Suddenly, Milner Field came into view, beyond the

gateposts so neatly and minutely drawn by Ronald Creswell. I walked some way before reaching a lodge house and beyond that a better view of the mansion, all turrets and towers of the sort where Rapunzel might let down her long hair and wait to be rescued by a passing knight. It also reminded me of the dreadful country-house weekends that my aunt occasionally enticed me to when trying to fix me up with a suitable man. Grand, Gothic, its windows glowing in the sunlight, the building trumpeted the news that Titus Salt Junior, youngest son of the late Sir Titus, spared no expense in creating a modern-day fairy-tale castle suitable for a wealthy merchant. Yet this spectacular and somewhat forbidding building gave off an air of melancholy that made me shiver. Bread is described as 'sad' when it has not risen. This mansion had risen magnificently, yet that same word came to my lips: sad.

It surprised me to see the tilting FOR SALE BY AUCTION sign, the wood creaking a forlorn complaint as I came closer.

A mansion such as this did not need a notice of sale, like some modest cottage that might catch the eye of a passing pedlar done well for himself on the horses. As I walked through the gates, I felt a visceral sensation and the notion came to me of stepping into a world where I would never want to belong. I had a quick word with myself. You are here on business. You are here for a diversionary afternoon out. Wait and see this Ronnie Creswell. Listen to what he has to say, thank him for any hospitality extended, and then ask for a set of directions back to the village that will not put your stockings at even greater risk.

The closer I came to the mansion, the more forbidding it looked. I was glad to reach the Lodge, also fine in its way but on a more human scale, giving off an air of normality and of being a place fit for people who knew how to laugh and smile. A shoemaker's last propped open the door.

All of a sudden, I expected a warm welcome.

LONG AGO

When men came to knock down the manor house, Nick felt sorry for the old place. It had its date above the door: 1550. Nick went to see what he could find. He could tell that the men liked watching the house fall. The man in charge let Nick chop broken floorboards, fetch and carry and run errands.

That night, they had a good fire and rabbit stew. Nick sang 'A-hunting We Will Go'. His grandmother had now told Nick the story from long ago, the story of the young shepherdess, the story of her bones. The girl was thrown down the well by a bad king who came hunting on a white horse in the days when there were still boars and wolves in England.

The well ran dry when the builders piped the spring water a different way. Nick felt sorry for the empty well and its bones. He began to give the well and the shepherdess flowers every Sunday.

The cleverest builder put a pipe in the ground and a tap. It was for the builders themselves, for Nick and his grandmother and for thirsty passers-by.

He ran home to tell his grandmother about the tap. She lay

pale and cold and still. Nick knew about death but thought it happened outside, where you might see a bird with its head bitten off, or a baby squirrel fallen from the nest.

He sat with his grandmother for a long time. He sat with her until the builder called Jack came to look for him.

A man in black came to the hut. He said that Nick must go to school in the village with the mill workers' children. He would learn numbers, reading and writing. At age nine, there would be a job for him in the mill. Nick lodged with a family in a tall house on Victoria Road near George Street. He slept top to toe with the other children in the room at the top. The man of the house would come into the room on pay-day evening and look out of the tall window. The children told Nick that the man was a spy, posted by Titus Salt to look out of the window and write the names of workmen who staggered home drunk from Shipley.

Nick missed his grandmother. He missed his hut. He missed the builders. Every Sunday he went to their old hut and to the well with flowers. Taking buttercups, he found his way back to the place where his grandmother was buried. It puzzled him that there were so many different names on her gravestone, the names of strangers. He could read their names. At the Golden Light, they had taught him his letters and gave him stories.

While he was reading the names on his grandmother's gravestone, a thin woman wearing a man's jacket set down a big pickle jar almost filled with leaves and flowers.

She turned to Nick. 'Here, lad, squeeze your buttercups in this jar so they'll last.'

'Thank you.' Nick put in as many of his buttercups as would fit. 'Why are there so many names on the stone?' he asked.

'It's called a paupers' grave, for them who can't pay for a private plot or a family plot.' She pointed to a name. 'That's my mam, Agnes Routh. They bury us poor people by the dozen, but we're in good company.'

'That's my grandmother,' Nick said. He did not say her name because of not liking to think of her in that place.

THREE

Millwright and now Maintenance Manager David Fairburn would never leave Salts. Though he would not admit it, David loved Salts Mill. He had loved it ever since his big sister wheeled him by in his pram on the way to the park. She told him to put his hands over his lugs, but he cupped his hands so as to hear 'that' noise better. Better than a brass band, better than his dad playing paper and comb. As he grew, he could separate sounds that others found a deafening wall of noise. He knew the whirr and drumming of engines, the bassoon of looms, hearing music in the thud and slam. Clogs on stone flags, and then the drumbeat of clogs on iron, clogs on wood.

When he started work, at first he felt afraid. He was twelve years old – nobody had asked to see his birth certificate. He could not find his way about the place. To understand what he was being told, he needed to watch lips. But he soon learned to tell by the sound of the shuttle when a loom needed attention. A racket to others told David a story.

The smooth running of the mill depended on the

maintenance men, headed by himself and Ronnie Creswell. David had trained Ronnie. He was glad that his former apprentice had done so well and caught the boss's eye. That was no excuse for going AWOL on some private business, probably connected with Ronnie's hush-hush opportunity to take over maintenance of the village houses. This wouldn't have interested David.

One day and one evening a week, David had attended the technical institute in Bradford. At eighteen, he had built an 850 horsepower steam engine for the spinning sheds and warping and winding departments by dismantling lesser engines and starting from scratch. By the age of twenty-one, he was teaching a night-school class at the technical institute where once he sat in the front row. Even the older geezers had not resented David's promotions. They knew his genius, respected his skill. David never lost his rag. He'd explain, he'd show, he'd explain again. He was given charge of Ronnie Creswell, a promising lad, as apprentice.

David taught Ronnie about the machinery and the lad took it in. But it was the fabric of buildings and materials that Ronnie cared about. He took to joinery, plumbing and electrics. Ronnie's Uncle Nick had done that work and, though now old, confused and his sight fading, there was nothing Nick and David, together or apart, couldn't drill into the lad.

Ronnie could now show David a thing or two. This did not divide them. They worked together, keeping all in order and good running, sharing certain tasks such as care of the reservoir in the subterranean depths under the mill.

Lately, there'd been a bit of needle between David and Ronnie. Nay, say it like it was, they'd come to blows in the yard at the Woolpack. They had sorted it out but there was still an edginess. It was over Dorrie, David's youngest sister. Ronnie looked out for her and she looked up to him, had a soft spot for him. The Fairburns and the Creswells were like family. They'd gone outside to meet a pal who was bringing them a couple of beers.

Ronnie said, 'When I danced the quickstep with Dorrie . . .'

'What?'

'Is she all right?'

'What do you mean?'

'Summat she said. Is she courting someone?'

'No.'

'Only . . .'

'What?'

'I couldn't help noticing, she's got a bit of a bump.'

David couldn't say why he suddenly thumped Ronnie. He just did.

Ronnie thumped him back and then said, 'Sorry,' as if he'd started it.

None of that got in the way of them doing their job.

They had worked a full day that first Saturday in August. Saturday was the day they checked the reservoir together. David was there in good time because he knew Ronnie had arranged to meet someone at the South Lodge. He hadn't said who or why. David supposed it must be something to do with people coming to view Milner Field mansion.

By the iron door that led to the deeps and the reservoir, David took the log card from its slot by the door. He saw that Ronnie had initialled it and must be down there. David checked the door. He swore. This was more than careless. To leave the door to the reservoir unlocked was reckless. Ronnie should have waited for him.

When the door closed behind David, the world became silent for the briefest splash of time. Then his boots clattered on the iron staircase, echoing in the vast space. He went to the controls gallery. The smell was almost right – rainwater, brick and ironwork, lubricating oils that kept mechanisms in good order – but there was something else he could not place. It was something like the smell of a big cleaning day, to do with dusting and polishing, a sweet scent.

There had been no rain for two days but he saw, before he got halfway down the staircase, that the level was too low. The overflow gate was partially open. That explained the lower than expected water level. David walked round the balcony to the control panel. He noticed a lever was in the wrong position. He righted it. He turned the wheel, bringing the gate down. Something was different, a movement of air, a change in the atmosphere.

He ought to be able to hear Ronnie, or see him.

'Ronnie!' Knowing himself to be alone did not stop David calling again, even as his first shout echoed back to him.

He looked into darkness where the gallery wove round the immense space. At the bank of lights, he flicked every switch.

Again, his call came back to him, each echo growing fainter. R-o-n-n-ie! R-o-n-n-ie!

A sick feeling came over David, as if he floated on a rocking boat. Ronnie had played some trick. They almost always did this job together on a Saturday, checking the levels, checking the dials.

When he saw a cap floating in the water, David knew someone had been in here messing about. It was with a sudden burst of relief that he thought, Ronnie doesn't wear a cap. This was just some prank. He went to the telephone and dialled security. 'Harry, are you on your own?'

'I am.'

'Send duty security down.'

'What's up?'

'I don't know. Just send someone.' He replaced the telephone. The air felt wrong, some breeze that shouldn't reach here, a sound the water ought not to be making. You're imagining it, David told himself, but he knew that was what a normal person would say, a normal person not finely attuned to sounds and smells.

At a halfway point, the reservoir formed a kidney shape that had concealed the body now floating into view. David blinked, thinking his imagination was playing a trick. The body came nearer, as if making its way out to the canal. Dark hair was flattened against the scalp. David could not take in the sight. It was unreal, a dummy, a Guy Fawkes in August. He reached out with the long pole but could not make the hook meet his prey. Slowly, the body began to sink.

He reached so far he almost toppled over, but the hook caught in the cloth. He pulled. He struggled, his hand slipping, grasping. The sound was of gently lapping water. He caught that scent again. His sister wore Lily of the Valley when they went to the dance. It wasn't that, but something like that.

Behind him, he heard the clatter of boots on iron.

David did not turn to see who came. His voice sounded strange to himself, as if he were the drowned man. 'Help me! It's Ronnie.'

FOUR

As I knocked on the propped-open door of the Lodge, I thought I heard someone calling. It was the dying notes of a song. Whoever was singing had not heard me. Realising I was not expected, I knocked louder, and prepared to explain myself. A woman started to sing 'Bye Bye Blackbird' with enough gusto to raise the roof. I took a peek around the door. The voice was coming from upstairs. The unseen artiste could certainly hold a tune and must like the song because she forgot a verse and started again. I timed it right. When she belted out the final 'Blackbird, bye bye!' I didn't give her time to start again but knocked once more, willing my knuckles to imitate a hammer.

Light, rapid footsteps on the stairs told me the singer had heard my rude interruption. Moments later, the footsteps came to a stop in the downstairs room. After a brief pause, during which I heard a bare whisper of sound, a well-made woman in her forties appeared holding a tabard that she must have just pulled over her head because of its unsuitability as apparel fit for answering the door to a visitor. I admired that in pulling it off she had not disarranged her crimped fair hair or disturbed the neat collar on her blue cotton blouse that, paired with a navy skirt, seemed eminently suitable for greeting visitors.

She had bright blue eyes, a broad, friendly face, and a smile that seemed to say she expected me. I said hello and apologised for the interruption. Some awareness clicked for her, though of what I did not know. 'Good afternoon, madam.'

'Good afternoon. I'm Mrs Shackleton.'

'Mrs Creswell.' She glanced beyond me as if expecting I would be the first in a long line, setting me to wonder whether Ronnie had invited a whole batch of persons to hear his interesting information about the past.

'I'm here to keep my appointment with Mr Ronald Creswell.'

There was a flicker of hesitation. 'So, you're not here for the viewing?'

'No.'

'And the agent; he isn't with you?'

'No.'

'Ah.' She scratched her ear. 'Ronald is my husband. He said nothing about a visitor.'

'The letter is from Ronnie, your son?'

She raised her eyebrows in puzzlement. 'Ronnie?' The friendliness evaporated. 'You'd better come in.' She moved the shoemaker's last so as to open the door wider.

I was tempted to say that I'd wait and look at the garden until Ronnie arrived. Her glance beyond me towards the main entrance made me realise that she wanted me out of sight, in case legitimate visitors turned up. I had disrupted her routine. A strange woman claiming to have received a letter from Mrs Creswell's son must leave the way clear for potential buyers of the mansion, ready to imagine themselves in sole possession.

I stepped into a neat clean kitchen. Mrs Creswell waved me to an upholstered chair by the fireplace. 'Sit yourself down. Ronnie won't be long.'

I thanked her and sank into the seat, glancing at a framed watercolour above the fireplace, a scene by the canal, children waving to a man on a passing coal barge. In the room beyond, a telephone rang. She went to answer it, leaving the door between the two rooms open. From the one-sided conversation, I gathered that the expected viewing party had changed its collective mind and would not be coming. She came out looking crestfallen, remembered my existence and said suddenly, 'Did Ronnie tell you Milner Field is for sale?'

At that moment there was a thud in the empty fire grate. We both turned to see something black and feathered. It was a dead crow. It brought with it a fall of soot.

Mrs Creswell turned pale. She put her hand to her heart.

'Oh my good God, not here,' she said. 'Let's have no bad omens here.'

'The poor bird just fell into the chimney,' I said, knowing that a superstitious person might see this bird as a harbinger of death.

If she heard me, she made no sign, but seemed to talk to herself. 'Not here,' she said again. 'It happened in the mansion last week. A bird in the chimney, that one was dead.'

I thought the bird's wing was broken. The one eye I could see was still bright. It seemed to gleam in my direction. I tried to sound matter-of-fact. 'Ronnie will bury it for you when he comes.'

She was still staring at the crow. At the same moment, we both gasped with surprise and shock as the crow moved, and then stood. Neither of us spoke. We simply watched as the dazed bird nodded its head, pecked at its wing, while looking at the tiled hearth as if taking a measurement. It then strode to the open door, not swaggering in a crow way but swaying. And then it was gone.

If anyone had told me a story about a crow falling down a chimney and dusting itself off, I would have been hard pressed to believe it. We were both taken aback, Mrs Creswell much more than I. She looked shaken.

It would have been crass at that moment to ask about the curse, but I hoped that Mrs Creswell would say something.

When she didn't speak, but just stared after the bird, I said, 'It's just one of those things, Mrs Creswell. A bird in a chimney; it could happen anywhere, anytime.'

She did not answer. I supposed at Milner Field a crow down the chimney might take on a sinister significance. 'It survived because of its size and strength,' I added.

With a great effort, she forced a smile and said in a reassuring voice, 'Nothing bad has ever happened to people in the Lodge.'

'That's all right, then.' The kindest thing seemed to be to divert her.

There were photographs on the mantelpiece: one on the left of Mr and Mrs Creswell in their wedding clothes. In the centre of the mantelpiece were five children, all young. I asked about them. 'Which is Ronnie?'

'That's Ronnie, taken when he was twelve.' The bright-eyed boy in the picture stood to attention, giving the appearance of trying not laugh.

'Those are my middle two boys, Stephen and Mark, they work away. And that's Nancy, who's still at school.'

'They're all bonny,' I said. 'And who is this young chap?' The photograph at the other end of the mantelpiece appeared to be from an earlier era. It showed a boy, about ten years old, done up in a blue buttoned jacket with white lace collar and cuffs. Just like Ronnie, he had a thatch of pale hair and a cheerful look on his face. 'I can see a family resemblance to Ronnie.'

'Everyone spots that. His name was Billy. Sadly, he died young, not long after this picture was taken.'

'A long time ago, by the picture?'

'Oh yes. The only living person who remembers him is our Uncle Nick. Ronnie pestered Uncle Nick on and on to know about Billy, just because he looked like him, one of those obsessions that kids sometimes get. He wanted to know why Billy died so young, why he didn't grow up.'

'How did Billy die, if you don't mind my asking?'

'A tragic accident. When the mansion was being built, he found a way in there. He paid a high price for his mischief. He fell down a shaft from a great height. No other child owned up to being there. Ronnie had this morbid curiosity about how and where it happened.'

I thought of the accident described by Mr Duffield: a little boy trespassing in Milner Field and falling to his death. It unsettled me to see that child's photograph. Before Mrs Creswell had time to say more, a man in workman's overalls that were so wet he might have had a bucket of water thrown over him rushed into the room, stumbling over the shoe-maker's last. His hair was clumped, as if he had been trying to tear it out.

'David, whatever's the matter?'

'Where's Mr Creswell?'

'Where he always is.'

'I'll fetch him.'

'Sit down, for heaven's sake. Tell me what's wrong.'

He didn't sit down but stood silently, looking at Mrs Creswell, his fists so tightly clenched that his knuckles turned white. He went to Mrs Creswell, took her very gently by the shoulders, and led her to the other fireside chair. She allowed herself to be lowered into it.

He said, 'There's been a terrible accident.' He stepped back from the chair, putting a distance between himself and his own words, which hung heavily between them.

Mrs Creswell looked at him blankly. Slowly the colour drained from her face. 'What? What sort of accident?'

'I'm so sorry, Mrs Creswell. They didn't want me to come, but who else should tell you?'

Her lips trembled as she spoke. 'Tell me what?'

'Ronnie is drowned.'

She shook her head. 'Don't be silly. No. You must be mistaken. Not Ronnie, Ronnie wouldn't drown.'

'I wish he hadn't gone down there on his own.' He looked at me blankly and then asked again, 'Where's Mr Creswell?'

Mrs Creswell stared at him, not answering.

David said, 'I'll fetch him.' He turned to me. 'You'll stay with her?'

I nodded. 'Yes.'

He took a deep breath, straightened his back and hurried out of the door, once more tripping over the shoemaker's last.

'He's been drinking, or something,' Mrs Creswell said. 'Or Ronnie's played a trick. I think they fell out.'

I was tempted to agree, to say, *Yes, that'll be it.*

The kettle had been boiling for a minute or so. It had reached that stage where the lid rattles in protest. I said, 'You stay put, Mrs Creswell, I'll make that tea.' She was shivering. I picked up a crocheted shawl from the back of her chair and placed it around her shoulders. I took charge of tea-making, finding sugar, taking the brandy flask from my satchel. I wanted time to go backwards. I wondered whether Ronnie's story about having something of interest to tell me was not to do with the past. Perhaps he feared some harm might come to him, or that he might harm himself. But why me, who had never heard his name before the letter arrived? I mashed the tea, stirring it, wanting it to turn strong quickly. I reached for the tin tray, to carry everything in, and then took it to the table.

Mrs Creswell seemed to have recovered herself a little. She said, 'David's wrong. He gets things into his head. Ronnie likes to play a trick.'

I could not think how to reply, but she beat me to it. 'Someone would have telephoned if anything was amiss with Ronnie, wouldn't they?'

'You would think so.' I poured. 'I'm going to put sugar in yours, all right? And a dash of brandy, if you've no objection.'

'David's left me in no fit state. What's got into him to come saying something like that?' She picked up her cup.

'That's what we'll find out, Mrs Creswell.' The man's voice came from the doorway.

I turned to see a uniformed police officer. He stepped into the room. 'Mrs Creswell. It's good that you are sitting down and you have someone with you.' He glanced at me, and then back at Mrs Creswell.

Her hand shook. The cup rattled into the saucer, spilling tea.

The officer said, 'I come bearing bad news.' He looked at his shoes, and then back at her. 'I'm very sorry to tell you that Ronnie was brought up from the deeps of the mill, from the reservoir. Nothing could be done to revive him.'

She leaned forward, her mouth dropping open, her blue eyes big and startled. Suddenly, she came to her feet. 'Take me to him.'

'He's been taken to the hospital.'

'The hospital? Then—'

The officer realised his mistake. 'There's no life in him, Mrs Creswell. Being taken to the hospital, that's the way it's done.'

The light went from her eyes. I thought she might fall and went to steady her.

David appeared in the doorway, ushering in a wiry, weather-beaten man of forty-five or fifty, his face lined, his eyes weak and watery. His hands were gnarled – gardener's hands. This must be Mr Creswell, his house. No one would have thought it. He looked out of place, marooned in the middle of the room.

The policeman put a hand on his shoulder, saying quietly, 'Ronald, go to your missis. I'm that sorry I can't imagine.'

Mr Creswell did as he was bid, going to Mrs Creswell and putting a veined hand on her shoulder. She let his hand stay there for a long minute before shaking him off, stepping away from him, shaking her head. 'We found work, and we lost everything.' She turned on him, thumping his chest. 'We should never have come to this accursed place. I thought it was just the mansion and I kept out. But a curse doesn't care about walls and dividing lines. It's here in the Lodge, in the air we breathe and the ground we walk on. There's no escape.'

Mr Creswell put his arms around her and drew her to him. 'Nay, lass. Them's stories. Them's old tales.'

The officer said, 'It's not your fault, Mrs Creswell. All that about Milner Field being cursed is superstition. Accidents happen.'

Mr Creswell responded sharply. 'No such thing as an accident when a man attends to his work.'

At that moment, a girl of about ten came through the door, sidling round the officer. She clutched at Mrs Creswell, saying, 'Mam! What's wrong?'

Mrs Creswell drew the child close. 'Nancy, we've had some bad news about our Ronnie.'

'I know,' said the child. 'I went to the mill and they said, "What are you doing here?" I said I was looking for my brother. They took me to Uncle Nick and they didn't tell me, they told him. He said I should come home to you.'

Mrs Creswell kissed the child on the head. 'You're a good girl. Go back to Uncle Nick.'

'He said come to you.'

'And I say go to him. Go to Uncle Nick. Tell him we'll be moving in with him. Tell him we won't spend another night under this roof.'

FIVE

I uttered my condolences, shook hands with the Creswells and left the house. The officer followed me out, elbowing David to come with him. Once outside, he said, 'You'd no call to come here, David.'

David's eyes blazed. 'Who else should break such news to Ronnie's mam? He was my apprentice and my pal. I need to be here.'

The constable spoke sharply. 'The sergeant wants you back at the mill. We'll go together, when I've spoken with this lady.'

The little girl stood on the path, arms held stiffly by her sides, watching me, making no move to go to the village as instructed by her mother. I was about to speak to her when the police officer loomed, taking a notebook from his pocket. 'Good afternoon, madam, I'm PC Beale. Your name and address, please.'

I gave him my card, the one that had my address and telephone number but did not mention my occupation. He glanced at it and tucked it in his notebook. 'And you are here because . . . ?'

'Ronnie Creswell wrote and asked me to come. There was something of interest he wanted to tell me.'

'What sort of something?'

'His letter gave no hint.'

'Do you have the letter?'

The truthful answer would be, *Yes, in my shoulder bag.* I wanted to reread it. What might I have missed?

I answered with a half-truth. 'I brought what I needed, directions from the railway station to Milner Field, but the letter was unusual and I can tell you exactly what it said. The writer and I have never met. His letter came out of the blue, saying that he had information from the past that would be of interest to me. He asked me to come here today, to the South Lodge at Milner Field, and that he would be here a little after six o'clock.'

'About the past, you say? Are you some sort of medium, madam? Do you have anything to do with spiritualism?'

'No.' I decided against playing questions and answers. 'I don't know where Ronnie found my address, but it may be connected with my occupation. I undertake inquiries, as a private investigator.'

'Do you now? Well, you won't be needed here, madam, but we shall need to take a look at that letter.'

'Then I'll be on my way, Constable Beale. I will have the letter sent on to you care of your headquarters. My father is chief superintendent at Wakefield and I shall be seeing him tomorrow.'

It was time for me to go. This seemed heartless, but if I were quick I might follow the policeman and go back to Saltaire by a way that didn't take me through a wood.

That plan was not to be. As PC Beale and David set off

at a trot, little Nancy barred my way, her face a blotch of misery.

'Do you want me to walk with you to the village?' I asked.

'Not yet.'

'What then?'

'Pamela is in the orangery.'

'Who is Pamela?'

Nancy seemed unable to answer. For a moment I wondered if Pamela might be an imaginary friend. Not that I had given it a great deal of thought, but I assumed imaginary friends moved on when a child approached double figures. It was a relief when she started to cry and I could hold her and stroke her hair. 'I came to see Ronnie, but now I must go. Will you let me walk you to your uncle?'

She broke away. 'But Pamela doesn't know. She's Ronnie's sweetheart, waiting for him in the orangery.'

I felt a sudden pain in my chest. My 'Oh!' came out as a gasp. 'We must fetch her to the house, to your parents.'

Nancy shook her head. 'Mam won't want her there. She doesn't like her, and Mrs Whitaker doesn't like Ronnie. But they're engaged.'

She looked up at me, aware that this plan would no longer become reality, but unable to find other words to tell this secret. Ahead of us, the evening sun gave a shining light to the panes of glass in the domed orangery. Beyond it stood the mansion whose earlier fairy-tale quality when seen from a distance now gave way to an oppressive grey gloom. Nancy ran ahead, and then stood sentry by the orangery's oval glass door until I caught up with her.

She opened the door. We stepped onto a mosaic floor in a space flooded with evening sunlight tinged forest green and with the whisper of exotic plants. As I closed the door behind us, there came a sudden burst of music. Someone had put on a gramophone record.

A cheerful, squiffy-sounding voice began to sing, 'I belong to Glasgow, dear old Glasgow town.'

Nancy smiled. 'Pamela's here. This is where we dance and we sing along with Will Fyffe.'

'Nancy,' I asked quietly, 'why were the parents against Ronnie and Pamela marrying?'

'Because Pamela Whitaker's life is planned. Ronnie can't afford to keep her.'

We walked closer to where the sound came from.

A big bonny lass, wearing a white lawn dress, red sandals and red scarf tied gypsy-style around her head came twirling from behind a mass of shiny dark green leaves. We stood motionless, watching her spin towards us as she sang, holding out her arms to Nancy as she came closer. 'When I've had a couple of drinks on a Saturday—'

She came to a sudden halt. 'Nancy? What's wrong?'

Nancy ran to her, bursting into sobs.

Pamela picked her up and hugged her. 'Daft lass, what is it? What's the matter?'

In that part of the orangery, there was nowhere to sit. This tunnel of green was a broad passageway from one place to another, from the garden to a door that led into the mansion. For Pamela, it would be forever transformed, as the pathway from before to after.

Pamela carried Nancy towards the scratch-scratching sound of the needle on the gramophone record.

Nancy had stopped crying. She was whispering into Pamela's ear. When she turned to look at me, Pamela's face had turned to stone.

I nodded a confirmation of Nancy's words.

Still holding Nancy, Pamela slid onto the cast-iron bench at the side of the gramophone.

I lifted the cabinet lid and raised the needle arm, replacing it in its holder. I took the record from the turntable, returned it to the paper sleeve and cover, and looked for the gap on the shelf.

Pamela took a hanky from her pocket and dried Nancy's tears. Now she turned to me, her face drained of colour except for two dark red spots on her cheek and a nervous blotch on her throat. 'Who are you?'

'My name's Kate Shackleton. I don't know Ronnie, but he wrote to me. He asked me to come here today because there was something he wanted to talk to me about. He didn't say what.'

'Then it can't be true, about Ronnie? There's been a mistake, or someone's telling lies.'

'I was talking to Mrs Creswell when a workmate, David, came to break the news to her. PC Beale wasn't far behind. I'm so sorry, Miss Whitaker. It seems that there was some kind of tragic accident in the basement of the mill.' I could not bring myself to say the word reservoir. Somehow that seemed too far-fetched. I had never heard of a building with its own reservoir in the foundations. In my mind's eye, I saw a vast stretch of water that made me shiver.

Pamela swayed slightly. She blinked and seemed not to see or hear. I knew that feeling of spinning out of the world into a sickening void. She gripped Nancy's shoulder so hard that the child winced, and then she released her, saying, 'They didn't want us to marry.' The venom in her voice turned the words from a statement into an accusation.

She was shivering and shaking. My coat was light, but I took it off and wrapped it around her.

With me on one side and Pamela and Nancy holding hands, we made our way back through the orangery.

Nancy had to run back for Pamela's bag. 'Will you go to the Creswells, Miss Whitaker?' I asked.

'Not now. I can't.' Hands shaking, she took the bag from Nancy. 'And if I drive, I'm going to kill someone.'

'Let me.' It would have sounded like an offer to kill someone for her had I not reached out and taken her keys. 'I'm an experienced driver. I'll get you home.'

A Bugatti sports car was parked by the side of the mansion. I climbed into the driver's seat. 'You'll need to give me directions.'

Nancy clambered onto Pamela's lap.

I said, 'Nancy, your mother said you must go to your uncle. Will you tell me the way?'

Nancy gave directions to the village and her Uncle Nick's home. We stopped by a three-storey house with a big upstairs window. Nancy hesitated.

'Do you want one of us to come in with you?' I asked.

'I can go in on my own.' Nancy climbed out of the car and then turned back, looking from me to Pamela and from Pamela to me as she asked her question. 'Mam kisses hurts better. Might she kiss Ronnie better?'

Pamela couldn't speak for weeping. From Nancy's face, it was clear she knew the reply to her question but hoped for a different answer. She looked to me.

'Kissing back to life would be a very big miracle,' I said. 'There are no very big miracles left in the world, only small ones.'

Nancy rooted herself to the spot.

Pamela got out of the car. She picked up Nancy and hugged her, and then pointed to the window where an old man stood. 'Go up to Uncle Nick. He'll answer your questions.'

Nancy disappeared inside the house. Pamela and I waited, until she had time to run upstairs. When she appeared at the window, we waved. A stooping, grey-haired old man now stood beside her.

'That's the Creswells' Uncle Nick,' Pamela said. 'He will take care of Nancy.'

LONG AGO

When he was just a boy, Nick started work in the mill. He was quick and clever. He had worked with the builders who knocked down the manor house and were building the mansion. He fetched and carried there. He knew how to look sharp and take orders and he slept in the hut. Now he slept top to toe in the room with other children. Two of them kicked and one cried in his sleep.

What Nick liked best was going to the schoolroom for a half-day, and that was because of Miss Mason, his teacher. She had shiny black hair and eyes the colour of cornflowers. She smiled when she called the register and looked at each child who said, 'Present, miss.'

The day a new boy started, Miss Mason moved them about so that the boy could sit beside Nick. His name was Billy Creswell.

'You are relations,' she explained. 'Nick, your grandmother was sister to Billy's grandfather.'

They were the same height. Nick had a thin face and dark hair. Billy had a round face and fair hair. Sometimes they walked, together with a few others, along by the river to the weir, a proper big weir by the wool-washing building. They paddled and took turns with the fishing rod. There were things about Billy that Ronnie didn't like. Billy liked to watch a fish gasp. He threw worms on a fire. When a boy with a crutch came to the weir, Billy wanted to see the stump of his leg.

One Sunday, Nick was on his own, walking by the canal. He imagined a bargeman might tell him to hop on. He would have an adventure to tell when he got back. Someone further on was throwing stones at a duck. The duck flew away. Nick guessed who was throwing stones.

Suddenly, Nick heard a cry. It was nearby. He went to see. It was Miss Mason. She had fallen. Nick was on the path. Miss Mason was on the bank. She must have slipped. Her face looked different, all squidged up as if she was hurt. When she touched her cheek, blood on her fingers made a streak. He wanted to keep on walking, pretending he hadn't seen. It wasn't right to see her on the ground. She turned, and saw him, and called to him. He came to a stop.

'Nick, come here.' She drew her skirt around, she slid her arms over her stomach and over her legs and was all hunched up. 'I want you to do something.'

'What, miss?'

'Go to my house. Fetch the big coat from behind the door. Fetch a towel from the hook by the sink.' He did not move. 'Go on. The door's unlocked. I'll wait here for you.'

'Are you all right, miss?'

'I slipped, that's all. If you see anyone on the towpath, don't say anything. Don't say I slipped. I'm just sitting here.'

'Yes, miss.'

He thought he heard someone and looked round, but it

was only birds taking flight from an ash tree. He knew that Miss Mason lived in the first cottage because when it was her birthday, she invited her class to come to her garden and have lemonade and a slice of cake.

He stepped into the house, almost on tiptoe so as not to disturb anything. It was so neat and clean, with the net curtain at the window and a jam jar on the table with pencils and pens. He closed the door, so as to take Miss Mason's navy blue coat from the hook. He put it on a chair and looked for the towel she wanted. Just as he lifted it off the hook by the sink, the door opened.

It was Billy, with snot on his nose. He wiped it on his sleeve. 'What you nicking, Nick?'

'I'm nicking nowt.'

'The coat won't suit you, give us it.'

'Get lost.' Nick pushed past him, awkwardly holding the towel and the coat. He knew why Miss Mason wanted the big coat. There was blood on her skirt and something else that he didn't want to see, something that shouldn't come out of a person, out of a sheep maybe, a little lamb. Women had babies, but babies cried or moved, and he had heard no cry and saw no movement. Nick spoke roughly to Billy, telling him to skedaddle. Nick had permission to be in the house. Billy didn't.

Billy said, 'We'll see who knows what's what, clever clogs.' But he left.

Nick hurried back to that spot on the river. He didn't know where Billy had gone and he didn't care.

Miss Mason was sitting up. Nick bobbed down behind her and she put her arms in the coat. She took the towel from him. 'Turn away, Nick.'

43

He turned away.

The sky was the blue of Miss Mason's eyes. He was used to seeing her smiling. He didn't want to look at her.

She said, 'Give me a hand up, please.'

She didn't pull on his hand, just seemed to steady herself with one hand on the ground and the other on his arm. Then she bent down and picked up the towel, which was bloody and had something wrapped in it.

She didn't ask him to, but he walked beside her as far as her door. She put her hand on his shoulder and pressed too hard. At the door she said, 'Can you keep a secret?'

'Yes.' He knew he could keep a secret. Only he knew that the bone from the well, the shepherdess's bone, was buried by the mansion gatepost.

'I won't be in school tomorrow. A neighbour will bring a note. It will say that I slipped on the canal bank. You can say that you saw me slip and fall, and that you walked me back, and that I put my hand on your shoulder.'

'Yes, miss.'

She squeezed his shoulder. 'You're a good boy, Nick. There's no one else I would trust.' She went inside and closed the door behind her.

Nick waited. He did not want to go. He did not want to stay.

When he heard Miss begin sobbing, so loudly, and funny sounds in her throat, Nick turned away and walked back along the canal. He was glad there was no sign of Billy.

Now Nick knew this would not be a day when a bargeman shouted, 'Hop on!'

SIX

In the time it took for Nancy to go into the three-storey house and appear at the window with her uncle, a small crowd of children had gathered to admire Pamela Whitaker's motor car. As I set off to drive her home to Bingley, a couple of boys hung on to the back of the car until we reached the main road.

'Turn right,' Pamela said, her voice flat. 'Though I don't care where I go now.'

I drove until we approached a substantial house of local stone whose tall gates stood open. 'This is it.'

I drove through the gates, stopping by the front door. A man was looking out through a downstairs bay window. When Pamela made no attempt to move, I went round to the passenger side and opened the door.

She got out, saying, 'Thank you.'

'It's the least I can do. I'm so sorry.' And then, most annoyingly because people are entitled to their own grief without others snatching at it, I had to blow my nose.

I watched her, holding herself very straight, throwing back her shoulders as she walked to the door.

45

The man I'd seen at the window was opening the door, and opening his arms to her. He must be her father, and by his gesture he already knew of Ronnie's death. Pamela recoiled from him, and I heard her say, 'Don't touch me. You'd rather Ronnie was dead than see us wed.'

An older woman wearing a long black skirt and cardigan appeared. It was the kind of house where they kept on the nanny.

Pamela's words chilled me. Had the parents really been so opposed to her having anything to do with Ronnie that they would be glad to see him drowned? Why had he sent for me? I couldn't have come any sooner. Ronnie had set the date, time and place for our meeting. Did someone know I was coming and step in first to silence him? That seemed ridiculous. I was giving myself a part in a tragedy that wasn't mine. Besides, he would have told someone why he sent for me. Few people keep everything to themselves. If his letter to me had any connection with his death, someone would come forward.

For now, my work was done.

I had been so slow walking from the door to the gate that by the time I got there, the man of the house caught up with me. 'It was good of you to drive my daughter home. Where do you live? My chauffeur will take you.'

I gave him the cold shoulder, thinking of his disregard of Pamela and Ronnie's feeling for each other. 'Thank you, but that won't be necessary.'

We had passed Bingley railway station. I had a return ticket in my pocket.

Having missed a train, I waited on the draughty station platform for half an hour, along with a group of factory girls, busy shedding the day's tedium with chatter and laughs, dolled up for a night out, carrying dancing shoes in finely made drawstring bags. One of them said that she didn't know why she was bothering to go. She had fallen in love with the man who played trumpet in the band. Since she couldn't dance with the trumpet player, she had no heart for dancing.

I was glad to be home. Mrs Sugden and I sat at the kitchen table. Over our supper of home-grown salad, bread and butter and slices of ham, I told her about the events of the day. When the food was cleared, she asked to see Ronnie Creswell's letter again, feeling sure she would divine some secret meaning from his words.

She read aloud that intriguing sentence: "'I have something to tell you, a story about the past that I know will be of interest to you. Please trust that I cannot say more at present.'" She put down the letter. 'Whatever might he be talking about? Perhaps something important enough that someone wanted to silence him?'

'I don't know. But copy it into the ledger. I promised to send the original to the police for their files. Perhaps Ronnie knew something that he didn't feel able to tell his nearest and dearest, something that might put them at risk. If that was the case, something life and death, why didn't he show more urgency about wanting to see me?'

'Might Ronnie Creswell have confided in anyone?'

'He may have spoken to his fiancée, but she's in no fit state to be asked.'

'It doesn't sound a sensible letter to me. Might the balance of Ronnie's mind have tipped? Might he have taken his own life, or set himself some dare that failed?'

'He had too much to live for. He was good at his job, had a

beautiful girlfriend and prospects, a lovely family. Wanting to tell me something indicates that he had information he didn't want to put down on paper. I'm thinking he knew something that would be incriminating, or destroy a reputation.'

If I were right, that person must have a secret or a reputation worth keeping. That would usually indicate someone at the top with a lot to lose, someone at the mill perhaps.

'His girlfriend brushed off her father when he met her at the front door.'

'That'll be it, then. They have someone lined up for her and the maintenance man was in the way.'

'You could be right. Once the police have his letter, they may be able to come up with something. The inquest will be reported.'

'In the Bingley or Keighley paper, or the *Telegraph & Argus*, maybe, but what's the betting the Leeds papers won't notice the death of a working man from far-flung Saltaire?'

'What's far-flung about a dozen miles?'

'Local people want to know what's happening on their doorstep. What's Saltaire to them or them to Saltaire?'

'I'd say the death by drowning of a young man with his life ahead of him merits a paragraph.'

'It's tragic all right, but if dark-horse Ronnie Creswell and his beautiful fiancée kept each other under wraps, her parents will shut down the story to protect her reputation, unless that's outweighed because she's a tragic figure and someone has a picture of her looking glamorous that's worth putting in the paper. What's her name?'

'Pamela Whitaker, but we're not investigating. The police are on the case. That's why I must let them have this letter. I'll take it with me tomorrow for Dad to pass on.'

'I'll copy it into the book now.' She paused at the door. 'Jim Sykes called by earlier.'

'Oh?'

'I told him you were still out. He asked when you would be back, but he was reluctant to say what he wanted so I didn't press him. He said I could make out an invoice for the Hunslet job. There were a few loose ends to tie up, but he would take the invoice with him on Monday. Oh, and he's ready to start again as soon as another job comes in.'

'Good.'

'Only the thing is, I could see there was something he wanted to talk to you about. You know when a person tells you something isn't important, and you know very well that it is?'

'Yes.'

'That's what he said. He wanted a word with you, but it would wait. He was his usual well-turned-out self in his Montague Burton suit and the cricket club tie, but he has bags under his eyes. It took him three goes to make his cigarette lighter work. There was a look on his face that made me ask him what's wrong?'

'Did he answer?'

'He said, "It's nothing. I shouldn't have come. Everything is under control."'

'Then obviously it's not.'

LONG AGO

Nick walked back along the canal with the sound of Miss Mason's sobs in his ears and in his head. He felt like someone who could no longer see or hear, not caring whether a barge came, not caring whether he saw a rabbit. He was glad that he could not see Billy. Billy had gone. He wouldn't dare tell.

Nick walked along, looking at the ground, looking at his clogs that were too tight and hurt his toes. Just as Nick wondered whether he should carry his clogs and walk barefoot, he heard a sound that made him jump.

'I know a secret. I know a secret.'

Billy suddenly rose up from behind a clump of nettles. 'Go on, what did I miss, mister knight in shining armour?'

'Nowt.'

Billy started to laugh. 'Who will I tell first?'

'No one.'

'Miss won't cane me no more.'

'She never has.'

'But she thinks I'm stupid, that's why she put me next

to you. Now we're two witnesses to a dead baby, and she's not married.'

'Shut up about it.'

'What's it worth?'

Nick had nothing to offer, except that he knew his way into the mansion, and no other kids did.

'Will you keep quiet if I show you somewhere special?'

'Where's that then, teacher's pet?'

Nick looked at Billy, wondering what to do, or what to say to shut him up. Billy was the same height as Nick, but there was more meat on him. He was off his guard, and he was threatening Miss Mason.

Nick watched as Billy bent down to pick up a stone. He liked to have a stone handy, ready to throw if he saw a cat.

Nick said, 'I know a place where we can jump across where there's no floorboards and we swing on rafters, see secret passages.'

Billy dropped the stone. 'Go on, then.'

Nick led the way.

The workmen's tools and kettle were in his grandmother's hut. Nick knew the way into the mansion from the cellar. He knew where the foreman kept the key. Not all the floorboards were down. He and Billy didn't speak at first, though there was no one to hear. The watchman had a hut by the gate. He only came into the half-built mansion if he was bored.

Nick and Billy took turns to jump between rafters. Where the staircase would be finished off next week, they walked sideways. They did jumping dares and drop-down dares, bending their knees to break a fall, just the two of them, their secret.

Billy kept pretending to fall, or to be scared, and then he

laughed. The shaft where the dumb waiter would go had a shallow wheel with a groove and rope. There was a ledge where the cupboard part of it would be slid in. None of the builders had put in a dumb waiter before. Jack had told Nick it would be easy.

As Billy was swinging on the ledges where the dumb waiter would go, he called to Nick, 'We come here every Sunday from now on. We'll charge a penny for people to come.'

'We'll get in trouble. You'll break that ledge, leave it.'

'We come here every Sunday, or I'll tell.'

Billy was swinging with both hands and kicking the inside wall. All of a sudden, he gave a little yelp and took one hand off. He must have hurt it, a spell of wood.

Suddenly he was slipping. He reached out his hand and said, 'Nick, help!'

Nick grabbed Billy's wrist. 'You'll tell. You don't keep your word.'

'No, I won't tell—'

As Nick let go of Billy's wrist, the t-e-l-l became a scream and an echo of that scream, lasting all the way down to the ground.

SEVEN

Jim Sykes had called at Batswing Cottage on Saturday afternoon, to give Mrs Shackleton the news about Rosie being taken into hospital. He should have remembered that she would not be back from Saltaire, but it had slipped his mind, what with everything that was going on and with the bombshell dropped by the doctor. Mrs Sugden had let him in. He could have told her about that morning's events but Jim was not a man for telling a story twice when once would do.

Saturday morning had started well enough. Jim went over to Hunslet to tie up the loose ends of the investigation. The job was done and dusted, resulting in recovered goods, an employee sacked without a reference, but no police involvement. For the employee, it was a lucky escape. For the business owner, it was a satisfactory conclusion, with security tightened.

All that remained was for Mrs Sugden to send in the invoice.

That morning, Jim had taken a cup of tea and a slice of toast up to Rosie. She told him he shouldn't have put jam on the bread because she'd put on too much weight. Their daughter

Irene was staying over at her friend's house and going straight to work from there. Irene knew her mam was unwell, but the boys were kept in ignorance.

Rosie had seen their own doctor. He examined her and couldn't say precisely why she was having the pains. He asked all the usual questions about was she regular, and had anybody else in the family had an upset tummy or stomach pains? Might she have strained a muscle at work or while carrying heavy shopping?

She took the pills and waited for the pains to go away.

When she came home from work early on Friday, doubling up in pain, Jim decided enough was enough. He told her she could give up that job. The works' doctor at Montague Burton knew she wasn't swinging a leg. He sent her home to rest, and told her to see her own doctor.

Jim told her she took on too much and she shouldn't. The pains were her body's way of telling her to stop. They managed well enough. They were luckier than most, Irene in a good job, and the boys working.

Rosie went to bed early with a hot drink and said she'd be all right in the morning.

It was when Jim came back from Hunslet and she was still lying there that he decided something must be done. She was pale and claimed to be cold, but her hands were warm. The tea was half drunk and the toast half eaten.

'How's your tummy?' he asked.

'It's not as bad.'

Jim knew that meant it was still the same. 'What can I get you?'

'When you boil the kettle, fetch me some Indian Brandy in hot water.'

The kettle was already boiled. He took Rosie her Indian Brandy, which she swore by, and a damp facecloth and a comb. He emptied the chamber pot and, without telling her, set off for the doctor. Then he wished he hadn't emptied the chamber pot. The colour of her wee might have told a story.

The doctor had finished his surgery for the day. He came back with Jim. Jim went up to announce the doctor, expecting Rosie to complain, to say there was no need for the doctor.

To his surprise, she said, 'I suppose we better let him have another look at me, see if he can get to the bottom of it, if that's not too coarse a quip.'

The doctor examined her, and asked the familiar questions. Once more, he could come up with no new explanation. She saw that he was at a loss. The doctor did not know what to say.

As it turned out, he did know what to say. He went downstairs and said to Jim, 'I'm going back to the surgery. I'll telephone St James's. I'm not saying there's something dangerous or life-threatening or anything of that sort, but I want a second opinion on Mrs Sykes, and I want her to be taken in today if they'll find a bed.'

'Have you told her, Doctor?'

'No. I thought you would.'

'Then we best do it together if it's all the same to you. I don't want Rosie refusing point blank. You'll hold more sway than me in something like this.'

The two men went up the stairs. The doctor pointed out that it was frequently the case that a second opinion could be helpful. These pains had gone on long enough.

'But it's Saturday,' Rosie said.

Neither Sykes nor the doctor queried the significance of the day of the week, but the doctor said, 'That's true. You may not be examined until Monday. Meanwhile, you will have rest. The nurses will take good care of you. They will record your pulse and your blood pressure and note your symptoms. You will be in good hands, Mrs Sykes.'

Back downstairs, the doctor said, 'I believe you've kept up your hospital fund contributions?'

'I have.'

'They wouldn't turn Mrs Sykes away, but that does help. I'll send for an ambulance. We don't want her clambering on trams.'

'I'll drive her there.' Sykes felt suddenly awkward. The doctor had come on foot. Perhaps he didn't have a car. Rosie would know.

When Sykes came back from taking Rosie to the hospital, glumness took a grip of him. They had taken her from him with no ceremony. He was given a number. If she was kept in, he should look for her number in the hospital list in Monday's paper, or come to the gate and read the notice. Visiting day was Sunday. It would be too soon for him to come tomorrow, but if she were still here the following Sunday, they would have issued a visitor pass by then.

Sykes attempted to object. They were taking his wife and telling him nothing, but for once, he couldn't find words. He kissed her on the forehead and watched her being wheeled away.

When he got home, Irene was there. She had decided not to go to the dance. 'Where's Mam?'

He explained.

'Why didn't you tell me?' she exploded.

'You weren't here.'

'Why didn't you say you didn't know what was wrong? Why did you both keep saying indigestion, constipation, cramps.'

'It might be.'

'You should have talked to me.'

'You're not a doctor.'

'No, but the women at work, they know every female complaint under the sun. Having a cup of tea in the canteen is like attending medical school.'

'And what they don't know they make up.'

Irene bounced about in sullen silence, making egg on toast for the pair of them. Finally, she said, 'We can go see her tomorrow. Sunday is visiting day.'

'We don't have a pass.'

'Dad! Get a pass.'

'How? It's an office matter. They have procedures.'

'Go see Auntie Kate. She knows people in that hospital. She knows a ward sister. She knows a matron.'

Jim just stood and looked at her.

She looked back at him. Her shoulders dropped. She came over and kissed his cheek. 'Poor Dad. You've turned helpless and hopeless. I'll go.'

'You will not.' Jim picked up his jacket. At the door, he said, 'Don't expect me back in a hurry. We'll have cases to discuss.'

'You mean you're going to the Chemic Tavern?'

'I mean I'm going to see Mrs Shackleton about how I got on in Hunslet and how she got on in Saltaire.'

'And what else?'

'Ask if she can wangle a hospital pass for us to see your mother at St James's tomorrow.'

*

57

Mrs Sugden had told me that Sykes had called earlier in the day and would call back later. It was about eight o'clock when he knocked on the door.

Usually, when we have our discussions, Mr Sykes, Mrs Sugden and I sit at the kitchen table, or the dining table. That Saturday evening, we sat in what Mrs Sugden likes to call the drawing room, where we have two comfortable chairs and a sofa with a drop-down arm. One look at Sykes and I wanted to point him to the sofa, click the little lever to release the arm, tell him to lie down, and throw a blanket over him.

He told us about Rosie being taken into hospital. Since this was Saturday and visiting day was tomorrow, there had been no time for him to be issued with a visitor pass. His daughter Irene had been telling him off for not insisting, and for coming away without a pass.

We were waiting for a telephone call from my friend Angela, a hospital sister. Meanwhile, I attempted to distract his attention by telling him of the events at Saltaire and Milner Field. This worked up to a point, and to give him credit he took it all in and asked a few pertinent questions about the letter writer, Ronnie Creswell, and about the workmate who had left the scene to hurry to Ronnie's mother and break the sad news. Not that the tragic business was our immediate concern. The police were well and truly on the case.

We stuck to business. Sykes produced his note of charges for the firm in Hunslet. He had spent a week undercover at the company, keeping track of missing goods and reporting the culprit to management. Mrs Sugden took his notes and put them in her typing tray, ready to make out an invoice.

Why is it that the telephone only makes us jump when we are waiting for a call and expecting it to ring?

It was Angela. There would be a visitor pass at the porter's office tomorrow. She had called at the women's ward to see Rosie Sykes and could report that she was comfortable, and very happy to be receiving visitors tomorrow. She would like to see Mrs Shackleton first.

I passed on the message. It cheered Sykes to hear that Rosie was comfortable and resting. 'She's looking forward to seeing you tomorrow,' I added. 'Oh, and I'm going to pop in first for a quick hello.'

Sykes looked suddenly taken aback. 'What is she going to tell you that she won't tell me?'

I had no idea, and so came up with an explanation so plausible that I congratulated myself. 'Rosie knows I'm going for tea with my parents tomorrow. I'll be setting off early afternoon and will call at the hospital on the way. Also, she probably wants me to bring something or other that you wouldn't want to ask for in a chemist's shop.'

He brightened. 'You could be right.'

'Of course I'm right.'

He nodded. 'That's it, then. Rosie wouldn't want to worry Irene. We made the mistake of not telling Irene about Rosie's trouble and now she's suspicious. She's turned into the Inquisitor General, thinking we're holding something back.'

'The visitor pass will be for two. Bring Irene. I'll be there on the dot, in and out of Rosie's ward within ten minutes. I'll see you at the entrance and give you back the pass.'

Sykes's sense of relief was palpable. While Mrs Sugden told him her two stories about mysterious ailments that vanished just as quickly as they arrived, I brought out the whisky decanter and poured us each a small glass.

Relieved of his fears, Sykes wanted to know more about

my visit to Saltaire. I gave him chapter and verse, up to driving Ronnie Creswell's distraught fiancée, Pamela Whitaker, home to Bingley.

Sykes became so engrossed, upset at the news of a young man's tragic death that he let his tea go cold. And then he asked, 'What sort of car does Pamela Whitaker have?'

'A Bugatti.'

Sykes let out a whistle. 'Never! And that's Whitaker's daughter's. I wonder what his chauffeur drives him about in.'

'Do you know Mr Whitaker?'

'I spoke to him briefly once. Whitaker is a good business-man, a friendly fellow and straight-talking. He owns three mills in Bradford and one in Halifax. You couldn't have a better man for chairman of the board at Salts.'

'Why does he need three mills in Bradford?' Mrs Sugden asked.

'Because each mill handles a different process. Mill owners all made the same mistake, way back, starting up with every process under one roof, spinning, weaving, finishing. When the businesses grew, they ran out of space. Whitaker's three mills now do different processes. That's what was so clever about old Titus Salt. He had several mills across Bradford. He became disgusted with the housing and working conditions and hit on the idea of bringing all the processes together under one roof, creating the biggest and most advanced mill in the world. Of course, he could do it: he had the brass.'

Mrs Sugden looked thoughtful. 'Just going back to this sudden death . . . How's a mill owner who can afford to buy his daughter a sports car going to feel about that daughter taking up with a young maintenance man that a mill owner will regard as a grease monkey?'

'Good question,' Sykes said. 'Whitaker is a self-made man; he may recognise qualities in the lad.'

Mrs Sugden adopted her wise-owl look. 'Or else it's *Romeo and Juliet* all over again. Two families both with the same idea that a match should not take place. If that isn't a recipe for foul play I don't know what is.'

This is the trouble with we self-made investigators. The sharp point of suspicion pierces the soul, worst possibilities push their way in and the mind expects to meet the heart of darkness. I felt sure that did not apply in the tragic case of the late and much missed Ronnie Creswell. Yet Mr Creswell Senior's words stayed with me. 'Ronnie's father refused to believe it was accidental. He said, "There is no such thing as an accident when a man attends to his work."'

Sykes felt obliged to put the opposite view. 'Workplace accidents happen all the time. Owners always want to keep them quiet if they can. Was young Creswell on his own in the reservoir?'

'I don't know. It was a workmate who came to break the news to Mrs Creswell.'

The way Constable Beale had led away David Fairburn hinted at suspicion, but that is a default position for policemen. It seemed to me unlikely that a guilty man would rush to break the news to his victim's mother, unless that man was a very good dissembler, or wanted to get his side of the story in first.

EIGHT

At 1.50 p.m. on Sunday, I joined the queue of patients' relatives awaiting admission to St James's Hospital. The line began to move slowly towards the main door and then to the inner gate and the turnstile where the uniformed porter checked passes.

I climbed two flights of stairs to the long high-ceilinged ward with standard iron beds on either side, regulation-distance apart. Then followed the business of treading the ward, ignoring patients who already had someone at their bedside, looking left and right with quick glances, giving a small nod and smile when inadvertently catching someone's eye. Through an open window, I heard the clip-clop of a horse and cart and the sound of someone calling in the grounds.

I spotted Rosie Sykes before she spotted me. She wore a bright white nightgown trimmed with lace and a pink and white crocheted shawl around her shoulders. She was putting in her teeth. Like most women who had babies, she had been advised to have her teeth out when her first child came along, being given two good reasons: the baby would take all the calcium and absence of teeth would save the expense of dentistry.

'Hello, Rosie.'

She smiled. Her eyes shone. 'Thank you for coming. I know you're off to Wakefield.'

'Glad you asked for me. Are you comfortable?'

'I am now. Not everyone gets their own teeth back when they've been whisked away for washing.'

'Well, that's good. Hang on to them.'

'I like that somebody else makes the bed. I was glad not to be gazing out towards the cemetery, but having it at my back is worse. I can feel it gawping.'

I looked out. The view was of the hospital grounds, Beckett Street and the cemetery. 'Gawp back. Tell it to lodge its claim elsewhere. Now, how are you feeling?'

'I'm doing well. Your friend popped in to see me just before lights-out last night. She was kind and reassuring.'

'You're in the best place and you look well rested. That can be half the battle.' I had brought a few things for her: a new facecloth, mint humbugs. 'Check with the nurse before you eat the sweets in case they want to monitor your diet.'

She thanked me, and then sighed. 'You must be wondering why I asked to see you first?'

'*I* wasn't wondering. Jim was. I told him that you might want to ask me for something from the chemist. Was I right?'

'Well, I'd like some Beecham's Pills. I'm feeling bloated and uncomfortable.'

'As it happens, I've brought some. Do you want one now?'

She smiled in gratitude and nodded. 'I'd like two, please.'

I passed her a glass of water. 'Hold out your hand. No one's looking.'

She swallowed the pills. 'You once said, people would sooner give reassurance than a straight answer.'

I had no recollection of having said that, but listened as Rosie went on talking. 'Now I'm just waiting for the blow to fall. You were a nurse. Do you think they'll put off telling me something if it's bad?'

'No, I don't. You'll be told, and nothing should be kept from you. If there's anything the doctor says that you want translating, ask the ward sister.'

'What's worrying me – well, coming in here sets you thinking. The kids think they're grown up but they're not. If anything happens, if I don't come out of here alive, will you keep an eye on them, and keep Jim busy so he doesn't brood?'

I took her hand. 'Oh Rosie, of course I would. But that's not going to happen. You'll be fed up of being poked, prodded and asked questions. Don't be afraid to ask questions yourself if you need to.'

'They tell you nowt in these places.'

'That's when there's nothing to tell. Make the most of the rest. Ask the ward sister if there is anything you ought to know. If there is something, it won't be kept secret.' I opened my bag. 'I've brought you postcards and stamps. You'll probably be out of here before you have time to make use of them.'

'I hope you're right.' She nodded. 'They won't let you take your own medicines, but I swear by Beecham's Pills.'

I stood and made ready to go. 'Rest and don't worry. Mrs Sugden's making a Sunday dinner for Jim and the kids.' I took her hand. 'I'll give him back the visitor pass before he climbs the drainpipe to see you. If you are still here next Sunday, I'll call again.'

*

Jim Sykes was seated on a bench in the hospital grounds; Irene was beside him, holding a bunch of flowers.

Sykes stood. 'How is she?'

'Looking rested, and can't wait to see you.' I handed Sykes the visitor pass. 'She knew I wouldn't turn up without sweets.'

Irene said, 'I'll remember that for when you're in there, Dad. Jelly Babies?'

'Less of your cheek.' Sykes handed the visitor pass to his daughter. 'Go join the queue and don't go in without me.'

Irene was bright and capable, but Rosie would not want to burden her with worries about her health. Irene had worked in the offices at Montague Burton and was courting a steady lad who worked as a presser. I must remember to warn her that if she married and had a baby, she must not listen to any doctor who told her the baby would take all her calcium and she had better have her teeth pulled. That happened to so many women who were deemed to be too poor to pay for dentistry. Now here some of them were, on Rosie's ward, enjoying a rest and hoping that their own set of false gnashers would be returned to them.

Sykes said, 'What did Rosie want?'

'To make sure you all have a proper Sunday dinner.'

I would not tell him about Rosie's worries. Although I had tried to reassure her, what I learned when nursing is to listen to the patient.

Suddenly Irene was waving to her dad. The queue was moving. I took out my car keys. 'Now I'm going to Wakefield to see my mother and dad. You're all set for Monday?'

'I am. All I have to do is deliver the invoice and walk round with the manager who'll take responsibility for security.'

After a few steps towards his daughter, Sykes turned back. 'Is Rosie keeping something from me? Only that's a reason she would ask to see you.'

'She's not keeping anything from you. She would tell you if something was amiss.'

Sykes was about to say something else. His quick glance told me he thought I was holding back, but he tipped his hat and hurried to join the visitors' queue.

I walked back to my car. Ronald Creswell's letter asking me to call on him was safely tucked in my bag. Giving it to my father to forward to the local CID was not simply for convenience. I felt a proprietorial interest, and a wish to find the truth for those left behind. I also could not shake off that itchy curiosity to know why Ronnie had picked me out and what he might have told me.

NINE

After Sunday tea, Mother, Dad and I took our dog Sergeant for a walk to the local park. We found a bench to sit on. I had given Dad Ronnie Creswell's letter, to be passed on through official channels to Shipley CID. He would do it, no questions asked. All the same, I told them about my visit to Saltaire and Milner Field.

Mother isn't interested in crime and detection, unless it's staged at the Wakefield Opera House or on a cinema screen. She has occasionally involved herself in a case, but only when it entailed a visit to Betty's Tea Rooms or an opportunity to unmask a villain in a theatrical manner.

Yet she was aghast when I told them about Ronnie Creswell's mysterious letter and tragic death. She forgot to throw the dog's ball. 'His poor mother. I've lost my sons to Canada, but to surrender a child to the Grim Reaper is beyond imagining. There'll be no way of comforting her. Is she religious?'

'I don't know. I do know that she had persuaded herself that the curse of Milner Field applied only to the mansion, not the lodge where they lived.'

'A curse?'

'Ask Mrs Duffield. She'll tell you all about it.'

'Withdraw, Kate. Do not involve yourself.'

'I'm not involved. I just wish I'd had chance to talk to Ronnie.'

Mother said, 'It surprises me anyone still lives there. I wouldn't.'

'It's the Creswells' livelihood, or was.'

'She won't stay on now.'

'You're right. She's ready to up sticks and go, leave her house, her job, everything, in case something happens to her other children.'

'How will they live?' Dad asked.

'That's all I know. I spent more time with Ronnie's little sister Nancy. She took me to the orangery where Ronnie's fiancée was waiting. It was terrible. Nancy broke the news. Pamela was devastated. I drove her back to Bingley in her Bugatti.'

'A Bugatti?' Mother raised an eyebrow. 'She's from the top drawer?'

'She's a mill owner's daughter. Ronnie was a maintenance man.'

'Goodness. In the two-penny novels it's usually the other way round. The pretty mill girl catches the eye of the boss's son.'

Dad said, 'Ginny, when do you read two-penny novels?'

'You don't have to read something to know the story. The girl's parents wouldn't have approved.'

'They didn't, from what Pamela said.'

'Her mother would have taken it badly. Not that I'm speculating, but I expect her mother must have had other plans for her.'

'Mother, you're not suggesting they would have had Ronnie done in?'

'Don't read anything into that, Katie,' Dad said. 'Your grandmother reacted badly when I came on the scene. When your mother took me home, we were six for lunch and the table was set for five. Guess who wasn't to be fed?'

'You never told me that!'

Mother made a dismissive gesture. 'That's history now!' She turned to me. 'I demand to know more about this curse. You must have a theory, Kate.'

'I do. About sixty years ago, a bonny little boy, a relation of the Creswells called Billy, died in an accident while Milner Field mansion was being built. That incident would be enough for mothers to order their children to stay away. Parents would have told their children whatever story was needed to frighten them off.'

Dad nodded. 'Stories are either forgotten or retold with knobs on.'

'Ronnie – the young man who drowned – seems to have been obsessed with the story of the little boy's death. There's a strong family resemblance between Billy and Ronnie. It's a far-fetched possibility, but I wonder if Ronnie, who must somehow have known I'm an investigator, wanted me to look back through the records and see whether after all these years I might uncover the truth about Billy's death.'

Dad asked, 'How old was Ronnie?'

'Twenty-two.'

'No!' Dad shook his head. 'Twenty-two, full-time job, a girlfriend who drives a Bugatti. The past for that poor lad would be last Christmas, not some long-ago family accident.'

*

As I reached the smoky city I called home, I discovered that my trusty Jowett had a plan of its own. Instead of taking me my usual way to leafy Headingley, I found myself on Albion Street, passing the newspaper building. Sunday. Newspapermen would be producing tomorrow's paper, but my librarian friend and his wife would be at home.

Delivering Mother's back copies of *The Lady* to Mrs Duffield gave me a perfectly legitimate reason to pay another call. If Mr Duffield, a mine of information, knew nothing about yesterday's death at Saltaire, no one else would.

The story of the curse on Milner Field could be an ideal cover for all sorts of dirty deeds and otherwise explicable misfortunes.

I thought back to knocking on the door of the Lodge, and hearing Mrs Creswell singing 'Bye Bye Blackbird'. She and Pamela, with her gramophone records and 'I Belong to Glasgow', would have been a mother- and daughter-in-law made in heaven. What idiocy to have come between the young couple.

TEN

News of Ronnie Creswell's death saddened and intrigued Mr Duffield. We sat in their garden again. Mr Duffield had not heard about the accident at Milner Field. That did not prevent a new line of speculation. 'It may be that the young man who lost his life through a moment's carelessness knew something, or thought he did; the origin of the curse, for instance. You would be his intermediary, a lady of good standing who would take his theory to the Bishop of Bradford.'

'It would have been interesting to know his view of the curse,' I replied, 'but Mrs Duffield has already come up with a powerful theory that the mothers of the shepherdess and the dead boy cursed the land and the mansion. I'm coming to the conclusion that "the curse" became a catch-all explanation for misfortunes.'

My praise of Mrs Duffield's 'powerful theory' gave her the impetus to interrupt. 'There's something you must see,' she said, producing a copy of *County Lady*. 'You can take it with you and pass it on to your mother when you've finished with it.'

Mr Duffield watched as his wife opened her magazine. He remembered he wanted to make a telephone call and left us to it.

Mrs Duffield pointed to the picture of an attractive, smartly dressed woman, pen in hand, seated at an antique writing desk. 'This is Mrs Whitaker. The Whitakers hosted a May fancy-dress ball at Milner Field. Tell me this: if businesses are feeling the pinch and Salts is desperate to sell the accursed mansion, why did Mrs Whitaker open up the place to throw a big fancy-dress ball? That must have cost a fortune.'

'I don't know,' I said. 'Do you have a theory about why they would put on a ball when everyone is watching the pennies?'

She pointed to the article alongside Mrs Whitaker's photograph. 'According to Mrs Whitaker's account, the ball was a great success. She sent this report with photographs to *County Lady*. She describes the costumes, the music and dancing. Mentions prominent families and young people enjoying themselves. It smacks to me of a mother bringing out her daughter. There's a picture of Pamela Whitaker as a shepherdess, standing by the son of Foxcroft Carpets as Napoleon Bonaparte. Turn the page.'

I turned the page. Sure enough, there was a photograph of Pamela Whitaker, dressed as a shepherdess, grasping a crook, looking slightly bored and wearing a forced smile. Beside her a slight, dapper young man with a small moustache stood to attention. He wore a French Emperor costume, complete with a slightly-too-big black felt bicorne, epaulets, sash and black boots.

Mrs Duffield went on, in an anxious-to-be-believed voice, 'I know a coming-out ball when I see one. Pamela Whitaker

72

was put on the marriage market that day. Her mother left it a little late. She is twenty-one.'

'Interesting,' I said.

'Fascinating,' Mrs Duffield corrected me. 'The young man is a Foxcroft. Mrs Whitaker's sister married into the Foxcroft family, so the families are close. Kevin is Mrs Whitaker's godson. As I read the situation, the women are determined to keep wealth within the family. A marriage between Pamela Whitaker and Kevin Foxcroft provides the perfect way to hand on assets to the next generation.'

Mr Duffield had returned from making his telephone call. He prefers to be the person who holds the floor. 'I can't keep up with these dynastic combinations,' he said. 'I'm too old. I do know that Foxcroft's didn't become the leading carpet manufacturers they are today without treading carefully, not stepping on too many toes and knowing when to put the boot in. If the son of Foxcroft Carpets was the parental choice for Pamela, Ronnie Creswell would have been the fly in the ointment.'

Mrs Duffield does not always second her husband's opinion, but today she did. 'Being a self-made millionaire takes mad courage. Mr Whitaker wouldn't want his daughter to marry down. Once a family's on the up and up they like to stay on that trajectory.' She picked up her copy of *County Lady*. 'I'll read you the account of the ball before you take it, Kate.'

As Mrs Duffield cleared her throat to speak, Mr Duffield quickly pushed himself up from his chair and announced his plan of escape. 'The duty editor was engaged. If he hasn't heard about this tragic death at Salts, he should.'

Mr Duffield hurried away, leaving Mrs Duffield free to read aloud to me the entire report of the ball.

Ten minutes later, Mr Duffield came back, trying not to look pleased with himself. He made the announcement from a standing position, his hands on the back of the garden chair.

'That took a bit of doing. I managed to get through to the deputy editor. He was sufficiently interested to contact Shipley police and squeeze something out of them. The constabulary are playing this close to their chest, but he has confirmation of a death. They wouldn't give a name. Investigations are ongoing. A man was taken in for questioning.' He sat down. '*The Herald* might be first off the mark on this. Thank you, Mrs Shackleton.'

Suddenly, I wished I hadn't told him anything. There ought to be no hurry to intrude on tragedy and grief. We sat in silence for a moment.

'How sad that you did not speak to that ill-fated young man,' Mrs Duffield said. 'I sat with a dying friend once. She had last words to say but simply couldn't get them out.' She turned to her husband and spoke sharply. 'If you have any last words, speak sooner rather than later.'

'I shall be sure to speak the next time I feel a headache coming on. Please do likewise, my dear.' He continued before Mrs Duffield had time to silence him: 'I did hear something else about Milner Field, not in relation to the death. There is a rumour about the Whitakers.' He nodded towards his wife. 'It's in connection with that party of yours.'

'It wasn't my party. It was a ball. I couldn't picture myself invited to a fancy-dress ball held in Milner Field.'

'But your instincts were correct, my dear. Rumour has it that an announcement had been expected, of the engagement of Pamela Whitaker and Kevin Foxcroft.'

'I knew it!' said Mrs Duffield. 'That picture of young

Foxcroft and Pamela Whitaker will be reproduced for the announcement of the engagement, how the lovers' knot was tied at the Milner Field fancy-dress ball. Such an announcement would be a counterweight to stories about a curse. They would drag up the old stories about royal visits and tree-planting and some ignoramus would be enticed to make a bid for the place.'

What story did the picture of Pamela and Kevin Foxcroft really tell? I wondered as I drove home. If the fancy-dressed couple had romantic feelings for each other, Pamela would have been Empress Josephine. If they were chums, Kevin Foxcroft might have dressed as a shepherd or a joke big bad wolf.

As maintenance man, Ronnie's only role in the business of a grand fancy-dress-cum-marriage-market ball would have been to ensure that no plaster fell from the ballroom ceiling.

I decided not to think about this again.

As I let myself in the front door, the telephone began to ring. It was Mr Duffield.

'Ah Kate, glad I've caught you. Something else about the night of that party. Had a call back from the sub. He gets lonely on night duty.'

'What does he say?'

'On the day of the party, there was a theft or a burglary at Milner Field. He couldn't make up his mind what to call it. Valuables went missing. One of the serving wenches hasn't been seen since. Turns out that she's a jail bird, with a record for shoplifting, snatching bags and stealing from employers.'

'Was much taken?'

'Enough, I think. The family silver. They were insured.'

'Was there an arrest?'

'No. Suspect number one simply vanished.'

ELEVEN

On Monday morning as the hall clock struck nine, the telephone rang. I was at the kitchen table, reading the morning paper. Mrs Sugden rarely betrays extreme emotions, but when she came to find me she trailed an air of excitement.

'Mr Whitaker's secretary is on the telephone from Salts Mill. Mr Whitaker wishes to know whether it would be convenient for him to call on you this morning or this afternoon. He wants to thank you for driving his daughter Pamela home from Milner Field on Saturday.'

I gave Mrs Sugden the nod. 'I'm working at home today. He can call any time up to four o'clock.'

For two reasons, I did not believe his 'calling to thank me' story. Firstly, he had thanked me on Saturday. Secondly, since he had found my telephone number, and presumably my address, he or his wife could have written a note or sent a bunch of flowers.

Our neighbours know a little about my occupation. Their curtains twitched only slightly on Monday afternoon when a chauffeur-driven Bentley stopped at the front gate of Batswing Cottage.

'He's here,' Mrs Sugden called from the hall. She had taken up a polishing-the-furniture post in the drawing room so as not to be caught on the hop. She times her door-opening duty to perfection, striking a fine balance between not keeping a visitor waiting too long and startling them by flinging open the door before they knock.

'It's all right,' I said. 'I'll go.'

Mr Whitaker was about five feet ten inches tall with an athletic build, dark hair, and a small moustache. He was expensively turned out in a superb suit, but the first thing I noticed about him was the sadness in his eyes.

Usually, I would have shown him to a comfortable chair, or, if he appeared extremely businesslike, taken him into the dining room that doubles as an office. Yet there was such an air of gloom about him that I didn't want him spreading it about. I must have hit the right note when I said, 'It's a lovely day. Shall we sit in the garden?'

He perked up, suddenly seeming almost cheerful, and ready to carry a tray. In the kitchen, we decided on dandelion and burdock.

'I haven't drunk this for years,' he said as I poured two glasses. His brief sparkle of glee lasted until he placed the tray on the garden table, which is made from the trunk of a tree that had to be felled. I pigeonholed him as one of those people who can be happy and sad at the same time, a state I regard as more common than people might think.

Our back garden borders Batswing Wood. I call it that because when we came to look at the house I found a leaf in the shape of a bat's wing. I pressed that leaf in a dictionary and see it whenever I look up a word.

Mr Whitaker squeezed himself on one end of the garden

bench. When I sat on the chair, he spread himself out, putting an arm across the back of the bench, as if measuring or claiming it.

We did one of those ease-yourself-in chats, talking about how much faster it was to travel by train. Through the kitchen window, I could see Mrs Sugden practising her interrogation techniques on the chauffeur. I hoped she was getting somewhere because Mr Whitaker seemed happy to sit watching a butterfly land on the buddleia and bees from our neighbour's hive make free with the lavender.

Eventually, I asked, 'How is Pamela?'

He shook his head. 'Devastated.'

'It was a stupid question.'

'Not at all. You've reminded me to say thank you from my wife and me, for bringing Pamela home.'

'I did what anyone would have done.'

His sup of dandelion and burdock went down the wrong way. He choked, coughed, took another sip and blinked himself back into shape to talk about Pamela. 'Since the tears and her one-sided shouting match, Pamela's not speaking to us. She's packed a bag and left.'

'Why does she blame you?'

Whitaker shrugged. 'We're nearest. We opposed the attachment to Ronnie, she says. She seems to think that if we hadn't been against him, he would have been in a different place that day, doing something else.'

Perhaps she was right, I thought, but said nothing. If he had come for consolation, he was with the wrong person. Mills are dangerous workplaces. There would be repercussions from Ronnie Creswell's death. The police would investigate. Factory inspectors would be informed. The Creswells might make a claim against Salts Mill. I was surprised Mr Whitaker had time to sit in a garden.

He looked about, and across to the wood. 'I like your garden. Ours in Bingley is a manageable size, one man for the upkeep. At Milner Field, we have a regiment, and enough garden huts to accommodate a small army. The mansion has more rooms than I've counted, and one person living there.'

On Saturday I had taken against Mr Whitaker, on Pamela's behalf. Now I decided to give him the benefit of the doubt. There seemed to be a desperate edge to this need of his to go all around the houses rather than come to the point, if he had a point for being here.

'Who lives in the mansion?'

'The estate manager, Aldous Garner. He occupies one wing, although now his tenure will be coming to an end I believe he often stays elsewhere. He oversees the dry rot, peeling paper and falling plaster.'

'Don't let the auctioneer hear you.'

'You're right. I'm being indiscreet. I must go on hoping there's someone out there who will fall in love with the place. A person of means with more money than sense and an inattentive guardian angel.' He bit his lip. 'Where was Ronnie's guardian angel on Saturday?'

A silence held between Mr Whitaker and me. The breeze dropped. A quiet magpie ambled in a circle and then strutted towards the hedge. Every note from the birds in the wood sounded bright and clear. It was not an uncomfortable silence but I began to think he had come on a whim, or to escape whatever was going on in Saltaire.

'Mr Whitaker, am I right in thinking you are here because there is something you want to tell me, or ask me?'

He nodded. 'I admit that there is something I want to put to you, Mrs Shackleton.' He looked at me closely, as if trying to guess how I might answer. 'Losing Ronnie has knocked the stuffing out of me. I'd better say how I know of you. It's through Hector Gawthorpe of Braithwaite's Mill.'

Hector Gawthorpe was the endearingly gauche young man who married Tabitha Braithwaite, a friend from my VAD days.

I deliberately kept quiet. Let Mr Whitaker tell me what he needed to say.

'You'll know Mrs Hector Gawthorpe as Tabitha Braithwaite, daughter of Braithwaite's Mill in Bridgestead.'

'Yes, of course.'

Tabitha had engaged me to find her missing father. Mill owner Joshua Braithwaite did well out of the war, and then disappeared.

'Hector Gawthorpe is a regular at the Wool Exchange. He pinned your business card on the noticeboard.'

I groaned. 'When?'

'Oh, years ago, shortly after he married Tabitha.'

Whitaker gave a rueful smile. 'I thought it out of place to pin a lady's name and details on that board. I took it down, but put it in my wallet, just in case. Hector saw me take it down. He said that he admired you. He thought had it not been for you, Tabitha would have gone on putting off their wedding.'

Lovely, kind Tabitha. We once worked on the same ward, during the war.

'And did you give my card to Ronnie Creswell?'

'No. I don't know how he came to know about you.'

'You kept my card a long time. Why remember it now?'

'Because I need help. When you drove Pamela home and

80

she told me your name, your card came to mind. The police are investigating Ronnie's death. I'm more cut up than I can say. I didn't let on to Pamela because it would have been premature, but Ronnie reminded me of myself when I was his age. We have no son. I harboured hopes that Ronnie might join the business. I'd already talked to him about setting up a separate company to take over maintenance of the housing stock in the village.' He came to a sudden halt, leaned forward and cupped his chin in his hands.

I prompted. 'You thought highly of him.'

He nodded. 'I was waiting to see how Ronnie shaped up. Now the rug's been pulled from under me. Things are falling apart in our corner of Worstedopolis. All mills are going through difficulties, but we are rocked to the core by Ronnie's death.' He paused. 'Why did Ronnie ask to see you?'

'I wish I knew. He said he had something important that I should know, something about the past.'

'And you have no connection with him?'

'Not that I'm aware of. Did he always live in Saltaire?'

'Yes. He's Saltaire born and bred. Odd, isn't it? Sixty years ago the village didn't exist. Now we've three generations who've never known anything else.'

'Why would Ronnie ask to meet me on a Saturday evening? It's an odd time to make an appointment.'

'We're back on a six-day week at present. It's feast or famine. On Sunday, Ronnie was set to play a cricket match in Roberts Park.'

I felt sure that Whitaker did not know such details about all his workers' timetables. He still had not come to the point about why he had come to see me.

He snatched the unspoken question from me, saying,

'You're wondering why I'm really here, though it is to say thank you.'

'I'm sure you'll tell me why you're here.' I felt my stomach churn. Part of me did not want to know. He should leave the matter to the police and the coroner's inquest, and rely on his wife and colleagues, not come to a stranger.

Images of the Creswells came into my mind's eye like moving snapshots: Mrs Creswell, the confident woman who opened the door of the Lodge, crumpling when David Fairburn broke the shocking news; little Nancy, puzzled and pale; and the silent Mr Creswell, his narrow shoulders stiff as a coat hanger, his mouth glued so tight shut that his few words shot from his dry lips with the hardness of a bullet.

Whitaker sighed. 'Overnight, we've become a different place, different people. I don't know where to turn.'

Any response would be inadequate. I heard myself say, 'I'm so very sorry.'

He nodded an acknowledgement. 'Everyone in Saltaire knows everyone else. You can walk around the village for half an hour and not see a stranger. Even the walkers cutting up to the moors are familiar faces. It's as if a blanket of sorrow suddenly wrapped itself around the factory and the streets. People look at each other differently. I saw it in church yesterday, and during the silence we held in the park when the cricket match would have started.'

'You have a village in mourning.'

'If you'd known Ronnie, you would have appreciated his qualities. If I'd pushed on more quickly with the maintenance company plan so that he had his name on a company board above a building, Josie – my wife – would have been able to

82

say to her family and friends that he had a business. She could have kept face.'

'Did you tell Josie your plan?'

'No. I wanted to be absolutely sure. Also, it seemed too soon. I didn't even tell Pamela. I thought it best not to be in a rush, to keep my own counsel. Now I'm thinking that if I had said what was in my mind, things might have been different. Pamela wouldn't have fled to her grandmother and be refusing to speak to us, at least.'

Ah, that's it, I thought. He won't show weakness at home. He puts on a brave face in the boardroom. He thought of me because I was there on Saturday, saw and heard the worst. He has decided to rely on my discretion.

'I have no appointments today, Mr Whitaker. You can talk to me. If you think we can help, tell me how.'

'I don't know where to start.' He looked utterly miserable. 'I don't trust anyone. I don't trust myself.'

'You trust me or you wouldn't be here.' I walked across to the back gate that opens onto the wood. 'Take a turn around the wood. Listen to the birds.' I snapped off a sprig of rosemary and handed it to him. 'Take a sniff and take your time.'

He took it, sniffed, and smiled. 'Are you a herbalist as well?'

'No, but my housekeeper-cum-assistant knows her plants.'

He had the wood to himself. Often the local children play there. Today they must have gone further afield.

I watched him begin a circle of the wood. Batswing Wood is compact, like a little bit of long ago left behind when the houses were built. Whitaker finished his first circle. It was ten minutes before he came back to the bench, with something to say, but not quite ready to spit it out.

We sat down again. 'Think of it as one, two, three,' I said. 'What comes first?'

He hooked one forefinger into the other to count on his fingers. 'One, Pamela has left home, won't speak to us, has gone to her grandmother.'

'It's natural. That could be worse. Give her time.'

He hooked his middle finger. 'The police questioned our maintenance manager David Fairburn on Saturday. As you'll know, he found Ronnie. They asked David not to leave the village. He has been told to report to Shipley police station this evening at seven. How he'll work today with that hanging over him I don't know. If they have suspicions of foul play, I want them to find the right man, and I can't believe that man is David.'

'Next,' I said. I could see that he was taken aback that I made no comment, but I wanted the full picture.

He hooked his third finger. 'You'll know that Ronnie's mother was our housekeeper. Unsurprisingly, she has left the Lodge. My wife advises me to bring in an outsider who will be discreet, so that there will be no tittle-tattle about Milner Field being an unlucky house. Is there anyone you can recommend? This isn't something I want to burden the estate manager with.'

'Because?'

He hesitated. 'Because, to be honest, he is going through the motions. I don't blame him. His job will come to a natural end when the mansion is sold. He worked with Ronnie on a plan for a separate company for the housing stock, giving him pointers and some ideas, but it was Ronnie who did most of the work. Garner has other plans. I believe he has another job lined up and that he is spending part of his time away from Milner Field.'

'Your estate manager must have been upset by the burglary on the night of the fancy-dress ball?'

'How do you know about that?'

'When I knew that Ronnie wanted to see me, I made enquiries about Milner Field.'

'Are you always so thorough, Mrs Shackleton?'

'Yes. Regarding a housekeeper, the only housekeeper I could recommend is my own. Now, Mr Whitaker, what is the last thing, the thing you are holding back because it seems too difficult to say and you hate to think about it?'

He leaned forward. 'What have you heard?'

'Only what you've just told me.'

I knew whatever he had to say next would be the longest item.

He did not hook any fingers this time, but said glumly, 'We're on a six-day week because we're completing a contract for Montague Burton.'

'That's good, isn't it? What is the difficulty?'

'We've worked with Burton's for years but now there's the possibility they are not going to renew our contract. I suspect someone is about to undercut us. The only way to do that would be through dirty tricks, finding out confidential information about our quotation and specifications.'

'Industrial espionage?'

'Yes.'

'Do you think there might be a link between these dirty tricks and Ronnie's death?'

'I hope to God that's not the case. I feel sure Ronnie would have come to me if he got wind of anything underhand, and so that horrible thought has crossed my mind.'

'Have you told the police?'

'No. It seems too far-fetched.'

'Tell the police. There may be no connection, but tell them.'

'But if there is a connection, would the police find it?'

'Are you asking for professional assistance?'

'Yes.'

I was able to reassure him. 'All this seems overwhelming to you, but it is not. Everything is manageable. My colleague Mr Sykes has just completed an assignment. He could investigate any industrial espionage. Relevant findings would be reported to you and to the police if appropriate. My housekeeper Mrs Sugden is very good at her job, gets on with people and is a good organiser. She doesn't suffer fools gladly and she would have the mansion as good as it could be.'

'So you would be able to take this on?'

'It looks possible,' I said, confident that Mrs Sugden could be persuaded that we should engage a professional decorator and knowing that Sykes was keen to start work again.

Mr Whitaker's relief was palpable. 'And what about David Fairburn?' he asked. 'It could be difficult for me if it's known I back David, when he is being questioned by police about Ronnie's death.'

'Well yes, he would be questioned. If you believe David Fairburn needs representation, I highly recommend a solicitor, Mr Cohen. If he is available to be at Shipley police station this evening when David is interviewed, it would be fortunate for David. You can speak to Mrs Sugden about our terms and conditions and about contacting Mr Cohen. His fees are somewhat higher than ours.'

He gave a sigh of relief. 'You make it sound so simple.'

'Good, because it can be.'

'And will you come to Milner Field?'

'You don't need me on the premises. Mr Sykes and Mrs Sugden, if they say yes, will do an admirable job. They'll talk to me. We're each other's sounding boards. You can be sure I'll keep an eye on things. That's factored into the fees Mrs Sugden will quote you.'

'Mrs Shackleton, you would be the linchpin. Everything you have said makes sense. If Mr Cohen is available, will you brief him for me so that I am at arm's length? You, Mr Sykes and Mrs Sugden could stay in the mansion, in the Tower or the Lodge, unless you are anxious about the curse.'

'I am not anxious.'

'Talking with you has given me confidence. Ronnie's death has knocked me off my perch. It doesn't make sense. The police were too quick to treat David Fairburn with suspicion. I have a horror of things going from bad to worse. I want to know the truth, whatever that is. Please say you'll come. It surely can't be for too long and engaging you and your colleagues could be the best investment that I make this year.'

This was turning into the most multi-faceted assignment we had ever been offered. Expecting Mrs Sugden to go to Milner Field alone might be beyond the call of duty for her. Concern about Rosie had frayed Sykes at the edges. Uncovering industrial espionage can be tricky. This was perhaps a three-handed job after all. Besides, my own curiosity, and my desire to try to fathom what Ronnie Creswell had wanted to tell me, drew me towards Saltaire and Milner Field.

I took a deep breath. 'Mr Whitaker, as I see it, here is what you are asking us to do. Mr Sykes is to look into the possibility that someone has access to confidential business information and has used this to bid against you for a contract you felt confident would continue. This means looking into who may have found a way to infiltrate the company. Linked to that is your fear that Ronnie Creswell's life was cut short because he found out something that he would have passed on to you had he lived.'

Whitaker looked utterly miserable and downcast. 'That's about the size of it.'

'You must tell the police your suspicions, give them the full picture.'

'I will.'

'Assuming someone is spying on Salts, you want Mr Sykes to find out who, why and how, and put a stop to it.'

He nodded. 'If he can.'

'You and he will need a story to explain why Mr Sykes is at the mill. To avoid suspicion, you should spread the word that he was engaged before Ronnie's death.'

'That won't be hard. There could be half a dozen reasons for bringing a man in on a temporary contract.'

'You have viewers coming to see Milner Field prior to the auction. You want it to be seen at its best.'

He nodded. 'Mrs Creswell had cleaners working with her. My secretary says they will stay on if someone takes charge.'

'There must be someone local who could take over?'

'I no longer know who I can trust.'

'I will talk to Mr Sykes and Mrs Sugden. Now, on behalf of your employee David Fairburn, do you want me to enquire whether Mr Cohen could be present when the police interview him?'

'Yes. And I want you to be at Milner Field too, Mrs Shackleton. Find out the truth of what is going on, and the truth about Ronnie's death. He was good at his job, and too careful to have had an accident.'

He was hesitating, again. There was something else. 'You are thinking about Pamela?'

'You read minds. I believe she would see you, talk to you, as the person who brought her home.' He took a small note-book from his pocket and jotted down an address.

'I should like to see her, but I won't be a go-between.'

'I wouldn't expect that, but if you do see Pamela, would you be so good as to call and tell my wife? Josie is feeling set adrift by everything that's happened. Oh, and thank you for suggesting a solicitor for David Fairburn.'

I stood. 'Let's go inside and draft a formal arrangement.'

TWELVE

I briefed Mr Cohen over the telephone. He was somewhat handicapped, having broken his arm slipping on the squash court. This gave me a legitimate reason to be in the interview room with him, to act as amanuensis.

He had one more question.

'On Saturday, what was your impression of David Fairburn when he burst in on Mrs Creswell to tell her that her son was dead?'

I had seen David Fairburn so briefly at Milner Field. 'My impression of him was of someone swelled by shock or panic. If he were a balloon, he would have burst. He was out of breath. He blurted out the news quickly, as if he couldn't believe it.'

'Fairburn wanted to tell the lad's mother before anyone else did?'

'Yes, that was my impression.'

'Or get his story in first.'

'I wouldn't say that.'

'Anything else?'

I thought for a moment. 'It was as if he felt culpable, which, given he was the older of the two, would make sense. Ronnie started as David's apprentice. He may have felt responsible for him, and for not being there at the time of the accident.'

Even as I spoke, I realised there could be other explanations for that air of culpability.

In a cold, whitewashed room with barred window, we took our seats at a square table. Heavy footsteps in the corridor came close, and then continued. Cohen looked at his watch.

He nudged my foot with his. 'If I do that, be particularly alert.'

This annoyed me. 'Do you think I'm going to nod off?'

'I mean you to stare particularly hard at whoever spoke last.'

I hoped he was having me on. Staring at a person while writing was not a skill I had ever practised. 'And if I nudge your foot, it means slow down. I don't want to have to scribble at high speed.'

The bold-faced clock on the interview-room wall was one of those that lets you know when it reaches the quarter-hour, not by a chime but by a noisy click-tick.

Several more minutes passed before the door opened. A tall young officer, looking slightly awkward, his hand on David Fairburn's arm in what appeared to be an almost affectionate manner, nudged David towards the table. He introduced himself as Constable Harrison. David Fairburn looked pale and subdued.

The constable was younger than David. He addressed our client in a friendly voice. 'Mr Fairburn, sit on the opposite side to your solicitor.'

The constable's tone encouraged me. If he had picked up any hint of guilt, he may have let the 'mister' slide and used only David's surname.

Mr Cohen introduced himself and said, 'Mrs Shackleton is here to take notes because I can't.'

'Hello, Mr Fairburn,' I said, and then gave my full attention to the blank legal pad.

David wore a good suit – his wedding suit, I guessed. He touched his well-ironed shirt cuff.

His wife had ironed the shirt. She wanted her husband to be presentable. She told him to let his cuffs show. I suddenly had the absurd thought that he would have worn a buttonhole at his wedding. What season was that, what flower, a daffodil, a carnation or a rose?

To Mr Cohen, Constable Harrison said, 'Sergeant Balcon will be joining you later, Mr Cohen; about fifteen minutes.'

Mr Cohen gave a nod of acknowledgement. I noticed that he extended the fingers of his right hand that protruded from the sling, and then closed his fingers, forming a fist. This could have been because he needed to stretch his cramped hand. Yet something in the way Cohen shifted his position slightly and, unseen except by me, repeated the action and made a fist, alerted me that he may be preparing himself for a sparring match.

What had he picked up that I had missed? Mr Whitaker had said that David Fairburn was here by appointment, giving the impression that he was here as a witness, nothing more.

Cohen cast a kindly avuncular look at the young constable. In the tone of voice that might just as well be saying, *Here's a thrupenny bit. Go buy a poke of sweeties*, he said, 'You may leave me with my client now, Officer.'

The constable hesitated slightly before standing and taking himself back into the corridor.

Mr Cohen began his questioning with the confidence of a man who has spent hours boning up on Saturday's tragic incident.

Within a few moments, we knew that at age fourteen Ronnie Creswell was apprenticed to David Fairburn, who was then twenty-five years old. David was now thirty-three years old, married with two children, and sharing a house with his parents. His father still worked in the mill and his mother in the canteen. He had three sisters; the youngest, Dorrie, still lived at home. The Fairburns and the Creswells were friends. They went to the same chapel.

I took notes as if a life depended on it, because that may be the case.

According to David, he and Ronnie had got on well from the start. Ronnie was bright and willing, had learned a lot from helping his dad in the gardens at Milner Field. Without being taught, he knew how the factory boilers worked because they were larger versions of those that heated Milner Field's hothouses.

After his initial enthusiasm, Ronnie was less keen to work on the mill machinery. Over time the two of them worked together less, with Ronnie working on the fabric of the buildings. They shared responsibility for the reservoir, however, undertaking regular inspections and maintenance between engineer's visits. An engineer inspection had taken place last week.

'Describe this reservoir for me,' Cohen asked.

'The tanks hold five hundred thousand gallons of rainwater that feeds the boilers. On top of the warehouses, there's a smaller tank, holding seventy thousand gallons, drawn from the river in case of fire. We check that, too.'

David braced himself to give yet one more account of finding Ronnie's body, and raising the alarm. He had spotted bruising and a cut to Ronnie's cheek and jaw. The police had tried to make something of this, David told us. They had made inquiries and found out about a falling-out between David and Ronnie when the two men had stepped outside on a Friday night when they were at a dance.

I took it that 'stepped outside' meant that there was fisticuffs, but when Mr Cohen pressed him David said, 'You can't buy beer in Saltaire. We went outside to meet a pal who was bringing us a couple of beers to take round the back.'

My handwriting grew in size and swirl as I wrote faster to keep up. I was about to raise my hand for a pause when Mr Cohen said, 'Tell me why and how you and Ronnie came to blows.'

David Fairburn remained silent. I looked up from my note-taking and gave David a hard stare. He needed to be straight with his solicitor if he wanted to walk free. What was he keeping quiet about?

David clamped his jaw. His breathing became heavy. At least he had not given an outright refusal.

Mr Cohen said, 'You were friends with Ronnie for a long time. Did you exchange blows on the day he died?'

'No!'

'Did you play any part in his death?'

'No! We were friends.'

'Friends fall out. What did you quarrel about at the dance?'

'I'd rather not say.'

'Don't you think your old friend would want you to tell

something, however personal or embarrassing it may seem to you, for the sake of arriving at the truth?'

'It's not just concerning me and Ronnie.'

'I didn't suppose for a moment that it would be. I can't put names in your mouth. Don't waste precious time, Mr Fairburn. Chivalry is admirable, but do not leave some poor female with the blight on her life that you saved her reputation at the cost of your life.'

David looked across the table, his eyes wide, his hands shaking. 'It's private.'

'You must be straight with me. Your friend's death may have been an accident. Is that what you think?'

'I don't know. Ronnie was always careful. It was a routine job. I can't think what could have happened.'

'Then we must consider possibilities, including another person at the scene of the death.'

'Nobody would have harmed Ronnie. He was popular; everybody who met him liked him. He stuck up for his work-mates, was captain of the cricket team, on the up and up in his job. '

'That's three reasons he could have made enemies. Tell me what caused you to quarrel.'

'It wasn't even a quarrel.' David took a deep breath. 'We went dancing every Friday night, me and my wife and sister, and Ronnie, and others, friends of ours. Some of us had taken ballroom-dancing lessons. Ronnie and my sister Dorrie were the ones who turned out to be good at it. Pamela was a good dancer, too, according to Ronnie, but she never came. She couldn't.'

'Why not?'

'She and Ronnie played their cards close to their chests. It would have been the talk of the mill, the talk of the village, if it came out that they were—'

'That they were what? Mr Fairburn? Don't make this a guessing game.'

'They planned to marry, permission or not.'

The penny dropped: David Fairburn knew of Ronnie and Pamela's plans and kept their secret.

Cohen's sigh seemed designed to indicate the unimportance, the triviality, of David's admission. 'So Ronnie came because he liked dancing and because it threw gossips off the scent of his liaison with Pamela Whitaker?'

'I suppose so.'

'Who did Ronnie dance with?'

'With my sister, Dorrie, and my wife, and with any girl that was sitting out.'

'Did the quarrel that wasn't a quarrel concern your sister?'

David turned a shade of pink. 'My wife had them paired up, but it wasn't like that. They were friends, more like family. Our parents have been friends for years.'

'So you were close. What did Ronnie say about your sister that upset you?'

'We were on the bottom steps, waiting for our pal and the beer. Ronnie had already narked me by saying he thought Mr Whitaker might be giving him more responsibility and, if so, he still wanted us to go on working together. He was getting above himself, jumping to conclusions. He then said not to take this the wrong way and he meant no harm, but he'd noticed a change in Dorrie. She wasn't her usual self, and when they danced up close . . .' Ronnie stretched out his fingers on the table and looked at the back of his hands, and then he looked up. 'It was as if he'd hit me in the stomach because I knew what he was getting at. He'd no call to talk to me like that about my sister. He was saying Dorrie was in trouble. I punched him. I don't know why I did it. He punched me back, just a reaction. That was it. I was angry.'

'So you were on bad terms?'

'No. He said he was sorry. He hadn't meant to interfere, and probably he was wrong. He thought because she was my sister, she was his sister as well.'

'Did you believe him?'

'Yes. I was mad because he thought he knew Dorrie better than we did.'

There was a tap on the door. A young constable announced in a hushed tone, 'The sergeant is on his way, sir. Five minutes.'

'Shut that door!' Cohen blared.

The door quickly closed.

'Am I in trouble?' David asked.

'Did you and Ronnie Creswell usually go down to the reservoir together?'

'We had a timetable, officially took it in turns, but if he was going down and I could be there I was, and the same for him. If there'd been a heavy rainfall, we'd join forces. That Saturday, Ronnie was working on one of the houses at the top of Victoria Road. He sometimes lost track of time.'

'But he hadn't forgotten?'

David hung his head. 'No. I saw from the docket that he'd signed for going down there, but not that he'd come out. The door was unlocked, which it should never be.'

'Who else had access to the keys?' Cohen asked.

'Me, Ronnie and the security officer. We signed out the keys from security.'

'Has anyone else been in that area during the past week or two?'

'Yes. The Water Board inspector and his apprentice.'

'Who else?'

'No one that I know of. Oh, security, I suppose.'

'And who is the father of your sister's baby-to-be?'

'She won't say. My wife says leave her for now.'

'Why was Ronnie the first to know about your sister's condition?'

David shrugged. 'My wife might have known. If she did, she didn't tell me. I suppose it was because Ronnie has always known Dorrie, and they danced together. They've been dancing partners since we all took lessons. And before you ask, there's nothing more to it than that.'

As he opened the door, the sergeant greeted Mr Cohen and sat beside him, opposite David. He nodded to me, giving me a hard but not unfriendly stare. Do they teach these things on police training courses? 'Today we do the hard stare in the morning, and the mild-mannered Tell-it-all-to-your-Uncle-Jack stare in the afternoon.'

The sergeant placed a manila folder on the table. 'We have some results from a preliminary post-mortem report.' He glanced at David. 'This gives us considerable information about what took place before Ronald Creswell's body entered the water.'

Cohen hadn't nudged my foot, but I stared at the inspector. So did David, but with no change in his puzzled expression. He had the detached air of an observer who did not believe that this could be happening, and to him.

'Perhaps you need to do a little more talking, Mr Fairburn,' the sergeant said. 'You admit to punching your unfortunate workmate on the jaw.'

'That was over a week ago,' David said.

'The deceased had a fresh bruise to his right jaw, marks on his throat and wounds to his left temple and cheek from a blunt instrument.' He looked across at David. 'Do you have anything to add to your previous statement?'

David ran his hands through his hair. He leaned forward ready to speak, to blurt something out. His mouth opened but he couldn't find words. He shook his head in a gesture of disbelief. 'If you're saying I hurt Ronnie, that's mad, that's crackers.'

Mr Cohen sighed. He ignored the sergeant and spoke to David. 'Mr Fairburn, I am here to represent you. You need say no more at present. Sergeant Balcon is doing his job and I will do mine.' He turned to the sergeant. 'My client has made no secret of the brief fisticuffs between himself and his old friend and workmate. They made up. He has also said that his workmate was already dead when my client went into the reservoir area. I require a copy of the post-mortem report. I request that my client now be allowed to return home to his family. He has cooperated with your inquiries.'

'That won't be possible, Mr Cohen.'

Mr Cohen scratched his ample right eyebrow. 'On what grounds are you detaining my client?'

'His fingerprints were at the scene of the crime and—'

'Of course his fingerprints are there. It's his place of work. Have you identified other sets of prints – the Water Board inspector and his apprentice, visitors to the mill, security staff?'

'Inquiries are ongoing.' The sergeant turned to David. 'David Fairburn, pending further inquiries, I am detaining you overnight for further questioning.'

Before Mr Cohen had time to intervene, David said, 'You can ask me questions until Domesday. It won't change anything. Just let's get it over with.'

Mr Cohen remained quiet for half a minute. 'My client has expressed a willingness to cooperate. My junior partner will attend during your morning interview, which must not be before eleven o'clock. Kindly arrange a telephone call to my office at nine a.m. to give the time of the interview.' He turned to David. 'It is noble of you to cooperate, Mr Fairburn. Do not answer further questions without legal representation. Is that understood?'

'Yes, sir.'

At the desk, Mr Cohen made formal requests for the documents he required.

Constable Harrison waited to speak to him. He looked a little uncomfortable. 'Sir, I'm to inform Mrs Fairburn that her husband is detained. Is there anything I might pass on from you?'

Mr Cohen took a business card from his top pocket. 'Please tell Mrs Fairburn that Simon Cohen Esquire will act for Mr Fairburn. Mrs Fairburn must feel free to telephone my office during business hours.'

We walked to our respective cars. Mr Cohen's driver opened the door, helped the solicitor into an astrakhan coat with a fur collar, and buttoned him in.

Cohen caught up with me as I was about to start my car. 'There's the question of timings, Mrs Shackleton. My client says that he recovered the body of his colleague just as the body was about to sink. We'll know from that timing how long Mr Creswell had been in the reservoir area, and at approximately what time the perpetrator left the area, leaving the door unlocked. If we can locate David Fairburn as being elsewhere during the period immediately prior to his entry and the sighting of the body, that could be of value.'

'Anything else? I'm going to Saltaire tomorrow.'

'See what you can find out from David's pregnant ballroom-dancing sister . . .'

'Dorrie.'

'That's the one.'

THIRTEEN

White light from the corridor shone through to the cell. The light penetrated David's eyelids. He felt cold enough to shiver, though he was no softie. The narrow plank was hard and uncomfortable. David turned his face to the wall. If this was what having a solicitor did, he would have been best without one. A solicitor must make you look guilty.

Tom Harrison had told him to hand over the laces from his shoes. He'd then taken David's suit, folding it carefully, saying, 'I'll put your suit on coat hangers.'

Hearing Tom say that, just for the seconds the words took to say, made David feel better, the words, the kindness behind them. But then he said to himself, What are you thinking? You're in a cell, like a criminal. It cheers you up that two-left-feet plodder Tom Harrison will hang up your good suit?

Much good it had done him, turning up respectably dressed. He ought to have worn work clothes. They would have been warmer. Beryl was good at ironing. She only once scorched something and that wasn't her fault. He couldn't remember what it was now, only that she was upset.

What would she be feeling now? He'd let her down. He'd let himself down and couldn't put his finger on how this had happened.

Who was it? he wanted to know. Who got Dorrie pregnant? Pity she never took a fancy to Tom, a police constable, job for life, comes with a pension. Tom would have taken good care of Dorrie. Perhaps it might still happen. He should have listened to Ronnie. He didn't ask Dorrie anything. He said nothing to Beryl, because he did not want to know, could not bear to think about what Ronnie had said. With Ronnie gone, David couldn't imagine Dorrie or Beryl or himself ever wanting to dance again.

David had been given one damp blanket. It smelled of someone else's sweat, stale tobacco and old booze. The picture that came to David with the smell was of a quiet, polite tramp screwing his courage, knocking on a door, asking for a cup of tea and a slice of bread.

Soon it would be Tides week. Factories closing down for the annual summer holiday, suitcases packed, kids excited. Why is it you can never find last year's bucket and spade? It was left behind, that's why. How could they have been so extravagant as to leave something behind? A holiday turned you dizzy and giddy, that's why. They would still go, for the sake of the kids.

Ronnie had thought about giving Blackpool a miss this year, but in the end, he and Dorrie didn't want to miss the dancing, having practised the tango for weeks. This might have been their last blast of glory. 'You haven't booked a bed,' David told Ronnie when he decided to come after all. 'You won't get in anywhere.'

Ronnie just laughed. 'I'll find somewhere.'

He would have, too, squeezed in by their obliging landlady. She would have made someone double up.

The picture came to David of Ronnie in the water, his dead eyes, and then of the seaside, Blackpool, the two of them rolling up their trousers, gingerly stepping into the water, pretending to be old men. Oohing and ahing about the cold and their rheumatics, until they had everyone laughing themselves stupid.

David began to see faces. He didn't know who they were or why they came floating into view, but they were the faces that brought sleep. He watched them appear, and disappear, and then he followed them into troubled dreams.

FOURTEEN

The night was cool, the car freezing, the visit to David Fairburn in Shipley police station dispiriting. I arrived home shivering, Mrs Sugden helped me off with my coat. 'I heard the car. I've made you a hot toddy and I thought it was about time to finish off what's left of the spice cake.'

'What's the occasion?'

'No occasion. I thought you'd be cold after that drive.'

'I am.'

'You'll soon warm up. Oh, and Jim's here, and not his usual self.'

'I heard that!' Sykes came into the kitchen from the dining room.

We sat at the table, sipping hot toddies and eating cake and cheese.

Sykes's news was no news. He had bought an early edition of the local paper and looked for Rosie's patient number. The listing said simply, 'Comfortable'.

Just to be sure that there had been no change that might have appeared in a later edition, he had driven back in the evening to the hospital gates, and seen the same announcement.

'Nothing's happening,' he said.

'Nothing happening is good,' I reassured him. 'Rosie has postcards and stamps. You'd hear from her in no time if she had anything to report. And the hospital have our telephone number.'

'Only for an emergency.'

'Then there is no emergency and she is in a lovely ward with people to talk to.'

'I know. And before you ask, I'm ready for another job if we have one. If I hang about the hospital gates waiting for the notices to change I'll be done for loitering, and I have strict instructions on a postcard from Rosie not to turn down work on her account.'

'We do have a job, as it happens – in Saltaire and at Milner Field.'

I told them of my conversation with Mr Whitaker. Sykes perked up at the thought of investigating industrial espionage. Mrs Sugden looked daunted at the thought of housekeeping in a mansion.

'You'll have plenty of help,' I said, hoping that would be true. What seemed more concerning to me was the death of the young man who'd written to me.

'The police are investigating Ronnie Creswell's death as murder. I wish I could find out what Ronnie was going to tell me, and whether that information cost him his life.'

'He must have confided in someone,' Mrs Sugden said.

'Possibly his girlfriend. I will ask her. She accused her parents, but I think that was because she believed they could have been married by now and Ronnie wouldn't have been working on the reservoir on that day, wouldn't have been a victim. Mr Whitaker thought highly of Ronnie. He wanted someone of his skill and abilities working with him.'

Mrs Sugden hesitated. 'Well, you know I was going to do some decorating, but if I can help at Milner Field, that seems more important.'

'Yes, I know you had plans, but I'm glad you'll be there. This is a short-term, once-in-a-lifetime job. You'll be housekeeper, organising and supervising the cleaning in the mansion ahead of the auction.'

'Suits me.'

Sykes said, 'We have a very good painter and decorator on our street. He needs the work. Let him get on with the job.'

Mrs Sugden thought for a moment. 'I suppose that makes sense.' She picked up her pen and opened her exercise book. 'Count me in.'

I turned to Sykes.

He asked, 'What do we know about my part of the job?'

'Mr Whitaker, Chairman of Salts board, has a long-standing contract with Montague Burton that appears to be in jeopardy from an unknown competitor.'

'Right up my street.' Sykes took the police-style notebook from his top inside pocket. 'There aren't many textile companies big enough to step up and compete with Salts.' He frowned. 'I'm not sure who would try. What details do we have about the dirty dealings?'

'Talk to Mr Whitaker. But briefly, Salts supply suit material to Burton's. Whitaker suspects someone who knows a little too much about Salts' business has put in a bid to undercut them.'

Sykes scoffed. 'Then they're crackers. No one matches Salts' quality and capability.'

'Then it could be a ploy to persuade Salts to drop their prices. See what you can find out.'

Sykes would take a personal interest in this investigation. Rosie had worked at Burton's, as had Irene for a short time. His tailor's son worked in the share office.

I told them about David Fairburn's interview, and that he was spending the night in a police cell pending further investigations into the drowning of his workmate and former apprentice. 'The preliminary post-mortem indicates foul play. The police are keeping David Fairburn in custody, either looking for a confession or digging for evidence to build a case.'

'Is that because Fairburn is guilty?' Sykes said. 'They think Fairburn was jealous of a younger man outdoing him?'

'Mr Whitaker wants me on hand to look for the truth, just in case the police don't find it.'

Sykes is a restless man. This restlessness often takes the form of driving a good distance to some hostelry where he will talk to people and keep up his vast swell of contacts. 'I'll keep my ear to the ground,' he said.

'What about the curse on Milner Field?' Mrs Sugden asked. 'Should we be worried?'

Sykes shook his head. 'News headline: "Bad Things Happen To People Who Live in Spectacular Mansion." There is not a family in Woodhouse that hasn't had similar, and worse, misfortunes. Nobody calls that a curse. They call it life.'

FIFTEEN

The city centre of Bradford is basin shaped. Roads leading off to the villages and countryside are a steep climb. I drove past the cathedral and followed tramlines to Bolton Road, a street of modest two-up two-down terraced houses whose front doors open directly onto the street. Pamela's Grandmother Whitaker had clearly preferred to stay put rather than move out to green pastures.

If this was Pamela's bolt-hole, I understood why she and Ronnie Creswell broke through social barriers. Pamela could move between the comfort of easy living and the humble origins of her father's background.

I had made a careful choice that morning about what to wear for Milner Field. The costume with zebra-striped lapels, padded shoulders, belted waist and calf-length skirt was not entirely suitable attire for Bolton Road. I parked outside the door and kept my car coat on.

As the door opened, I caught the smell of baking. The elderly woman who answered my knock had a round pleasant face and the same blue-grey eyes as her son. She wore a long black dress, black buckled shoes and a flowered cotton apron.

'Mrs Whitaker?'

'That's me.'

'My name is Kate Shackleton. I spoke to your son yesterday and arranged to call on Pamela.'

Although I spoke quietly, Mrs Whitaker glanced behind her at the steep staircase. She opened the door wider. 'You best come in. Arnold came by to tell me you'd call.'

I followed her inside. Suddenly, being here seemed not such a good idea. Here comes a busybody, dressed to the nines and out of her element. We stepped through another door into the room that was both kitchen and parlour. A fire burned brightly in the grate, lit to heat the oven.

'Sit down,' she ordered, as she moved towards the stairs. 'Take off your coat if you start to boil.'

The rocking chair must be Mrs Whitaker's. I sat on a straight-back chair at the table that was set with condiments and a doily-covered sugar basin.

'I'll tell Pamela you're here, but she won't want to see you. She wouldn't see her dad.'

'Say I'm the person who drove her home on Saturday.'

The back door stood open. From the yard came the sound of a ball bouncing rhythmically against the house wall. Absurdly, I felt a shudder of misgiving that my being here might bring ill luck. I should not so much as whisper the name Milner Field.

I listened to the crackle of the fire and looked about the room, at the French clock on the mantelpiece, sharing the space with a country cottage made of fine china and with a sunshine-yellow thatched roof. The glass-fronted cabinet held a fine tea service and a brown glass rose vase with stems of thorns.

The ball stopped bouncing. A child came to the door, peered at me briefly and disappeared.

When Mrs Whitaker came back, she announced, 'You're honoured. Pamela didn't say yes but she didn't say no. Left at the top of the stairs.'

It was a box room with space for a bed and a chest of drawers, and with storage space in the wall above the stairs.

Pamela wore a white nightgown with long sleeves, her arms resting on the red eiderdown. She was staring at the ceiling, but turned to glance at me, appearing pale and exhausted, her eyes red from crying. Distraught as she seemed, my outlandish zebra lapel stripes held her gaze for a few seconds.

'Hello, Miss Whitaker.'

'It's Pamela.' She sighed. 'I ought to thank you for driving me home, but if Dad sent you, you're wasting your time.'

'I wanted to come and see you.'

'Why?'

'To see how you are, and to say how sorry I am for your loss.'

She said nothing.

'There was a reason for me to be at Milner Field on Saturday. Ronnie sent for me.'

'Why did he send for you?'

'I don't know. Perhaps I never will know.'

'Well, I don't know either.' She closed her eyes.

'Although I never met him, I feel that I was meant to be there on Saturday.' Now I was sounding creepily scary, the harbinger of death. I ought to tell Pamela that her father was paying me, but not now.

111

She jumped the gun.

'If you've been sent to drive me back to Bingley, you're wasting your time.'

'I wanted to see you because we parted abruptly. I'm not reporting back to your father. I deliberately said I wouldn't. I certainly haven't been sent to fetch you.'

'Good, because I'm not going back. Dad locked my car away. According to him, I'm in no fit state to drive, as if that would stop me leaving. I walked here.'

'It's a fair walk here from Bingley, isn't it?'

'It's no distance. Ronnie and I walked miles, on the moors on a Sunday. That's what I'll do on my Sundays now. I know places where I can cry my eyes out and scream at the sky. No one will hear.'

'If you scream, you'll have two dozen Bradfordians appearing from hill and dale. Bradford's full of people who love to walk, people with Wordsworth in their legs.'

She gave the nearest thing to a smile and then she asked, 'Have you seen Nancy?'

'I haven't been back, but I will.'

'Give her a kiss from me.'

'And Mrs Creswell, do you have a message for her?'

'No. She sided with my mother. Ronnie and I weren't suited, according to her.'

'She'll realise she was wrong.'

'Why are you going back to Milner Field?'

'I'll be there with my housekeeper. She's taking over from Mrs Creswell who left the premises on Saturday.'

'I feel sorry for her, but I don't know what to say.'

'Tell me about Ronnie. Because I wish I'd met him. I wish I knew what he wanted to talk to me about.'

At first, I thought she would not speak.

'We met in the orangery every Saturday evening. I knew he had something on his mind but he didn't say what. When I asked him, he said that he would tell me but not now. Thinking about it, I wonder if he was trying to put me off coming on Saturday. He said we'd see each other at the cricket on Sunday.'

'But he didn't put you off?'

'No. I just came along as usual. We didn't have secrets, or at least I thought we didn't.'

Her words made me wonder whether there was something suspicious or dangerous going on and Ronnie wanted to protect Pamela from hearing about it. When Mr Whitaker came to see me, he had expressed the fear that Ronnie's life was cut short because he found out information that he would have passed on had he lived – information about industrial espionage.

I waited and then, to change the subject, asked, 'How did you and Ronnie get to know each other?'

'We lived in Bingley when the Roberts family lived in Milner Field. We visited. I was bored and went out in the garden. That's where I met Ronnie, helping his dad in the gardens. I helped as well, dirtied my dress, but it was good fun. We liked each other. Turned out we were the same age, born on the same day.' She blew her nose. 'We talked about running away to Gretna Green to be married, but that was my idea. Ronnie didn't want to be underhand about it. He said we must do things properly.'

It felt too soon for Pamela to know that Ronnie's death was no accident. Yet she would find out. Such news should not fall bombshell after bombshell.

113

'Have the police been to see you?'

'An inspector came, with a woman constable. I couldn't talk to them. They went away again.'

'There's something your dad would have told you if you'd let him.'

She straightened up. 'What? What is it?'

'When you see your parents, or talk to the police, there's something they'll tell you. The preliminary post-mortem on Ronnie indicates that his death may not have been an accident.'

She leaned back against the bolster. 'What do you mean?'

'Someone else may have been there. The police are questioning David Fairburn.'

She let out a yell of rage. 'No! Not David. Never him.' She shook her head. 'It's them,' she said. 'They didn't want us to marry.'

'Who?'

'Mother, Dad, Mother's family. I've come into money from my grandmother, Mother's mother. That's what that weasel Kevin Foxcroft was after – oh, and me, of course, he always had an eye for me.'

The footsteps on the stairs were surprisingly quick for a woman of Mrs Whitaker's age. She and her annoyance filled the doorway, a little girl clinging to her skirt. 'What are you yelling about? I've had her next door waiting for a chance to be nosy. She's asking me who's committing blue murder.' Mrs Whitaker looked at me. 'What have you been saying?'

Pamela spoke quietly. 'She's been telling me the truth.' She turned to me.

'We know part of the truth,' I said.

Mrs Whitaker folded her arms. 'If truth comes with that kind of racket, leave it alone. I want peace and quiet.'

The little girl chipped in. 'And you want eggs and I'm off to the shops for you.'

Mrs Whitaker glared at Pamela. 'Time for you to frame yourself and come downstairs.'

Setting an example, Mrs Whitaker went back down the stairs. The child followed, saying, 'If there's a penny left, can I—'

I handed Pamela her dressing gown.

She nodded defeat and slid out of bed. 'Will you be coming back, Mrs Shackleton?'

'Do you want me to come back?'

'You're the only one who's been straight with me.'

'Give your parents a chance.' I made a move to go. 'You can reach me at Milner Field. And I'm so sorry for your loss.'

Downstairs, Pamela's grandmother was covering a pie on a plate with a white teacloth. She placed it in a wooden box, the kind greengrocers use.

'Arnold told me you're moving into the mansion.'

'Yes.'

'It's the millstone around my lad's neck.'

'I hope we'll make it look its best for the sale.'

'Are you off to Saltaire now?'

'I am.'

'Will you do something for me?'

'You want me to take something?'

'Give this pie to Mrs Creswell, with my condolences.'

'Of course.' Mrs Creswell would be overwhelmed with offerings. People would rally round. They would give and do what they could, filling bellies when the bereaved were not up to fending for themselves. Empty spaces in hearts would be left to kind words and time.

Mrs Whitaker came out with me to the car. She watched as I lodged her pie safely. She lived close to Saltaire and must have heard the stories about the deaths of the shepherdess from the Middle Ages and the little boy who died when the mansion was being built. She would have been a contemporary of that little boy.

'Mrs Whitaker, I have an interest in the history of Saltaire and the surrounding area. Who would know about local stories?'

Mrs Whitaker gave me a shrewd look. 'The schoolteacher. The Creswell's Uncle Nick also knows a thing or two about the place. He was living on the land as a boy when the mansion went up.'

LONG AGO

Nick thought he could breathe again. People saw he was upset about his cousin Billy Creswell's death. They asked him, 'Weren't you two together that day?' 'Only for a short time,' Nick told them, which was true.

It was known that Nick was often on his own, by the canal. Sometimes a bargeman would let a boy take a ride and walk back, especially if that boy said he wanted to be a bargeman. They might show him how to do things and tell a few stories, or just let a person come along for the ride.

But no bargeman waved back to him on the day he saw Miss Mason fall. It was not hard for him to pretend that Billy was never there, because Nick wished he hadn't been. Miss Mason did not take part in the questioning of children after Billy was found. That was left to the headmaster and a policeman.

Nick had nothing to tell. When asked about that day, he could truthfully say that he walked by the canal and that he helped Miss Mason as she walked back to her cottage after her fall. Later he went along to the weir and paddled with some of the others. That was true. It was just the bit about taking Billy into Milner Field that he left out.

People stopped asking. There was a service for Billy, and a coffin that Nick thought looked very small. He hoped Billy would not be too cramped. That side of the Creswell family left, without saying where they were going.

Miss Mason no longer smiled when she took the register. Mostly, she was sad. When they did exercises in the yard, she did not jolly them along in the same way or join in. She set them off and no longer seemed to care how much heave-ho they put into it.

And then one day, Miss Mason asked Nick and another boy to stay behind and sharpen pencils. She let the other boy go home first.

Then she said to Nick, 'A teacher can be the centre of much attention. The man next door does my garden. When he saw me digging, he came to help. The school thinks I have changed too much since Billy's death and should not live alone. A school clerk has come to share the cottage. She is into everything when I am not there.' Miss Mason's eyes were too mad and bright when she said, 'I am watched, watched, watched.'

Nick did not know what to say. He said nothing.

She said, 'I want you to dig a hole where something can be buried. Do you know a place where no one will look?'

'Yes.' Nick knew only one place for burying.

'Where is it?'

'At the entrance to Milner Field, by the old gates that came from the manor house.'

'That doesn't sound a good place. People come and go.'

'People who come and go don't stop to look.' He knew this

because he had watched, still worrying because his grandmother had told him to bury the bone near where he found it. He said, 'I buried the shepherdess's bone there a long time ago, before my grandma died.'

Miss Mason did not seem very interested in what was buried before. 'When shall I come?'

'The builders don't work on Sunday. Come at eight o'clock. The watchman goes inside to have his breakfast by the stove.'

'I shall come on my way to church. Afterwards, I will take you to church with me.'

'I don't go to your church, and my hands will be dirty.'

'I'll bring a damp cloth. Polish your shoes.'

'I don't have shoes.'

'Your clogs, then.'

Nick prepared the ground, using a workman's shovel from the hut. He dug carefully so as not to damage the bone and this time he dug deeper. He had with him two daffodil bulbs borrowed from the park. He said to the bone, 'You will have something like a baby for company.' The day was so quiet he could hear the silence hum.

Miss Mason came along in her Sunday clothes carrying a basket. She took a white cloth from the basket. Under that cloth was a leather bag with a white satin ribbon on the handle, tied in a bow.

It would have been odd for the teacher to carry an empty basket into church. Miss Mason placed her basket out of sight behind the bilberry bush and would collect it on her way back.

For Whitsuntide, Miss Mason bought Nick a pair of boots and two pairs of socks.

SIXTEEN

I arrived in Saltaire as Nancy was coming out of the tall house on Victoria Road. She held the hand of an elderly man, tall, slightly stooped and with a walking stick. Both turned to look at the car as I drew up.

I climbed out of the car. 'Hello, Nancy!'

Nancy beamed. She tugged the old man's hand, saying, 'Uncle Nick, it's her. The lady who drove me home.'

I introduced myself.

He scratched his cheek and peered at me. 'Pleased to meet you.'

I took the pie from the car and gave it to Nancy. 'Pamela's grandmother baked a pie for your mother. She sends her condolences.'

Nancy took the pie. 'Thank you. I won't be a minute, Uncle Nick.'

I blew her a kiss. 'Pamela sent you a kiss.'

Nancy blew a kiss into the air. 'That's to go all the way to Shipley.'

As Nancy disappeared with the pie, I turned to Uncle Nick. 'I was very sorry to hear about Ronnie's death. Such a blow for your family.'

He nodded so slightly that I wondered if he had heard. He simply said, 'You're moving into Milner Field.'

'I'm to keep an eye on the place for Mr Whitaker. I would say that it's until Mrs Creswell comes back, but I don't believe she will.'

'She'd sooner starve.'

I was unsure how to respond to that. When he did not speak again, I asked, 'Is there anything in particular I should know about the history of the place? I believe you lived there before the mansion was built.'

'I'm saving my breath for walking.'

'May I give you a lift?'

'Not alongside the canal you can't, unless your motor drives on water.'

Nancy reappeared. Uncle Nick took her hand. He turned to me. 'If you're after hearing bits of old history, talk to Miss Lee, the teacher. The kids broke up. She's the infant school-teacher but I saw her going into the factory schools.'

Without another word, he set off walking down the hill.

Nancy hung back for a moment. 'He's in a funny mood today. It's his old teacher's ninetieth birthday. We're going to see her. There will be cake.'

At the factory school, a caretaker directed me to a classroom. A slender young woman, her fair hair scraped into a bun, was taking down a map from the wall.

I tapped on the open door. 'Miss Lee?'

She turned, looking friendly enough, but surprised.

'Sorry to disturb you. My name's Kate Shackleton. Might I have a word?'

'Have two. Come and sit down.' She scooped up drawing pins and dropped them in a box.

There were rows of pupils' desks, a teacher's desk and one long, low table. Miss Lee sat on one end and waved for me to sit on the other, saying, 'I teach infants and juniors, just here to help. You may want to speak to one of the other teachers if it's about the factory schools.'

'Oh, I'm not here about the schools. The Creswell's Uncle Nick told me you are the person to speak to about local history, particularly Milner Field in years gone by. I'll be moving in there with my housekeeper, to take care of the place, until the auction. I was there on Saturday when the family heard the bad news about Ronnie.'

She listened, and sighed. 'It's so sad, and I do hope Salts manage to sell the mansion. It's such a shame for it to stand empty. I went there once and thought of so many different uses for that building. You could put on concerts. It could be a residential college or an orphanage or a hotel.'

'You wouldn't be put off by stories of a curse?'

'Don't attribute this to me, but if I were either selling that place or resident in it, I would do things.'

'What things?'

'Clergymen; I would have all denominations go around in turns and send the demons packing. Better still, I would sell the place at a reasonable price to an order of nuns or monks who would cultivate the gardens, grow grapes and apples, make wine and cider and walk about saying their matins, bringing an entirely different atmosphere to the place. If something bad happened to The Holy Ones, they could then believe it would take time off their spell in purgatory.'

'You're Catholic.'

'I've said enough. If you breathe a word of this, I'll be out on my ear.'

'I wouldn't dream of it.'

'At the end of term, I go slightly mad. What is it you want?'

'Tell me the story of the curse.'

'There are several.'

'Oh.'

'But there's one in particular that rings true for me. It was told to me by the previous teacher and has been passed on over the years since the school opened and probably before that, when people were dotted about scraping a living where and when they could. There is also a written version, in a book in the library at Milner Field, printed in the early years of the last century. It's an old tale and difficult to date. It may be from medieval times, or perhaps during the harrowing of the north, or when John of Gaunt was said to have slain the last wild boar. It tells of a royal hunt and a king coming across a tearful young shepherdess who had been grazing her sheep on the moors. Supposedly she had lost a sheep down a well.'

'That sounds unlikely.'

'Totally. Reading between the lines, it's entirely obvious this royal personage did his worst to the poor girl and then dumped her down there. The story goes that the king dismounted to tell her not to worry about a lost sheep. The jovial royal personage, "soothed her". After that the foolish shepherdess fell down the well, so the story goes.'

'It's not much of a tale.'

'The story has been passed on in different ways at different times. You won't want to know what I think.'

'Tell me.'

We heard footsteps in the corridor. Miss Lee waited until the footsteps passed. 'It might shock you that I say this, but I think that like lots of stories the shepherdess tale has the grain of truth, wrapped in pastoral shades to make it as sugary as Little Bo Peep losing her sheep. I think the shepherdess was running away from the hunting party, hiding from them. She was caught and was what they used to call "ravished" by the royal personage and then thrown down the well and forgotten. I've read what I can, tried to piece the story together.'

'I can see why such a story would be passed down, as a warning, as a remembrance.' I thought of Mrs Sugden, and her dire warnings that I might meet a mad axeman in the wood. Had someone warned the young shepherdess against strangers, huntsmen and royal personages on white horses? 'And is the well still there, Miss Lee?' I asked.

'Yes, but not in use. It was the main source of water for the Elizabethan house that was demolished to make way for the present building. When the mansion was built, water from the well was diverted along with water from another spring.'

'So the curse is thought to come from the rape and murder of the shepherdess?'

'Yes, and because her bones cry out for Christian burial.'

I felt a slight chill. 'And do you think the very ground is cursed?'

'Sometimes yes, sometimes no. I regard myself as a rational human being. Other times, I think that the catalogue of misfortunes experienced by every family that has occupied Milner Field can have no other explanation. The curse is on the land, and the mansion is built on that land. Simple as ABC.'

She slid from the table. 'Sorry. You came to be told everything would be all right. I've shocked you.'

'I'm not easily shocked.'

What Miss Lee told me chimed with the story from Mr Duffield, and with Mrs Duffield's belief that the girl's mother cursed the place.

But Miss Lee had shocked me, not by the revelations of a story that may or may not be apocryphal, but because her account of the shepherdess tale had the ring of truth.

I thanked Miss Lee for her time. As I was about to step into the corridor, I turned back. 'And have you heard of another story: a child having an accident during the building of the place?'

She picked up a pile of books and bent to put them in a cupboard. 'Yes, a schoolboy. I don't know the details. It must still be within living memory, but only just. You could try talking to the old people in the almshouse, or to the Creswells' Uncle Nick.'

'Thank you.'

'But to be honest, I don't think you'll get much out of them. It's one of those incidents people seem to have erased from their memory.'

I would approach Uncle Nick again, when he might be in a more talkative mood. It intrigued me that the story of the boy, still in living memory, had not been repeated to Miss Lee. Yet the shepherdess's story, from centuries ago, had become a folk tale.

Leaving behind the smell of chalk and children, I stepped

out of the cool classroom into the sunshine of the schoolyard. As I did so, I saw a familiar motor. Sykes was parking his Jowett near the entrance to the mill. He had seen me, and in turning round for a moment he let me know that. That was the extent of our greeting. He was here for his meeting with Mr Whitaker to investigate industrial espionage and had assumed his guise of secret agent.

SEVENTEEN

In the high-ceilinged office, Mr Whitaker was seated with his back to the tall window which had a neat row of well-tended plants on the sill. He rose and came round the old oak desk that looked as if it belonged to the middle of the last century.

The two men shook hands. 'I'm glad to see you, Mr Sykes.'

'Glad to be here. What a fine building. Your founder was a remarkable man.'

'He was indeed; and following on from the Salt family, we have a lot to live up to.'

'From what I've seen, you're doing a grand job.'

Whitaker sighed. 'So far, that's true. Now we're at one of those turning points when I'm not sure what the next step will be.'

'Well, let's find that step and take it,' Sykes said, with an encouraging smile. He immediately thought he sounded like a motor salesman urging a timid customer to take a test drive.

Whitaker walked to the open door of the adjoining office. 'Come and meet my secretary. She's the only person I've confided in. I don't want to alarm the board, and given what's happened, I don't know who to trust.'

The secretary, a solid woman with neat hair and a crisp white blouse, looked up from her typing.

'Mrs Harrison, meet Mr Sykes.'

'How do you do, Mrs Harrison?' Sykes reached over the desk to shake her hand, noting the surprise on her face as he did so. There were more plants on the shelf alongside dictionaries, ring binders and trade journals.

'Pleased to meet you, Mr Sykes. If there is anything you need, or want to know, just tell me.'

'Thank you.'

She picked up the phone. 'I'll have a pot of tea sent up.'

Sykes followed Whitaker back into his office. They sat opposite each other at the desk. Sykes took out his notebook.

Whitaker produced a letter from the drawer of his desk. 'This was the bombshell.' He handed it to Sykes. 'It's from the chief buyer, inviting us to tender for the contract which was previously renewed automatically.'

Sykes read the letter. 'There's no hint that your bid won't be successful.'

'No, but simply to have that invitation, rather than renewing on the same terms, is a warning.'

'Did you speak to the buyer?'

'I put in a telephone call to the purchase manager. That's how I know we have someone up against us.' He sighed. 'He's ex-army, higher echelons, learned civil-service speak. There's no direct "You have a rival", but I understood the code. They're looking at the same quality but at a lower price. They can't beat our quality.'

'What makes you so sure?'

'I took a leaf from Sir James Roberts' book. He travelled, learned Russian in his search for the finest raw materials. I retraced his footsteps. Followed his practice of having raw materials finished and spun on the Continent and brought here through Hull, to hide the specific and the regional origins. Anyone who matched our combination of yarns must have inside information, but that's impossible.'

'Why impossible?'

'It's a trade secret. My board of directors understand the need for confidentiality. Only Mrs Harrison and I know the details of our suppliers and finishers. We make payments through a Swiss bank.'

'You trust your secretary, Mrs Harrison?'

'Absolutely. She worked here as a girl, came back after she was widowed.'

'Where do you keep your paperwork?'

'In a locked filing cabinet in my secretary's office, and some confidential papers in this safe.' He indicated a sturdy safe.

'Could whoever else is likely to tender for the contract have come up with similar yarns?'

'It's highly unlikely.'

'Would another manufacturer, a member of the Wool Exchange, be able to look at your yarns and make a guess at the source?'

'I've thought of that. This may seem idealistic, but I don't believe that would happen. There's a code of honour among members. We support each other through good times and bad.'

'But . . . ?'

'We have some very clever men in the industry. Your theory can't be ruled out.'

'Where do you store the yarn?'

'We use a combination of yarns. The yarn that gives our material its sheen is the key one. Come on, I'll show you.' He went to his secretary's door. 'I'm taking Mr Sykes to the top room.'

'The tea's on its way.'

'We'll be quick.'

Sykes followed Whitaker along the corridor. He noticed that the whole place smelled of lanolin. Over the decades, the smell from the wool had seeped into the fabric of the building. A large lift hiccupped its way to the top floor where Whitaker led Sykes into a long room whose windowed ceiling let in the light. Workers were examining fabric.

Whitaker walked Sykes the length of the room. As he did so, he nodded, smiled and greeted the workers. They responded warmly, in a way they didn't have to and that told Sykes here was a boss they had regard for.

At the far end of the room were entrances to other areas, an archway and some closed doors. Whitaker took out a key and unlocked a door. He flicked on a light switch. 'Here's where we keep the yarn now. Since the letter from Burton's, I've taken extra precautions, though if there has been industrial espionage I'm closing the stable door after the horse has bolted.'

The bales of yarn had been placed against the wall. They were carefully wrapped, fastened and sealed with a die-stamped coin.

'If it's an inside job, there would have been other ways of taking a sample than meddling with a bale,' Sykes said.

'That's true.' They left the room. Whitaker locked the door behind him. 'Anything else you want to see?'

'Not unless there's something you particularly want to show me.'

'Then let's go back to the office and have that cup of tea before it goes cold.'

It was a puzzle, Sykes decided, as they sat at the desk, a teapot and a plate of biscuits between them.

Whitaker did not hurry Sykes to come up with suggestions or ideas. He talked of Ronnie Creswell and the shock of his death. 'We're like one big family, or that's how I see it. And I had such high hopes for Ronnie. I told your Mrs Shackleton. I have no son. Ronnie was a little rough around the edges, but he had great promise. He was hard-working and ambitious.'

Sykes did not want to ask the question, but it was necessary. 'Ronnie was a maintenance man, with access to the whole building?'

'He was, but if you're thinking he had anything to do with undermining me and the company, you're wrong. I wouldn't have stood in his way if he and Pamela still felt the same about each other in another year or so. I thought my wife might come round to the idea by then.'

'Did you tell him that?'

'I let him know that I regarded him highly and that he had a future here. Saying something outright would have been awkward, with my wife being set against him.'

'Would Ronnie have come to you if he had suspicions about underhand dealings?'

'I'm sure he would. He could be a firebrand, wanting a shorter working day and a shorter week for the workforce, but I think he understood why that might take time when we have mills closing left, right and centre.'

'Is there any other company in the West Riding who could handle the volume of work that you do for Montague Burton?'

'No. It would have to be parcelled out to smaller companies, with the risk of patchy results.'

'So either it's a bluff or someone has stakes in several mills that could take over.'

'That's a possibility, though it would be a risky choice for Burton's. The impact on us would be huge. Titus Salt's idea of creating a village was visionary, but it makes us a company town. If the company suffers, everyone suffers.'

'Then you have a good case for keeping the contract and Burton's will know that. Let me put out some feelers. I have one or two contacts who may be helpful. Meanwhile, I suggest you look at your figures, shave a little off the price. Arrange to meet the purchasing manager. Since you are both good at understanding codes and he seems sympathetic towards you, don't lose heart. If, as you say, this offer to undercut you comes from a smaller mill, a company like Burton's won't take the risk.'

'I hope you're right, Mr Sykes. It's Jim, isn't it?'

'Yes.'

'Arnold. You know my trade secrets, we might as well be on first-name terms.'

'Talking of secrets, whoever is in on this has inside knowledge of your methods and your costings. How secure is your office?'

'Utterly. Locked filing cabinets, a safe in Mrs Harrison's office, a safe in the corner there. People don't wander in and out. Mrs Harrison wouldn't allow that. She is security conscious. Her son is a police officer. No one comes in without an appointment and no one is left alone in here.'

It was a puzzle, but Sykes would not otherwise be here. He spoke with more confidence than he felt. 'We'll tackle this.'

EIGHTEEN

Growing old increased the distance to anywhere and every-where. Nick could have hopped and skipped along this towpath once upon a time. Nancy did that now, skipping ahead of him, and then back. The thought struck him that he might not come this way again. It had turned into a long walk. All those years ago, the walk was short.

The whole school had said prayers when Billy Creswell's body was recovered. There had already been a boy drowned and the warning then was not to go in the canal or the river, especially if you could not swim. At that time, the boys on one day and the girls on another were taken on a bus to a public baths and lessons began. The swimming lessons lasted a year, and were then forgotten. This time the warning was not to go near Milner Field, where the building work was still going on.

No one was warned about the dangers of not going near Nick. Nick had killed Billy, and played his part in swelling the curse on the land and the mansion by burying the shep-herdess's bone too far from the well. Nick had put out a hand to stop his cousin Billy from falling to his death, and then he had let go. All this came to him again and again, as the years went by and as words poured from whoever happened to be standing in a pulpit.

Not that he meant to do harm, but things happened when you didn't mean them to.

Daffodils bloomed each spring, covering and emblazoning his secret. Nobody knew about the bone from the well. No one knew about Miss Mason's baby.

The one good thing he did, always, according to the season, was to drop flowers down the disused well, and sometimes a branch with blossoms.

Many times he wished he had passed on the set of spare keys to the mansion's owners, as the builders told him. It was too late. He began to think of them as the keys to hell, presented especially to him.

Nick's hearing had faded. His eyes wove their very own lace curtains. He began to dream. In the dream, the doctor who said he could cure Nick's eyes took out those eyes, dusted them and gave them to someone else. That someone else could see everything that Nick had ever seen, so that all his secrets were out, and not just his secrets. The dream took him to the Chapel of Golden Light. The congregation spoke their declarations, a condemnation of Nick. *Murderer*, they said. Miss Mason was there. In the dream, his teacher was young, her black hair shining.

As he watched Nancy skip along by the canal on the way to Miss Mason's birthday party, Nick felt the warmth of the sun on his face, sensing light and seeing shadows. Nancy came back to hold his hand. 'Can you see the barge?'

'The shape of it, the shadow.'

'We're nearly at Jane Hill; not far now.' Miss Mason was the only person Nancy knew who had chocolate biscuits. She kept them in a tin that had a picture of a boy in a sailor suit.

Today, Miss Mason had birthday cards on the mantelpiece. Nancy gave her flowers. Uncle Nick gave Miss Mason a cake, iced with her name. The baker had made it specially and would take no money. It was not every day that someone, and a teacher at that, reached the age of ninety.

After their birthday tea, Nancy went out to play two-ball against the cottage wall.

Nick and Miss Mason sat inside at the table by the window, looking out onto the canal. Would they ever talk about that day? Nick wondered. About the day she fell, about fetching her coat, about the blood and the little bundle in the towel. He would not bring it up. If she did, and she wouldn't, would he tell her the other thing, the thing that he had told no one? Would he tell her about Billy Creswell, and how long his scream lasted as he fell down the shaft?

'I'm taking medicine,' Miss Mason said, 'which I never did, except what I made myself.'

'Are you ill?'

She croaked a laugh. 'More than half my pupils are dead and gone. The few that are left wait their turn.'

'Like me.' Nick still saw in her what he always did. Perfection; well, near perfection. 'What ails you, Miss Mason?'

'Old age. The delay annoys me. I'm waiting for God to take me, if he will.'

'He'd be mad not to, miss.'

'That's probably blasphemy, Nick.'

'But it's the truth. Only you won't see me in heaven.'

'For what you did for me, I will,' she said softly.

She doesn't know, Nick thought. But yes, she does. If she had never guessed, never put two and two together sometime, over all these years, she would have spoken Billy's name to me just once at least. She knows I killed Billy to keep him quiet. Forever quiet.

'There is something I must ask you,' Miss Mason said.

The sound of the rubber balls bouncing against the wall stopped.

Nick and Miss Mason waited. Was Nancy coming in? They listened.

Nancy must have dropped a ball. The rhythm of the rubber balls changed. Now three balls bounced against the wall.

'She found the ball that was lost.' Miss Mason took the deepest breath she could.

This is it, Nick thought. She does not want to die not knowing what else happened on that fine long-ago Sunday when I brought her coat to her on the riverbank, when I brought a towel for swaddling a small creature covered in blood, when she leaned on my shoulder. I feel her hand there still. 'What is it, Miss Mason?'

He waited for her to say that she knew Billy was by the canal that day, and that the two of them went off together.

When she asked, would he tell her? She would ask, *Did he fall or was he pushed?*

She said none of those things. He decided that she never would, and that must be for the best. Teacher knows best.

She said, 'I have one last request, Nick. Tell me again where you buried my baby.'

He did not answer.

'Have you forgotten?' she asked.

'You know where. You were there, by the gates at the entrance to Milner Field.'

'Sometimes I think it was a dream. Come early one morning and take me there. I want to see.'

It was a long time since Nick chuckled. It took half a minute to stop and to make sure he did not cry, and then he started to cough. When he recovered, he said, 'It would be the half blind leading the frail. Would your legs carry you to the mansion?'

'I don't suppose they would.'

Nick watched a barge go by. If a bargeman on that long-ago Sunday had said, 'Hop on', what might his life have been? There was Sally, the weaver who gave him a look. He might have married.

'Do daffodils still grow there, by the gates?' Miss Mason asked.

'Yes.'

'Phil Danby, the undertaker, he was one of my pupils, long after you. I took him in when his parents died. I helped him find an apprenticeship.'

'You helped us all.'

'When I am dead, Phil will ensure that my baby comes with me to the grave. One evening soon, Phil will come to you and ask you to walk with him. You must take him to the gates and point out where the daffodils grow in spring, and then he will know what to do when the time comes. Don't speak to him of that day.'

'I never have spoken of it. I never will. But I will tell Phil Danby that there is another bone in that same place, the shepherdess's bone. I must tell him because one day her bones may be recovered from the well. She will want to be all in one piece for Judgement Day.'

'Don't speak of Judgement Day. Tell Nancy to come in. I'll cut the cake.'

NINETEEN

The gates to the Whitaker house in Bingley stood open. I parked near the front door, the same spot where I had let Pamela out of the car on Saturday.

A young maid, dressed for the part in black dress, white apron and white peak cap, opened the door.

'Is Mrs Whitaker at home?' I asked, giving her my card. 'I'm Mrs Shackleton.'

She looked me up and down. 'Come in. I'll tell her you're here.' She opened a door onto a drawing room. 'Go sit in there.'

The room was beautifully done out in William Morris wallpaper and with stylish furniture.

Moments later, Mrs Whitaker appeared, dressed in a sage-coloured afternoon dress and jacket. It was easy to see where Pamela Whitaker got her looks. Mrs Whitaker had high cheekbones, long eyelashes and pale blue eyes, a little bloodshot and with dark shadows. To give Mrs Whitaker her due, she looked like a perfectly normal, reasonably disgruntled woman. It must be a blow to have a decamping daughter and feel blamed for the death of that daughter's sweetheart, but she smiled and said hello.

'Hello, Mrs Whitaker, I'm Kate Shackleton. Your husband may have mentioned me. I'll be holding the fort at Milner Field with my housekeeper, Mrs Sugden.'

'Josephine Whitaker.' She took in my impressive outfit at a glance and offered her hand. 'Arnold said you would call. Do sit down, I've asked for tea so hope you'll have a cup.'

'Yes, I will, thank you. Just a flying visit. I'll be meeting Mrs Sugden's train.'

'It's a relief to me that you could come. I knew I was right to suggest an outsider.' I sat down. She took a bag from the sideboard. 'Everything you need is in here. Mrs Creswell's paperwork, names and addresses of cleaners, and a set of keys.' She sat on the opposite sofa. 'I'm hoping the cleaners will stay on. Given the short time to make the place ship-shape I've put out feelers among friends, just in case they are able to recommend additional staff.'

'That will be helpful. I'll be in touch again as soon as we know what's what. Shall I ring you directly?'

'Please do. Let's not stand on ceremony. I'm very glad you and your associates are able to bring Arnold some peace of mind. And thank you for bringing Pamela home on Saturday.'

'Anyone would have done the same. I called on her today.'

'How is she?'

'Still shocked and grieving. Sometimes grief sends us flying.'

There were photographs of Pamela on the mantelpiece, and photographs of a boy. Mr Whitaker had said he did not have a son. I wondered whether they had lost a child? 'May I look at the photographs?'

'Yes, do.'

We crossed the room. There was Pamela in tennis dress with racquet, Pamela on the netball field and, much younger, in a ballet dress.

'You must be proud of your daughter.'

'Oh, we are. She was clever at school, good at dancing, and a daddy's girl. She loved to go to the mill with her father on the Saturday half-day.'

'And who is the boy?'

'Kevin Foxcroft, my godson. He will be calling soon. You might meet him.' She said this with a smile and warmth in her voice.

I wondered whether Josephine Whitaker was as opposed to the match between her daughter and Ronnie Creswell as Pamela thought. It wouldn't hurt to try to find out. 'I'm a stranger and don't know anyone here, apart from meeting Mrs Creswell on Saturday, but I was very sorry to hear of Ronnie Creswell's death. From what I've heard of him I can understand why he and Pamela were friends, both good at games. He was captain of the cricket team, I believe, and ambitious.'

There was a slight change in Josephine's manner, a stiffening of her shoulders. 'They were childhood friends.' She sighed. 'I have called on the Creswells, and sent condolences.' A flash of pity altered her look. 'They have other children but that won't lessen the blow. Mrs Creswell and I had agreed that Pamela and Ronnie would not be a good match. Pamela is our only child. We want the best for her.'

'Of course you do,' I said.

Our conversation came to a stop when someone tapped on the window. We both looked across. It was a slender young man with neat short hair and a small moustache. He was the boy from the photograph on the mantelpiece, Napoleon Bonaparte of the fancy-dress ball.

Mrs Whitaker's eyes lit up. She waved him to come in but he was already on his way. A moment later he was in the sitting room.

Kevin breezed in and went to kiss Mrs Whitaker on the cheek. 'Hello, Auntie. And who's this?'

'Mrs Shackleton, meet Kevin Foxcroft, my godson.'

Kevin greeted me warmly and came across to shake hands in a delicate fashion. His hands were pale and smooth and his nails well manicured. 'Pleased to meet you, Mrs Shackleton. It looks as if you cheered up my godmother, which is why I'm here. Aunt and Uncle had a dreadful shock at the weekend.'

'Mrs Shackleton knows about the accident, dear. She happened to be at the Creswells' on Saturday and now she has kindly arranged to come to Milner Field with her house-keeper and oversee what needs doing prior to the auction.'

'Why?' he asked, eyes wide with surprise.

'Mrs Creswell has given her notice with immediate effect.'

'Oh Auntie, I knew about that. I was hoping to surprise you. I talked to Aldous. He and I assumed that as estate man-ager he would take on the organising of housekeeping. We wanted you to have no worries on that score.' He turned to include me with the warmest of smiles, which may have been genuine. 'I'm sure Mrs Shackleton and her housekeeper will be admirable.' He gazed at me. 'Aldous and I would never have found such a lady.'

I stood. 'I'm pleased to have met you, Mr Foxcroft. Now I'm going to collect my housekeeper at Saltaire station.'

Mrs Whitaker rose to see me out. 'Kevin, I'll be back to talk to you when I've seen Mrs Shackleton out.'

I was already in the hall but heard Josephine Whitaker say, 'Kevin, you know about many things, but housekeeping isn't one of them. And before you ask, your Uncle Arnold is dead set against taking up your offer of a share in a fine young filly.'

'But you'll come and see her?'

'No. That would be a fine thing, wouldn't it? A death at the mill and Mrs Whitaker goes gallivanting to Doncaster Racecourse.'

Mrs Whitaker emerged and walked me to the door. 'Thank you for calling, Mrs Shackleton. I love your costume. Do you mind my asking where it came from?'

'It's a bit embarrassing saying this to the lady of Salts Mill. My aunt brought it from Paris.'

She sighed. 'Wonderful. I hope you and it will bring good luck to Milner Field. Oh, and Kevin is Foxcroft Carpets, so if any of the rugs are frayed and want replacing just say.'

'I hope the splendour of the building will be what catches the eye and the purse strings.'

As we were saying goodbye, the telephone rang.

Before I reached my car, the maid was calling to me. 'Telephone! Telephone for Mrs Shackleton. She's wanted by the police!'

Reluctantly, I went back inside.

Mrs Whitaker opened the door wide to let me through and maintain her distance. I guessed she did not know that I had been at the police station on Monday with Mr Cohen to take notes of David Fairburn's interview. I was the good fairy coming to the rescue of the housekeeping department.

Talking to the police may transform me into a suspicious character.

The maid handed me the receiver. Her look as she did so was somewhere between admiration and wariness. She stayed close enough to earwig.

'Mrs Shackleton speaking.'

'Mrs Shackleton, Inspector Mitchell here.'

'Hello, Inspector.'

'We met some years ago, in Bridgestead. This isn't about that case, of course. Would you be so good as to call at Shipley station? There is a matter we must discuss.'

The only Mitchell I remembered meeting in Bridgestead was the village bobby. Where had I put a foot wrong? I wondered. My immediate thought was of the letter Ronnie Creswell sent to me asking me to call on Saturday. Dad would have sent it on through the police service internal mail. It ought to have arrived. If not, I would have some explaining to do.

'Yes, of course. I'll be with you shortly.' I put down the phone.

Mrs Whitaker was waiting by the front door, too polite to ask what the call was about. We said goodbye, agreeing that it had been nice to meet. I left the house.

I thought that was it, but she must have thought of something else to say. I heard her footsteps. She caught up and walked with me to the car, saying, 'I'll just tell you something, if you don't mind. Something I can't get out of my head.'

'Of course.'

'Arnold said that Ronnie wrote to you about something that happened in the past . . . '

'Yes, but he didn't say what.'

'I've thought what it might be. I didn't want to talk inside.

I don't want Kevin to see how much Ronnie's death has shaken me.'

Kevin Foxcroft was watching from the window. I opened the car door. 'Let's sit in the car. Tell me there.'

We got in and settled ourselves.

Mrs Whitaker took a deep breath. 'Mrs Creswell and I were of one mind regarding Pamela and Ronnie. Their feelings were a combination of familiarity and infatuation.'

That seemed to me as good a basis as any for love, and better than most, but it was too late to say that now. I listened.

Mrs Whitaker straightened her skirt. 'I called on Mrs Creswell at the Lodge when I knew she would be alone, to discuss the situation. Like me, she had family photographs on the mantelpiece.'

'I saw them on Saturday.'

'There's a young boy, about eight or nine, had the look of Ronnie. I made the mistake of asking if it was Ronnie, done up in an old-fashioned outfit.'

'I saw it and noticed the family resemblance.'

'The boy was called Billy. Had he lived, Billy would have been in his seventies now. He was related to the Creswells' Uncle Nick. I found out afterwards that Billy died during the building of the mansion. He went missing one Sunday. He was found dead by the builders on Monday morning. He had fallen down a shaft. No child owned up to being with him, or having seen him.'

'How dreadful.' I did not tell her that I had heard part of that tale from Mr Duffield and the schoolteacher.

Mrs Whitaker continued. 'The coroner recorded accidental death and ordered a review of security. The boy's family moved away.'

'How strange for Ronnie,' I said, 'to look at a picture of a little boy with such a strong resemblance.'

'That is why I am telling you. Mrs Creswell said that the story of Billy fascinated Ronnie. He wanted to know about Billy. Their Uncle Nick couldn't tell him anything, but one of the old people in the almshouse upset Ronnie by saying that the death was no accident. There was a rumour that Billy didn't fall, he was pushed.'

I sympathised with Ronnie's desire to know about Billy. We all have something that gives us that itch, especially when the thing is unknowable. Someone must be able to unlock the truth, one thinks. Would Ronnie have asked me to investigate the death of a boy whose double he was?

Did Billy fall or was he pushed?

Did Ronnie fall or was he pushed?

TWENTY

I entered Shipley police station for the second time in two days. Last night, I had sat with David Fairburn as he was interviewed. Could my summons today be connected with that, or had my letter from Ronnie sent on by Dad not yet arrived?

The inspector wanted to see me. Mr Whitaker had said he would let the police know that Sykes and I would be in the area. Perhaps the summons indicated a change of heart by the force. Meddlers had been tolerated long enough. I prepared for a warning to keep the Shackleton, Sykes and Sugden snitches out of police business. There could be no objection to Sykes being engaged on a business matter by Mr Whitaker. Nor should bringing my housekeeper to Milner Field raise a question. My role as what Mr Whitaker liked to call the linchpin was less specific. I decided that the simplest way of explaining myself, if required, was to say that I was supervising my housekeeper and ensuring she had all the help she needed.

I waited my turn while an elderly woman reported a lost

dog called Jock, a mongrel mixture with the colouring of a Jack Russell and the height of a cocker spaniel. A young constable patiently noted details. He was able to reassure the woman because he knew of a brother and sister who were good at suddenly producing the right dog when a reward was announced. He would pay them a surprise visit and look under their kitchen table.

The woman with the dog lead and no dog thanked the constable and left the station.

I gave my name.

'Ah yes,' he said. 'I'll let Inspector Mitchell know you are here.' He picked up the telephone and pressed a button.

His call was answered. 'Mrs Shackleton here to see you, sir.'

The constable guided me through. He tapped on a door and opened it at the sound of 'Come in!'

There stood Mitchell, the village bobby now resplendent in inspector's uniform, a big man who seemed not a day older than when I last saw him. In my memory, he was preserved in aspic as the village bobby at Bridgestead, where there was so little for him to do that he had busied himself putting a ship in a bottle for his father-in-law's birthday.

He reached out to shake my hand. 'Mrs Shackleton, thank you for having the letter from Ronnie sent on, and please take a seat.'

I sat down. So it wasn't the letter he wanted to talk to me about.

Tea and biscuits were brought in. Inspector Mitchell poured.

I raised my cup. 'Congratulations on your appointment, Inspector. Quite a change for you.'

'Yes, indeed.' He spooned sugar into his tea with the same

slow patience as he had put the ship in the whisky bottle. 'It's Mrs Mitchell who deserves the congratulations. She coached me for the sergeant's exam; but of course Bridgestead wasn't a sergeant's posting. She coached me for the inspector's exam. Bridgestead will never be an inspector's posting.'

'You had the qualification but not the title or the remuneration.'

'Just what Mrs Mitchell kept saying. I did have one advantage. When you came and stirred up an old case – a case we would both probably rather forget – that put me in my superior's spotlight. I was allowed to share the quiet glory.'

'Quite right.'

'Two years ago, when an inspector had a sudden heart attack, I was remembered.'

'Deservedly.'

He smiled. 'Thank you. And so here I am, not so very upper in rank but upper enough for me.'

'And upper enough to know you'd find me with Mrs Whitaker.'

'Ah yes. I have my sources.'

I could see that he enjoyed being mysterious, but there would be no mystery to a telephone call to the mill and Mr Whitaker suggesting where to try. He was not a man to be rushed, but ambled to the point as soon as politeness permitted.

He clasped his hands and became more serious. 'I wasn't here when you came with the sharp solicitor with the broken arm.'

'Mr Cohen.'

'He has quite a reputation.'

'He does indeed.'

'David Fairburn has cause to be grateful to him and so do CID.'

'Oh?'

'Mr Cohen's dissatisfaction with the fingerprint result prompted CID to send in their fingerprint chap again. As well as Ronnie Creswell's and David Fairburn's prints, they have those of the reservoir inspector, his apprentice, the security officer and two other sets unidentified. One set belongs either to a woman or to a man with small hands. We're looking at the rotas and job sheets to see who else may have gone down there.'

'In a place the size of Salts, that will be a big task.'

He nodded agreement. 'Precisely. Our resources aren't unlimited. There has to be some narrowing down. Mr Whitaker told me that you and your housekeeper will be staying at Milner Field and that your colleague Mr Sykes will be working with him in connection with some business matters. It would be helpful for me and for CID to know whether there will be any overlap or useful information in connection with our investigation into Ronnie Creswell's death.'

In plain speak, he wanted to know if Mrs Shackleton, private investigator, and her colleagues were here to look into a suspicious death and stick in an oar that wasn't wanted.

'This is an unusual assignment for me, Inspector. I am here purely to ensure that when the day of the auction of Milner Field arrives, the auction room will be full of potential bidders who have seen Milner Field and are impressed by its grandeur, cleanliness and sheen. Mrs Creswell has understandably left her post. I and my excellent housekeeper, Mrs Sugden, are taking over. We're strangers here. I would not leave Mrs Sugden alone to cope with such an important task. If anything

150

at all strikes us as being of interest to the police, I will be on the telephone to this station, or driving up to your door, without hesitation.'

'Good. And if I can be of any assistance, just say the word.' He walked me to the door. 'Keep your ear to the ground, Mrs Shackleton. I remember your skill at making connections.'

'What's the situation with David Fairburn?' I asked.

'The finding of additional fingerprints in the reservoir area does not eliminate David Fairburn from the list of suspects, but it does mean that he is released, pending further inquiries. His solicitor has been notified.'

'Is he still here?'

'He's signing the discharge papers now.'

'I could drive him home?'

The noise of the engine prevented conversation, though David Fairburn was in no mood for talking.

As I pulled up in front of his house, he said, 'When will they drag me back?'

'I hope they won't. Is there anything else you can tell me that may help you, or may be used against you?'

'It was exactly as I said, and I didn't kill Ronnie. Thanks for the lift.' He moved to open the door and then hesitated. 'There was something that I nearly said and then forgot.'

'What?'

'The smell, the scent I caught a whiff of when I went down the steps at the reservoir, it was like Brylcreem.'

'That could be significant. When you did realise?'

'Just now, when Tom Harrison – PC Harrison – gave me the discharge papers to sign. He uses Brylcreem.'

'Call back at the station. Ask for that to be noted.'

'What? That I'm pointing a finger at Tom?'

'No. The smell. It could be significant.'

'I'm not going back there.'

'Just do it, Mr Fairburn, and wait a moment.' Across the street, curtains twitched.

'What now?' he asked.

'Someone is going to ask you this sooner or later.'

He turned his head away, as if to ward off a blow, looking so broken that I could barely bring myself to ask him. 'Is Dorrie at home?'

'What do you want with her?'

'I should like to meet her. Your family must be worried, and she has to go on working in the mill.'

'Leave my sister out of this.'

David Fairburn went inside, closing the door firmly behind him.

TWENTY-ONE

I met Mrs Sugden in the Saltaire railway station buffet. We lunched on cheese sandwiches, currant cake and cups of tea while she showed me the sets of direction cards that had arrived this morning from the motoring club. I have been teaching Mrs Sugden to drive. Preferring familiar roads, she was happy for me to drive us to Milner Field while she familiarised herself with the area.

As we turned the bend, Milner Field rose into view, turrets and towers reaching for the sky, windows sparkling in the afternoon sunlight.

The direction cards slid from Mrs Sugden's hands as she gasped in admiration. 'Whatever was Titus Salt Junior thinking when he built this place? Did he keep a harem?'

'I'm sure Titus was on the straight and narrow. His father's example gave him a great deal to live up to. Titus Junior needed to reach for the stars, dreaming of himself and Catherine hosting kings and queens, princes and princesses.'

'The great, the good and the not-so-good.' Mrs Sugden

gave one of her a-humphs. 'People would come, all right. They'd eat all, sup all and pay nowt, all the while looking down their snitches at a Yorkshire millionaire.'

I parked outside the Lodge.

'This is where the Creswells lived. Let's take a look. This will be your meeting point for the cleaners. Mrs Whitaker gave me the housekeeping files. You'll be able to keep them here once we've taken a look at them. Mr Whitaker invited us to stay in the tower part of the main building. It's self-contained.' I got out of the car. The door to the Lodge was unlocked. On stepping inside, I immediately sensed a change in the atmosphere between Saturday and today. The smell of ashes filled the room from the uncleared fire grate. Photographs of the Creswell children were gone, including the little distant cousin Billy, the boy who looked so like Ronnie. The clock on the mantelpiece had stopped at one. An air of abandonment clung to the rooms. The house had swallowed emptiness, and breathed it into every corner.

Our luggage, sent in advance, took up the centre of the parlour floor. I turned to Mrs Sugden. 'It looks as if someone thought we would stay here. Let's check that we're not missing anything and that you have what you need.'

Mrs Sugden went into the kitchen. I could hear her opening and closing cupboards and drawers.

I found a curt note on the mantelpiece, tucked under the stopped clock. It was written in an ornate style, as if the author had consulted a book on handwriting and made the most elaborate choice. There was a key in the envelope, but not for the Tower quarters. I read the note aloud.

Dear Ladies,

Welcome to the Lodge.

This key opens Milner Field servants' entrance. You will find necessary keys hanging in the housekeeping room, together with all that you require. Mrs Creswell, former housekeeper, intends to leave the village. I suggest you consult her before she departs.

The Lodge has been prepared. I trust you will be comfortable here rather than in the Tower quarters.

Sincerely,
Aldous Garner, Estate Manager

I gave a sigh. 'He thinks we're both housekeepers. No disrespect to your chosen occupation, Mrs Sugden. Aldous Garner doesn't know you. It's that old snobbery again, from someone who has a high opinion of himself and assigns two professional females to the housekeeper's quarters.'

I picked up the telephone and followed the instruction to dial nought. A male telephone operator answered on the instant. 'Operator, Mrs Shackleton for Mr Whitaker's secretary Mrs Harrison, please.'

The secretary answered promptly. 'Yes, Mrs Shackleton?'

'Hello, Mrs Harrison. I have keys and the housekeeping files from Mrs Whitaker and am in the Lodge. The estate manager has left a note assuming we are staying here. We need the key to the Tower and our luggage is here.'

'Sorry about that. I'll ask the estate manager to have your luggage taken over to the Tower, and for the door to be unlocked and keys supplied. Do let me know if you need anything else.'

'Thank you.'

Mrs Sugden emerged triumphant from the kitchen. 'Well, one person is hospitable. Here's a note under a dish signed Julie the Cleaner saying "look in the cupboard". Behind a packet of tea and half a cup of sugar she's left us a set of keys, including one for the Tower.'

'That's good of her.'

Mrs Sugden can sometimes be mercurial. 'This lodge would suit us, all in one place. Would we be cutting off our nose to spite our face by not stopping here?'

Sometimes, the truth is complicated. I kept it simple. 'We need to be closer to the heart of the place.'

With a young man dead, industrial espionage, fears of a curse, worries about the sale of the mansion and theft of the family silver on the night of the fancy-dress ball, it did not suit me to be in the South Lodge. We needed to be in the centre of things.

TWENTY-TWO

Mrs Sugden, practising her driving, drove us the short distance from the Lodge to the Tower, stopping smartly by the door. The mansion seemed less forbidding on this sunny afternoon than it had on Saturday. Perhaps over its sixty years of existence it had developed the knack of appearing benign when unwary strangers approached.

'Might I be showing prospective buyers round?' Mrs Sugden asked. 'I don't think I'd ever find my way about.'

'Someone from the auctioneers will do that.'

We entered a dark porch with a high window where ivy had begun to finger its way across the glass.

Thirteen steps up a winding, creaking staircase led us to the entrance of the Tower quarters.

'It's a bloomin' lighthouse,' Mrs Sugden said as we reached an oak door. I turned the key.

We entered a high-ceilinged room and crossed to the shuttered windows. As we opened the shutters, the gloomy room turned into a magnificent space filled with light. It was sparsely furnished and smelled of soot. Mrs Sugden went to the fireplace. 'Chimney hasn't been swept.' She tried the sofa. 'This upholstery is similar to my new wallpaper. I'll be up to the minute when that decorating is done.'

'You have innate good taste, Mrs Sugden.'

'And your Paris costume right suits this room. Look, there's a cocktail cabinet and a piano.'

She went to the piano and tried to lift the lid. 'Oh, it's locked.' She attempted to open the door of the cocktail cabinet. 'Locked and emptied! This is like Goldilocks. Will the beds be too hard or too soft?'

'There will be two beds that are just right.'

We went onto the landing and up the next staircase, which led to two perfectly satisfactory bedrooms and bathrooms. The third staircase led to an unfurnished attic. A thick rope attached to a hook hung from the ceiling. Its end formed into a perfect noose. The window was ajar and the draught from the door set the rope swinging as we entered. Mrs Sugden shuddered. 'Gives me the creeps.'

I closed the window. 'It's only the cross draught,' I said. 'The noose is someone's idea of a joke.' A punchbag had been detached from the rope and stood in a corner.

As we made our way back downstairs, the doorbell rang, the door opened and there were footsteps on the stairs. Whoever it was knew we were there and ought to have waited. By the time we reached the apartment and went inside, that person was walking up the stairs.

I locked the door. 'Whoever it is needs to learn to knock.'

I went to stand by the window.

There was a knock and someone tried the handle. He must have seen the car outside. When the door did not open, he knocked again, more loudly.

Mrs Sugden opened the door. 'Hello, may I help you?'

'Am I speaking to Mrs Shackleton?' He did not try to hide the annoyance in his voice.

I was proud of Mrs Sugden. 'I'm Mrs Shackleton's housekeeper, who may I say is calling?'

He snapped his credentials. 'Aldous Garner, estate manager. I thought you couldn't get in.'

'Just a moment.' Mrs Sugden pushed the door almost closed and stood with her back to it.

'Let Mr Garner in.' I stayed by the window, slanted to the light that shone on my pearls.

She waited a moment and then opened the door and stood aside. Garner stared at me. Either he recognised real pearls or he knew a designer outfit when he saw one. It is a shame to have to impress people who don't mind their manners.

'Mrs Shackleton?'

'Yes, and this is Mrs Sugden, my housekeeper.' I glided across the room to the floral sofa. 'Do come in and sit down.' I lowered myself onto the sofa and indicated a chair.

He was dressed in country tweeds and wore brown leather brogues. His greying hair was short and neatly cut, his nails well manicured. I put his age at a little over forty and his suppressed irritation at near boiling point. I guessed that he had wanted to appoint his own housekeeper. Mrs Sugden and I were usurpers and that suited me very well. But a little charm was called for. I offered him tea or coffee, which he declined.

Mrs Sugden's *coup de grâce* was her move to the cocktail cabinet, saying, 'May I mix you a drink, sir?'

I laughed. 'Mrs Sugden's little joke. The cupboard is bare here. Our trunks have been placed in the housekeeper's quarters that Mrs Sugden will use as her HQ.'

It was Mr Garner's turn to try to charm. He apologised for the lack of supplies, and his mistake in thinking we would occupy the Lodge. I waved aside his apologies.

'What I should like, Mr Garner, is to see the rest of the mansion in the afternoon light.'

Once in the mansion, Garner became the perfect guide, letting the faded glories of each room dazzle their own story. There was oak panelling everywhere. Stained-glass windows softened the light. An immense organ was carved from oak. Chimney pieces were of alabaster, carved with ivy. Recessed arches for the comfort of classical statues spoke of no expense spared. There were obvious gaps in the rooms. The billiard room lacked a table. Wallpaper held its original colour only where a cabinet had been removed. Certain rooms felt empty, previous owners having laid claim to their loved belongings. In spite of the gaps and the overdone last-century feeling, what remained was breathtakingly beautiful. Yet the place reeked of sadness, and promise unfulfilled.

Mr Garner wanted to show me the library.

Mrs Sugden hung back. She called me to come and see a room that Garner had hurried us by.

Perhaps inspired by the vanished Elizabethan manor house, this room was designed as a Tudor hall, but on a more domestic scale. It was panelled, and with a narrow balcony, and furnished with elaborately carved table and chairs. I knew immediately what Mrs Sugden wanted me to see. It was not the ingenuity of the design or the antique furniture. The table had hosted a meal for four and not been cleared. There were lamb chop bones on the plates and dregs of red wine in glasses. Several empty bottles stood on a sideboard.

160

'What a beautiful room,' I said, ignoring the mess.

Mr Garner had strode on but now he doubled back. 'I'm so sorry that this was left in such a state. I must have a word with the scullery maid.'

Both Mrs Sugden and I ignored him. She picked up four plates and knives and forks and went to the dumb waiter at the end of the room. 'Once I open the windows there'll be flies in here if we don't clear up.'

She opened the door to the dumb waiter. As she did so a blast of cold air came into the room. She placed the crockery and cutlery inside, went back for more greasy dishes, and then quickly closed the door and sent the dumb waiter rattling down.

'You'll like the library,' Mr Garner said, ready to move on.

Not so fast, I thought. Mrs Sugden continued to clear the table. We would wait for her. I went to look at the sideboard. 'The carving is exquisite. Elizabethan, Mr Garner?'

'Yes, I believe so,' Mr Garner said, willing to be diverted, assuming that only Mrs Sugden, a genuine housekeeper, would care about dirty plates. I went on admiring the room until the dumb waiter came rattling back up from the cellar.

Mrs Sugden opened the door.

'Emptied!' she said triumphantly. 'It must be freezing down there, and who's doing the emptying?'

'The scullery maid,' said Mr Garner. 'She comes in for a couple of hours in the morning and in the afternoon.' He looked at his watch. 'She'll be off in five minutes.'

'One sees dumb waiters rarely,' I said, going to examine this one, trying to get my bearings so that I could be sure to take a look at the dumb waiter terminus when we explored the basement.

Mrs Sugden placed dishes and tureens inside and stepped back so that I could be the one to send the cupboard on its downward journey. When it had gone, I opened the door onto the darkness of the shaft, once again feeling that icy chill. Little Billy Creswell had fallen down a shaft to his death. What terror he must have felt. Could this be where he fell?

I imagined I heard a scream, but it was the mechanism of the pulley that needed oiling.

Mrs Sugden went on exploring. Mr Garner and I sat in the library where he poured sherry for us. This was my opportunity to discover what made Aldous Garner tick.

It suited him to play host. As he poured, he seemed to relax, saying, 'I half close my eyes, and imagine the glory days.'

I smiled, and encouraged his nostalgia for a world that had never been his. 'A butler would be pouring our sherry, and lighting your cigarette. Tell me, which decade would you have liked best?'

'Early on, when there were horses in the stables.' He became animated, leaning forward, giving the impression of grasping something more precious than a glass of sherry. 'Or the excitement of the first year of taking up residency.'

He smiled wistfully when I asked if he would stay on when the house was sold.

'I'd like to. I love Milner Field.'

'But?' I asked.

'It would depend on the buyer. If it's some vulgar person with more money than sense, then the answer is no.'

Remembering that Mr Whitaker hoped for just such a moneyed and senseless person with an inattentive guardian angel, it struck me that either Whitaker or his estate manager would be disappointed.

Mr Whitaker had told me that Garner was spending time elsewhere, and probably had plans to move on. I wondered how much we would see of him. 'Do you feel it's time for you to have a change?' I asked.

'I do, as a matter of fact. Until the auction, I'll be dividing my time between Milner Field and a cottage I've taken. Time to hand over the reins. Mr Whitaker would have liked me to take on management of the housing stock in the village, but that's not my line. I told him, and I can hear myself saying it now – look for someone younger. Ronnie Creswell. That's who I suggested, little knowing we would soon be mourning his loss. The lad came to me, asking me about my work, asking for tips.'

So Mr Garner knew that he was yesterday's man, giving way to the next generation. He ought not to have been on the way out, but something must have gone wrong for him. He was alert, with that energy that comes from wanting to see things done, alongside a certain languid laziness in wanting not to be the one to do it.

A little flattery would draw him out. 'You still have so much to offer, Mr Garner. You must know the estate better than anyone.'

He acknowledged his own worth. 'But the truth is, the farm runs itself. The gardeners know what they're doing. The mill doesn't want to throw good money after bad by doing any more than is necessary in the house and grounds, so there is not a great deal for me to do. It's fortunate that I have a plan.'

'I'm so glad. Are you able to tell me the plan?'

'I'm keeping this quiet until after the auction of Milner Field. I wouldn't want to give the impression of jumping ship.'

'That's very loyal of you.'

He favoured me with a confidential smile that I guessed was much practised. 'I'm keen on the sport of kings, have been all my life. There's an opportunity for me to manage a racecourse.'

'How wonderful. Which course?'

He tapped the side of his nose. 'I've said too much already. When it comes to saying goodbye to Milner Field, that will be the time to tell.'

'Well, congratulations. I'm glad things are working so well for you.'

He offered to fill up my glass and I let him, wanting him to do the same for his own glass, which he did, and his tongue loosened a little more. 'I have a share in a horse by the name of Sparky Lass. She will, we hope, surprise the world of racing.'

He was the second person that day to boast of a share in a racehorse. There could not be so very many people round here who would have a share in a filly with a vulgar name. What was the connection, I wondered, between Kevin Foxcroft of Foxcroft Carpets and Aldous Garner, the estate manager with expensive tastes? A love of racing. There was perhaps nothing more to it than that.

'Mrs Shackleton,' said Garner, with a sudden seriousness, 'you must let me give you supper this evening. Here you are finding out all about me, and I know nothing about you.'

'Thank you, but Mrs Sugden and I have much to do. Besides, there is very little to know about me.'

He leaned back in his chair as if to take a long-distance look at me. 'I find that hard to believe.'

'It pleases me to spend time at Milner Field, admiring the gardens and doing my bit towards a successful sale of the mansion for Mrs Whitaker.'

'That is very kind of you.'

'Thank you for the guided tour. I'll find Mrs Sugden and we won't take up any more of your precious time.'

The truth of Mr Garner's future dawned on me. Whether the mansion sold or not, Aldous Garner would be out of this comfortable job where he could entertain friends at his employer's expense. Mr Whitaker would be too astute to dismiss his estate manager in advance of the auction, but he would not forgive the loss of the family silver on the night of the ball, nor the run-down state of the mansion. The auctioneers would have checked the inventory of the wine cellar. Garner's days in a comfortable job were numbered.

Back at the Tower, we decided on what to do next. Mrs Sugden had looked through the cleaners' details. She said, 'Mrs Creswell wrote out the timetables. The person who went in with the cleaners and saw to it all is Julie who left us the note. She lives in the village on Ada Street. She'll be the one to gather everyone together, and make a start as soon as possible.'

'Do you want to go see her?' I asked.

'If it's all the same to you, Mrs Shackleton, I think you might be better placed to speak to Julie. It may be that she expected Mrs Creswell's job and I would be the one she would think took it from her. You could ease the way.'

'All right. I'll do that. And what about you?'

'I'll go by the existing rota and timetables.' Mrs Sugden was in her element, and one step ahead of me. 'It's elbow grease we need. The women ticked off the jobs they did. Gwyneth Kidd – the lass that didn't come back after the fancy-dress ball – got through more work than anyone else.

She lodged in Shipley. I could find my way to her last known address, and practise my driving.'

'It doesn't hurt to look, but apparently Gwyneth was last seen on the night the silver was stolen. She was suspected of being involved. The police wanted to interview her.'

'People don't always want to be interviewed by the police. If I'd been in charge of the cleaners, I would have wanted to know what happened to my best worker. A grafter doesn't suddenly turn into a thief.'

'Take the car, then. Do you want me to sit in with you?'

'No. I know what to do. Time for me to take the plunge.'

TWENTY-THREE

When Mrs Sugden set out on her solo driving practice, I set off for the village. As I passed the orangery, I heard music and stopped to listen.

A gramophone was playing Will Fyffe's music-hall song 'I Belong to Glasgow'. A clear young voice sang along, making a good attempt at impersonating a drunken man.

'I belong to Glasgow, dear old Glasgow town, well there's something the matter with Glasgow cos it's whirling round and round.'

Nancy Creswell twirled into view from behind a palm tree. She stopped twirling and singing when she saw me. Just for a second, I caught a gleam of hope in her eyes, as she looked beyond me for someone else. And then her arms dropped to her sides and her mouth turned down before she managed a greeting.

'Hello, Nancy. What are you doing here?'

'I had to come back to the Lodge for my coat and to Dad's hut to tell him to come home for his supper.'

'And have you done that?'

'I've told Dad and he'll come. I couldn't get in the Lodge. Door's locked.'

'I'll unlock it.'

'We never locked the door when the Lodge was our house.'

The singer on the gramophone suddenly stopped belonging to Glasgow, dear old Glasgow town. The needle started to scratch, scratch, scratch.

Following the sound beyond a palm tree, I removed the record from the turntable and put it back in its sleeve.

Nancy took it from me and placed it in the gramophone cabinet, closing the door carefully. 'I thought Pamela might come. It's her gramophone. We sang and danced, her and Ronnie and me.' She burst into tears. 'He's not coming, she's not coming, and now I wish they'd gone to Gretna Green.'

'Gretna Green?'

'That's what Pamela said they should do – to be married, no questions asked. She was sure but Ronnie wasn't.'

'I know. Ronnie can't come any more, but you'll always remember him singing and dancing. You'll see Pamela again.'

She shook her head. 'Not now. They'll make her marry Napoleon Bonaparte.'

'You mean the man who dressed up as Napoleon on the night of the ball? Kevin Foxcroft?'

'Yes, him.'

'Pamela loved Ronnie. She won't think about anyone else.'

I believed that to be true, but perhaps Kevin and the Foxcroft family hoped that with Ronnie out of the way Kevin would comfort Pamela and win her, and her fortune, on the rebound.

'I was going to be bridesmaid.'

'Come on. We'll call at the Lodge and get your coat and I'll walk you home. You can show me the quickest way to the village.'

I unlocked the Lodge door. Nancy retrieved her coat from exactly where she said it was, behind the pantry door.

'You can leave the door unlocked,' she said.

'Well, Mrs Sugden and I have moved into the Tower, so we will keep the Lodge locked, but just say if there's anything else you need.'

We walked back through the wood through a patchwork of shade and light as the sun fingered its way between branches.

Nancy took a coin from her pocket. 'Do you want to make a wish?'

'Yes.'

She tossed the coin, caught it and slid it onto the back of her hand. 'Pattern or plain?'

'Plain.' She revealed the coin, one side embossed with a lamb.

'Best of three?'

'Agreed.'

Nancy won, two out of three.

'I hope your wish comes true,' I said.

'I want to come back here to my own room. At Uncle Nick's, everyone is sad and squashed together.'

To divert her, I said, 'Tell me about the night of the ball.'

'Pamela looked prettiest. The men looked silly but it made me laugh. There was Robin Hood and Friar Tuck and kings, sailors, soldiers and a farmer with straw in his hair. We couldn't go in the house but one of the boys knew the way to the tunnel and we went along that and it was scary. Our Ronnie knew the tunnels. He wasn't scared.'

I wondered if Nancy simply meant the passageways used by servants, or something more secret and sinister. A tunnel might explain why there could have been a theft of silver on the night of the ball when everyone was otherwise occupied. 'How did Ronnie know the tunnels?' I asked.

'He did work in the house when the plaster fell down, stuff like that. He didn't tell Mam so I didn't snitch.'

As a maintenance man, Ronnie would have known his way around the mansion and the mill. Might he have found out something he shouldn't, something that cost him his life?

'What tunnel did you go in?'

'I'm not telling except it comes through the pantry cellars in the servants' quarters. There are different doors for going upstairs into the house, like to the dining room. We didn't go up the stairs, so we didn't go in the house. On the wall, there's a moving cupboard that takes stuff from the kitchen to the dining room. It's called a dumb waiter and there's a bigger dumb waiter for logs and coal. Roy had a flashlight and when he took us through the tunnel he told us what rooms was above. If he didn't know, and I could tell when he didn't know, he'd have a think and make something up.'

'How does Roy know all this?'

'His mam, Julie, is one of the cleaners. She's our mam's friend. We call everybody else Auntie or Mrs Somebody, but Roy's mam is just Julie. Roy was there to help wash up. He went in the kitchen. Nothing bad has happened to him, not yet anyway.'

'He sounds like a boy who can look after himself.'

'Mam was mad at me. She said she hoped I didn't go in the house. Well, I didn't.' There was anxiety in her voice now. She was looking up at me and stumbled over a branch.

'Don't tell Mam I went in the cellar. She'll think I went in the house.'

To take Nancy's mind off her mother's worries about the curse, I asked, 'Tell me what other costumes you saw on the night of the ball.'

'The waitresses for the night were done up as olden-day wenches with black skirts, white blouses with puff sleeves and mobcaps. Julie and Gwyneth and Dorrie Fairburn and a good few others was serving. Everybody had a good time. Later, when I was in bed, I heard cars. Some were leaving and then the police car came. Somebody stole some stuff. Mam and Julie felt responsible.

'Your mother wasn't in the house, though?'

'Oh no. She plans it all and writes it and tells people when to come, but she's religious about not setting foot in the place. Mr Garner understands.'

It occurred to me that Mr Garner would be glad to have an arm's-length housekeeper who would know nothing of his generous entertaining and incursions into the wine cellar.

'And Gwyneth, the cleaner who didn't come back the next day, was she the one who stole something?'

'They said she did. I saw her trip. Julie had sent me to look for Dorrie Fairburn. She was taking round trays of drinks but I couldn't find her. I saw Gwyneth hurrying off. She caught her skirt on twigs. I went to help her. Should I have told?'

'Going to help her was a good thing. Where was Gwyneth hurrying to?'

'She was getting a lift in a motor.'

Dorrie Fairburn missing, Gwyneth hurrying away. The night's excitements seemed to be among the servers, not the guests.

Nancy put her finger to her lips and shook her head to me. 'I didn't tell because I would have got into trouble for being there. Uncle Nick says, "Tell nobody nothing."'

But had Nancy told someone who would make more sense of the events than I could? 'Who have you told?'

'You because you asked and Uncle Nick because he keeps secrets.'

'I'm honoured you've told me. Now let's hurry, before your mother sends out a search party.' I felt a bit guilty about grilling Nancy. She was a great little talker. Being attached to her Uncle Nick made her sound older than her years. What secrets did her uncle keep and might they lead to trouble?

Nancy pressed her coin into my hand. 'I'll lend you this, for luck. Gwyneth said keep it safe, and don't lose it. She might need it back. I could have hidden it in the Lodge but not at Uncle Nick's. He's taken all the hiding places and there's too many people.'

'I'll look after it until you want it back.' I looked at the coin carefully, to show appreciation, before slipping it into my pocket.

She then seemed happy to walk back in silence. As we reached the park, I sensed a change in her. Two children were playing by the stream. They waved. Nancy did not wave back but hurried on. One of them called after her but she ignored him.

'Are they your friends?' I asked.

'I don't like them now. I won't play with them any more.'

'Why not?'

She sighed, a sigh far too deep. 'They ask me things. They say things. They want to know too much.' She kicked a stone.

'You're right to ignore them. They don't know any better.'

We walked in silence, until we reached the bottom of Victoria Road.

'My brothers will be coming.'

'What are their names?'

'Stephen and Mark. Stephen's nineteen. Mark is fifteen.'

'I'm glad they'll be here.'

It was good to know that the Creswells had two more children, though nothing would make up for the loss of Ronnie.

'Do they live far away?'

'A bit far. Stephen works on a farm. Mark looks after horses.'

As Nancy and I reached Victoria Road, and the sounds of mill machinery filled our ears, I thought of last Saturday, and Ronnie's words. If you arrive in Saltaire when the mill hooter goes, press against the wall or you'll be trodden flat by two thousand people coming out. Nancy's grip on my hand tightened.

How hard it must be for the Creswells to live within yards of the place where Ronnie died. From here, he would be home in minutes, but never again.

'Nancy, you told me about the cleaner, Julie. I ought to meet her. I saw from the addresses that she lives on Ada Street. Where's that?'

She pointed. 'It runs behind the mill canteen. It's the house with the pot dog in the window and geraniums on the windowsill.'

A girl, about Nancy's age, stood outside her house skipping, looking across, smiling at Nancy and waiting to be noticed.

Nancy, eyes front, ignored the girl. 'Walk me all the way up.'

'All right. I'll see you to your door.'

When we had passed the child who wanted Nancy to acknowledge her, Nancy said, 'She wants to be my friend. Her mother is making her a black dress. Ronnie's my brother, not hers.'

Nancy was too young to understand all those feelings surrounding childhood grief, that there will be others who feel the drama of it and want a share, without knowing the reeling shock of loss.

'Were you friends with that girl before?'

'Not really.'

'You do what you think is right for you, don't let her upset you.'

'Dorrie Fairburn came to see Mam. Pamela hasn't come.'

'She will.'

'I saw Gwyneth today but she didn't see me.'

'Where did you see her?'

'In the garden up by the North Lodge, when I went looking for Dad.'

If Gwyneth had come back, she must not know she was suspected of theft.

'Did you call to her?'

'No, and she didn't see me. She was already leaving, going out onto the road. And I can't say it. If someone doesn't know about Ronnie, I can't say the words. And Gwyneth doesn't know or she would have come to see Mam. Everyone else has.'

We had reached the house. 'Go on, then. Your mam will be glad you're back and that your dad is coming. Bye bye. Say hello to your mam from me. It's probably best if I call another day.'

But Mrs Creswell saw us from the window and beckoned.

Nancy groaned. 'Now I'm in bother. I took too long and she'll say I left my coat behind on purpose.'

TWENTY-FOUR

By the time we reached the house, Mrs Creswell was opening the door. Nancy waved her coat at her mother. 'Got it!'

'You took your time.' Mrs Creswell looked at me. 'Thank you for bringing her home. Chase her away if she comes again.'

Nancy's eyes widened with indignation. 'I went to see Dad. He said he hopes you're all right.'

'He said no such thing, now get upstairs.'

Nancy turned back on the second step. 'Dad won't sleep in the hut tonight. He'll come home.'

'Upstairs!'

Nancy disappeared.

Before she had time to close the door, I said, 'Mrs Creswell, Nancy is no trouble at all. I'm happy to walk her back and I will keep an eye on her if she finds her way to her old home.'

'Thank you. We were happy there.'

'And if there's anything at all that I can do or help with, please just say. My housekeeper is taking over your work for now.'

'It's all one to me. We won't be coming back.'

When she opened the door wider, I think it was more to do with not wanting neighbours ogling than to be polite. 'Come in. You'll need me to tell you what's what about the housekeeping.'

We stepped into a narrow kitchen on the ground floor. There was a smell of fried sausages. A door onto the back yard stood open. Mrs Creswell picked up the *Shipley Times* and swatted a bluebottle, expertly whacking it towards the door. 'They're clean here. There's a weaver and her two lasses on the middle floor and a young mechanic and his wife and babies on this.' She sat on a tall three-legged stool and waved at a straight-back chair. 'Sit down. Let me think what you'll need to know.' She clasped her hands, rubbing one against the other.

She looked exhausted. Her eyes were red from crying, her mouth turned down from misery. I would not learn much from someone who apart from never setting foot in the house was too distressed to think. 'Please don't trouble, Mrs Creswell. Mrs Sugden will muddle through. Your paperwork is clear.' I was reluctant to tell her that Julie was the person I intended to talk to. Julie went into the house and turned Mrs Creswell's instructions into action. She was the one who would show Mrs Sugden the ropes. 'And you have cleaners who have done the work before, perhaps one of them might come early?'

Mrs Creswell seemed relieved. 'Julie will see you through. She arrives before the others. Nancy will run down and tell her.'

'Thank you. That's kind of you.'

Mrs Creswell called up the stairs, 'Nancy!'

Nancy appeared again.

'Run to Julie. Say the cleaning is on for tomorrow and pass the word. She'll see . . . ' She turned to me.

'Mrs Sugden, in the Lodge, at twenty to eight for an eight o'clock start.'

Nancy nodded, and ran.

I thanked Mrs Creswell.

'I don't have to think about that ever again.'

I felt great pity for her. If she blamed herself for Ronnie's death, that was a terrible burden, and ridiculous. I hoped she would attend the inquest and that the coroner would be able to give an account that would be in some way helpful. 'If there's anything at all I can do, please just say. Anything you need.'

She shook her head. 'I'm well shut of the place. Would you ever see Mr Whitaker spinning or weaving?' She answered her own question. 'You would not, but the cloth is made and sold just the same. I did my job Whitaker-style.'

'You did your best.'

'My best wasn't good enough. Nor was my son good enough for the Whitakers.'

'It's not your fault.'

'Mrs Whitaker, Pamela's mother, that's who I blame. She said that Ronnie and Pamela weren't a suitable match. I went along with it. Pamela was brought up with everything a girl could want. She would soon grow tired of a working man. I didn't want to see my boy hurt; and now, well, having his heart broke would be nothing compared with losing his life. He could have lived with a broken heart. I warned him.'

She suddenly lost track of what she was going to say. Did she really think Mrs Whitaker was so opposed to Ronnie that she would have him killed?

'What did you warn Ronnie about?'

'Ronnie was organising the union, firing up the workers to argue for shorter hours. I told him not to. He said a ten-hour day one week and being laid off another wasn't fair. He said there'd be strength in numbers. He was a fly in Whitaker's machine oil. He was the spider in Mrs Whitaker's face cream.'

Her view of Mr Whitaker was at odds with what the man himself had told me, regarding Ronnie as someone who might come into the company, and be the son he never had.

This wasn't a good time or place, but Mrs Creswell may never confide in me again. I was about to ask her to tell me more when a wavering voice that I took to be the old uncle called down the stairs. 'Who is it? Who are you talking to?'

Mrs Creswell stood. 'I have to go. Uncle Nick had a long walk to see his old teacher. It's tired him out and set him on edge.'

The uncle appeared, carrying a bunch of keys. He rattled them in my direction. 'These are for you. I've had them man and boy and that's too long.'

Mrs Creswell stared at him.

'She doesn't want old keys.'

'What are they for?' I asked.

'For everything in Milner Field.' He thrust the keys towards me. 'I was given them when the builders finished. I forgot to pass them on.'

I reached for the keys.

Mrs Creswell's eyes widened. She glared at him. 'You've had them sixty years?' She turned to me. 'Oh, chuck 'em away, Mrs Shackleton.'

'Thank you. I'll take them off your hands.'

Mrs Creswell ushered her uncle back upstairs.

Grasping a set of heavy keys sufficient to unlock the Castle of Otranto, the Tower of London and the gates to the Seven Circles of Hell, I wished them good evening.

Sykes had seen me. He stood on the opposite pavement with that stance men have when they want to be noticed – legs slightly apart, thumbs in trouser pockets – and then turned and went into the mill yard.

I crossed the street and walked in that direction, following him.

'You all right?' he asked.

'Yes. That's the Creswell house. I walked Ronnie's little sister home and had a word with Mrs Creswell.'

'Poor woman.'

'She doesn't want Nancy anywhere near Milner Field, but Mr Creswell is still doing the gardens, and staying there by all accounts. The place is a magnet to Nancy.'

'I saw you with her and thought you might want a lift back.'

'Yes, I will. Thank you. Mrs Sugden has practised her driving by going to Shipley and following a lead. How is everything at home? Have you heard more about Rosie?'

'No change, but our Irene and your Miss Merton have the Milner Field and mill telephone numbers.'

'Then you can rely on them to ring here with any messages.' Miss Merton was our near neighbour until her brother became university vice chancellor and they moved a little way off into grander accommodation.

'Is there somewhere I can stay the night?' Sykes asked.

With the mood so sombre, I hoped no one saw me laugh. 'Are you joking? We're in an almost empty mansion. Garner, the estate manager, occupies his own wing of the mansion, when he is not living elsewhere preparing for a new future. Mrs Sugden and I occupy the Tower, which is self-contained. There's an invisible scullery maid who operates the dumb waiter. Mrs Sugden may have more news of her tomorrow. The Creswells' Lodge stands empty. You could stay there.'

He glanced at the keys Uncle Nick had bequeathed me. 'Is that your latest offensive weapon?'

I gave the keys a shake. 'Could be, but they're for the mansion. Creswell's Uncle Nick gave them to me. He's only had them sixty years.'

'A man after my own heart.'

'And has Mr Whitaker finished for the day?' I asked.

'Not yet. He's doing some paperwork. We spent some time calculating how much he might shave off his price to keep the Montague Burton order.'

The mill yard felt eerily quiet. The crane with its massive hooks hung still, ready to swing and lift bales up the side. I thought of the noose Mrs Sugden and I had seen hanging from the ceiling in the room at the top of the Tower. I told Sykes about it. 'It swung when we opened the door, caught by the draught between the door and the window.'

'Someone's idea of a poor joke,' said Sykes. 'I'll find a pair of ladders and take it down.'

'It did add to the eerie atmosphere. I felt a powerful waft of cold air by the dumb waiter in the mock-Tudor dining room at the mansion. It gave me the shudders to think that might be the shaft that the little boy fell down years ago, when the mansion was being built.'

'There'll be a logical explanation for the lower temperature,' said Sykes. 'The cold air will be from the ventilation system.'

He had parked the car beyond some empty bogies; a couple of smart company vans stood nearby. I thought back to the other mill, and my first professional case. That was on a much smaller scale, but whatever size company there would be trade secrets, the determination to stay on top, a powerful will to succeed at all costs, and that tribal desire to hand on something of value to the next generation. Did a larger company such as Salts mean there would be increased ruthlessness, a power struggle from within? The smallest family mill could harbour a murderer.

'What's really going on in the mill? Is someone in the company biting at Mr Whitaker's heels for the chairmanship?' I asked.

'That's one of the questions,' Sykes said as he opened the passenger door for me. 'Arnold Whitaker would have told me if he suspected that. It's unlikely that the other directors will be clamouring to take his place. He's very good at his job. It's easier for other directors to let someone else take the lead and carry the can.'

'Any breakthroughs?'

'I'm seeing someone later tonight in the Boy and Barrel.'

I didn't ask. Sykes guards his contacts as if they were crown jewels and a maharaja was about to ask for the return of his rubies.

'The truth is, if he doesn't have something for me, I'm stymied. I need to know who is behind the attack on Salts.'

'Attack is a strong word.'

Sykes raised his eyebrows. 'Not if you're on the receiving end.' He cleared his throat. 'Arnold Whitaker showed me his calculations and his last price and specification for the Burton's contract, which he'd expected to be renewed. When the purchase manager told him there was a question mark over renewal, he gave Arnold a little information from the rival quotation.'

'Isn't that unethical?'

'It would be if it wasn't so completely obvious that the rival had used Salts' figures, taken off a sixpence here, added tuppence there. They also promised the same quality yarn. Whoever wrote the bid has inside information. This is an attempt to put Salts out of business.'

'A clumsy attempt, from what you say.'

'It needs to be nipped in the bud or there'll be open season on big boy Salts. Smaller mills could set aside their differences, band together and try to step up to the mark.'

Sykes moved to start the engine and then changed his mind. 'There's something you could do, if you don't mind perhaps wasting half an hour.'

Sitting side by side in a car in a big yard with high walls somehow shut out all those fleeting thoughts that can scatter concentration.

'I'll gladly waste half an hour, especially if I can turn up some titbit of information that will help us put the pieces of the puzzle together. Mr Whitaker trusted me to find the truth about Ronnie's death. Well, if there is a single truth, I'm still chasing the revelation, and the links to what's going on at Salts.'

I was waiting for Sykes to tell me how I might find out something or other by 'wasting half an hour', but he was thinking of his own plans for later that evening. 'That's what I'm hoping to find out tonight in Bradford,' he said.

At least Sykes would be meeting a man in a pub. I felt I was chasing shadows, and obsessing about the night of the fancy-dress ball, and the feeling that something was going on. Well, of course something was going on. A party!

'Let's not rule anything or anyone out,' I said. 'Let's look for those connections. Ronnie was maintenance. He played a part in preparing the mansion for the ball. Industrial espionage doesn't spring up overnight. What if the idea of stealing a march on Salts by trying to cut in on their contract started as a chat on the night of the May Ball when the aristocracy of the woollen industry gathered at Milner Field? Who better to listen in than one of the so-called "serving wenches", and who might she tell? If Ronnie got wind of dirty dealings over a lucrative contract, he could be a marked man.'

'True,' Sykes said, 'but if Ronnie was a threat, why wait from May until August before doing anything about him?'

'I don't know. But that evening of the ball seems significant. On that night, there's a theft. The cleaners are there as waitresses. One of them, Gwyneth, isn't seen again, until today. Where did she go, and what has brought her back?'

'Who saw her today?' Sykes asked.

'Young Nancy Creswell, but from a distance. Mrs Sugden is going to Gwyneth's old lodgings. They might have passed on the road between Saltaire and Shipley. I will happily waste half an hour, as you put it, for the chance of a key that will fit a lock. So tell me.'

'All right. This is it, for what it's worth. There's a worker at Salts who asked to be remembered to you. When you were on the Braithwaite's Mill case, he was caretaker there. He wears a high boot.'

That was a long time ago, eight years, my first professional assignment. But I would never forget it. Sykes's mention of the caretaker with the high boot suddenly brought the man to mind. 'A thin, grey-haired chap in a brown overall. He must have had aches and pains from the steep steps he climbed between floors. He had a patient, quiet manner. He swept the floors with a brush almost as long as himself.'

'His current sweeping brush is the right length, but the description fits. You have a good memory.'

I was surprised that the man had remembered me, and associated me with Sykes.

Sykes said, 'His name is—'

'Charlie.'

'That's him. How do you remember his name?'

'The weavers would wave and call "Charlie" if they wanted something. I was pleased with myself for reading his name on their lips, but how did he know I was here?'

'He was on his tea break and saw you walking down Victoria Road earlier.'

I groaned. It had seemed a good idea to wear my Paris outfit. I ought to have known I would stick out like a zebra among ponies.

'Anyhow, he spotted me too and made the connection. He spoke but I couldn't hear a word he said, so he waited by the door for me.'

'He could have spoken to you, couldn't he?'

'You were the one who made an impression. Charlie Benson made a point of telling me he takes his grandson to the park of an evening. He was specific about where they would go, along the river to the weir, opposite a wool-washing building. He told me that he wants to talk to you, to the lady who was at Braithwaite's, he said.'

'Did he say what about?'

'No. But I could tell by how clear and insistent he was

about where he would be and when that this was something he regarded as important.'

'Is that why we're sitting in a stationary car? No one else has volunteered to talk to me. He may have seen or heard something at the mill. Something that would help you, or he may know about a grudge against Ronnie Creswell. He's bound to pick up on what's going on when he walks about sweeping.'

'Not when he's looking at the floor. Anyway, he would have told the police, or his boss,' Sykes said wearily. 'I'll tell you why I hesitated to take up your time. It was Charlie's twinkle when he mentioned his grandson. I think he just wants to show him off to you. He wouldn't expect me to be interested. But on the other hand, there just might be something in it, and I'm banging my head against a brick wall when it comes to finding out who has been up to dirty tricks at Salts.'

After Sykes throwing his wet blanket over Charlie's request, I had no great hopes of anything other than a 'How-do? Meet my grandson', but a walk in the park might clear my head.

TWENTY-FIVE

Nick sat in his chair by the window. The woman who had walked Nancy home crossed the street and began to talk to someone. Nick knew the woman's name five minutes ago. Now he had forgotten it. He was rid of the keys to Milner Field. That was an end of it. If anyone had known he had them, the questions would have started all over again. Were you playing with Billy Creswell that day, that Sunday? Who saw him? Who went to play in Milner Field? Own up and you won't be in trouble.

No one owned up.

After all these years, Nick half believed his own lie. He said he had not seen Billy Creswell that Sunday. Going to see Miss Mason today had brought it all back. He knew he would have the dream again, the dream of Billy's fall down the shaft, his scream. The voices, hurling the question, coming at him, fit to burst his skull. Did you see Billy that day?

But now it was ended. He had told Miss Mason where he buried what she liked to call her baby. He didn't know if it was a baby. He hadn't let himself look at it properly. But it was up to her now. It was up to her and the undertaker who would come and dig for the creature and bury it with her. The undertaker was probably lying. He would say something obliging for a quiet life and an extra shilling.

Nick sat in his chair by the window. Nancy was reading to him from *Comic Cuts*. Usually, he forgot all else when they were absorbed in the stories and the nonsense and the daftness that made them laugh out loud. This evening, he could not pay attention. Nancy appeared not to notice. She did not laugh very much but she did once or twice. Her mother had told her to read the comic and told Nick to listen. Nick laughed when Nancy laughed. When he forgot to laugh, she said, 'Don't you think that was funny?'

'Read it again; I didn't catch it.'

What troubled him was having handed over the set of keys to the mansion. He had given up what he had kept close for so long. 'Give the keys to the new person,' he had told Nancy.

'You've given them to Mrs Shackleton yourself,' said Nancy. 'Mam told me.'

He had spoken allowed, must be careful about that.

Mrs Shackleton was the woman who had twice brought Nancy home from Milner Field. He ought not to have handed that kind person the keys to hell. That was how he came to think of them.

It seemed like yesterday when he took the keys from the builders who were finishing off, saying yes he would pass on the spare set. He had meant to do it. He slid them onto his snake belt, bought with pennies he had saved from helping, from fetching and carrying. He pretended to himself he was the owner. After the builders had gone, he walked about the empty place, singing, calling, whistling, locking and unlocking doors. He was eleven years old and fearless. He would walk by the canal and someone would say hop on and he would go all the way to Liverpool and back. But no one said hop on.

It was by the canal that he heard a cry. He saw that Miss Mason had fallen and went to help her up. Nick saw the blood. Billy Creswell saw the teacher fall but he did not come forward to help. He hung back behind a bush. Miss Mason was all scrunched up, bent over, and making a horrible noise more like a scream than a groan. He wanted to turn away and run. It was not right for her to be like this. A grown-up, a teacher, she should be on her feet, like in the classroom or in the yard when they did exercises or played games. Or she should be sitting at her desk with her head to one side, deciding who to let speak, when too many children had their hands up.

Nick had not meant Billy Creswell to die. He only wanted him not to tell on Miss Mason. But he would have told, and now Billy would be waiting for Nick at the gates of hell.

Nick had kept the keys too long. It was too late to go knock on the door of the mansion and say, 'Here are the spare keys.'

He hid the set of keys. He tried to forget that they were the keys to hell.

Now he was rid of them.

He watched the lady with the keys and the man go into the yard. They came out in a car and drove down the hill. Something bad was bound to happen.

TWENTY-SIX

After a light shower of rain, the smell of grass in the park made me glad to be outdoors. Charlie Benson would be by the weir, he had told Sykes. A young couple walked into the park, pushing a pram, intent on the occupant's every breath. We exchanged 'Good evening's, the woman adding, 'Sometimes walking by the river is our only way to get him to sleep.'

'A good trick,' I said. 'Tell me, is it far to the weir?'

'Reasonable.'

Whatever that meant.

I walked on, listening to the murmur of the water, watching a dipper take a dive for food.

Charlie was standing back from the river. The weir was powerful, and noisy. The little boy stood on a miniature beach. He wore short trousers, carried a fishing net on a stick and took cautious steps.

Charlie saw me and nodded. 'Evening, missis.'

'Good evening, Charlie.'

He coughed, politely turning his head and putting his hand to his chest, leaning forward.

I said, 'I remember you from Braithwaite's Mill. The women called for you a lot. I read your name on their lips.'

He laughed. 'So they did. They were a fine bunch of lasses.'

'Mr Benson, pleased to meet you properly. I'm Kate Shackleton.' We watched the child stepping through a murmur of water, carefully trailing his net, making barely a splash. A movement of wings made me look up. A kite took off from the opposite bank, the underside of its wings a revelation of colour.

I let several long minutes elapse. He was not a man given to easy talking. It was a wonder to me that he had spoken to Sykes. He seemed anxious and was sweating. Perhaps he did not know how to begin, or was having second thoughts.

'You have a fine little lad there. What's his name?'

'Stanley. He likes to come here.'

'What brought you the couple of miles from Bridgestead to Saltaire, Mr Benson, if you don't mind my asking?'

'Wife wanted to be near our daughter. Daughter and son-in-law work at Salts. Wife works in the canteen. First time in us lives we make ends meet.'

'I'm glad things are working out.'

The child came splashing through the water, showing tiddlers, showing a tadpole.

'Good lad. Put 'em back.'

The child upended the net, and went back to start again.

'Do you allus come to a place when there's summat amiss?' Charlie asked.

'I came here because Ronnie Creswell wrote to me. Unfortunately, I was too late to meet him. Now I'm staying at Milner Field, helping out with a few things.'

There, I had put my cards on the table. Would he pick one up?

He sighed. 'It's a poor do that lad met his end.'

'You knew Ronnie?'

'He was sometimes here of an evening at the cricket pavilion. He showed Stanley how to hold a bat.'

Charlie rubbed his shoulder. The man was not well. Walking about the mill the whole day wasn't the right sort of job for a man with a high boot. He should be at home with his feet up.

'Let's sit on the bank,' I said.

He nodded. 'If I didn't have this boot, I'd take off my shoes and paddle.'

We settled ourselves on the bank and for several moments watched Stanley. It was a peaceful place. The roar of the weir made me think that whatever we had to say would be insignificant in the great scheme of things. But we were here to talk.

'Charlie, I think you have something in particular to tell me?'

'Wife said I should keep quiet. Tell 'em nothing.'

'But you think you should tell me.'

'Only if it's to you. Because I've spoken to the police once. I can't do it again, especially as it's summat and nowt. If I'm thought to be pointing a finger, we could lose us jobs. Would it be between us?'

I hesitated. 'Is it about Ronnie's death, or about something else going on at the mill?' I wondered if he had seen something suspicious that might link to the industrial espionage Sykes was investigating.

Charlie shook his head. 'Don't know what it's about, but it's fishy.'

'Every bit of information helps. You could tell the police.'

'The police spoke to me on the day Ronnie died, about who

I saw and who was and wasn't a worker, or anything out of the ordinary. I told them I saw the boss's wife, Mrs Whitaker, that day Ronnie died. It wasn't out of the ordinary except that she was wearing what they call slacks. She sometimes comes to the mill on a Saturday. She brings a plant, says hello to people and stays half an hour. She had the smart young chap who came in a car and was shown round the mill by Ronnie Creswell. He was there two Saturdays.'

'Do you know his name?'

'I do, but only because the weavers all knew that he's called Kevin Foxcroft and that he's intending to marry Mr Whitaker's daughter.'

'Was there something else to tell?'

'Last Saturday, I saw young Mr Foxcroft, on his own, go right up to the reservoir door and look at the slot where time cards are, where they tick off the inspections. He'd done that previously, when he and Mrs Whitaker were there for a much longer time, well over an hour. I remember the date because it was Stanley's birthday, last Saturday of June.

'Then this Saturday just gone, I went into the back yard to empty my sweepings, I saw——' He pressed his chest again and then put his hands first in one jacket pocket and then the other, looking for something. 'I've tablets that ease the tightness.'

'Don't talk just yet. Rest.'

He shook his head and caught his breath. 'I'm all right now, just hot.'

I helped him off with his jacket.

'Look for my pills. I can talk. Where was I?'

I checked his jacket pockets and found nothing but an old bus ticket. 'You were going to tell me what you saw when you went to empty your sweepings in the back yard.'

193

'A big bloke going through one of the doors in the back yard, just saw the back of him.'

'Mr Benson, I'm not keeping up. You've mentioned two Saturdays: one in June and last Saturday. When did Mrs Whitaker and Mr Foxcroft stay for more than an hour in the mill?'

'In June.'

'And this past Saturday?'

'They were there for a short time. But the young chap still went to see the time cards and I thought, Aye, aye, why does he care when the maintenance men go in and out of the reservoir?'

'Why do you think?'

'I thought he was spying. Same day, I saw the big fellow go through the door in the back yard.'

'What was suspicious about that? A lot of people must come and go.'

'That's what the security officer, Paul Bradley, said when I told him about seeing the man. And there'd been no comeback from the police about young Mr Foxcroft by the reservoir door. Paul said there were deliveries that day. Drivers are allowed to come in to use the facilities and all the drivers had been questioned. One must have gone in to use the lav.'

'You weren't satisfied with that explanation?'

'No. There's two doors. He went through the one that is usually locked. It leads to the basement. Paul said I was mixing up the doors and the driver had gone to the lavatory.'

'This sounds important. The police will certainly have taken note.'

'I didn't know who the man was at the time. He didn't look

like any driver I'd seen. After talking to Paul, I began to doubt myself, was it that door? But now I think I know who it was.'

'How, if you only saw the back of the person?'

Charlie gulped. He took out a hanky and wiped his brow. He was looking distinctly unwell. It was a good walk back to the village.

'Save your breath for now. We can talk later.' I took aspirins from my satchel and tipped one in his hand. 'Chew on this, and then swallow. When you get your breath, say the man's name.'

He took the aspirin. As he chewed, he put his fingers into his top pocket. He swallowed the aspirin, saying, 'I have my own pills. I took one at tea break.'

'Charlie, the man's name?'

'I don't know his name. If you go to the Congregational Church on Sunday, you'll see him.'

That was a let-down. I tried not to show my disappointment. 'How will I know him?'

'I recognise people by their gait, have done since I was a kid. If you have a foot and a leg like mine, you look at others and puzzle over yourself. This man, upright as a post, moves his arms marching-style, goes over a bit on his right foot.'

I had not known what to expect, but this Sherlockian observation was not it. If he had been born into a different walk of life, Charlie might have trained as a physiotherapist. 'You said there were two doors. What was unusual about the man using the one he did?'

'It takes you to the gallery of the reservoir.'

'The police would investigate that.'

'Not if security and David Fairburn, who both ought to know, said it was always locked.'

I glanced about. There was a group of men on the cricket pitch, practising throws. They paused to huddle over some discussion.

'Shall we start a slow walk back? We'll sit on a bench.'

He shook his head. 'Stanley needs his play.' A cool breeze came from the river. Charlie seemed to rally a little.

'Any road, if I say a name on the strength of the way a man can be upright and tilting at the same time as he swings his arms, I'll be in trouble. Paul on security made that quite clear. He knows the law.'

'Charlie, you know the man's name, don't you? You are keeping it back out of fear of being in trouble, losing your job?' He would not meet my eye, but looked away, towards the cricketers. 'Charlie, we are not in a court of law. You can tell me.'

'Be in the church grounds Sunday after the service. I'll give you the nod when he comes out.'

The little boy was still playing in the river. He had been joined by another child. They were laughing and splashing.

Charlie was swaying a little, not drunk or I would have smelled it. 'Are you dizzy?'

He nodded. 'Feel a bit sick.'

'Lean back against the slope of the bank. Take deep breaths. I'll be back in a minute. You need a cup of tea.'

Charlie leaned back, and then slumped over to the side.

He needed help. I ran. I ran for the cricket pitch faster than I had ever run. Two of the outlying players, poised to catch a ball, spotted me coming. The concentration of the rest of the men was such that one of them threw the ball just as I entered the line of fire.

'Gentlemen! Emergency! Charlie Benson, mill caretaker,

has taken badly. We need a stretcher to get him to the village and to hospital. Will someone please run ahead and say that he's coming?'

I must have used my VAD nurse voice because they sprang into action. A hand shot up and a tall young fellow raced up to me. 'What shall I say, miss?'

'Possible heart attack.'

He nodded and was off.

By the time I got back to Charlie, the mother of the little boy who had come to play with Stanley was standing on the bank, watching over Charlie.

Charlie was sweating profusely and holding his chest.

'You're going to be all right, Charlie,' I told him. 'The cricketers will carry you to hospital.' I produced another aspirin. 'Here, chew on this and then swallow.'

The woman who had brought her little boy said, 'And don't you worry, Mr Benson, I'll mind Stanley and see him home.'

Stanley was gripping his fishing rod. He was blinking and looked set to cry. 'It's all right, Stanley,' the woman said. 'Your granddad will be right as rain in no time.' She produced a bag of sweets. 'One each. We'll give your granddad a start while you take your time tipping your tadpoles back and then we'll go home.'

Five cricketers appeared, two of them with a stretcher. This must be a well-equipped cricket hut. Three men lifted Charlie onto the stretcher, one of them the joker, 'Owt for a free ride, eh?'

As they set off, Charlie looked up at me. 'Where's Stanley?'

'He's with the other little boy and his mother. She'll see Stanley home.' I patted his arm. 'Rest, Charlie. Save your breath.'

I walked on ahead, keen to get to the hospital and give an account of Charlie's symptoms.

Sykes was waiting for me by the park entrance. As we fell into step, hurrying to the hospital, I told him what had happened.

'Poor man. Lucky that you were with him and that you acted quickly.'

'I don't know about luck, but it's fortunate that Titus Salt provided a hospital for his workforce.'

'Charlie is clearly a worrier.'

'It's more than that. He was searching his pockets for pills. He was sure he had them and that he had taken one at his tea break. I don't know what medication he is on but I am guessing it is for a heart condition. It didn't help that he believes he wasn't taken seriously about what he saw as suspicious activity. He doesn't miss a thing.'

'Such as?' Sykes asked.

'On the day Ronnie died, he saw Kevin Foxcroft, Mrs Whitaker's godson, linger for a moment outside the door in the mill that leads to the reservoir. He says he was glancing at the time cards, as if to see what time Ronnie would be there.'

'He'd have to do more than glance. He'd have to take the card out and look. But why was Foxcroft there?'

'He sometimes goes into the mill with Mrs Whitaker on a Saturday-morning visit.'

'That's not a crime. Has Charlie appointed himself Salts Mill detective-in-chief?'

'So it seems. Also, last Saturday he saw a man entering a door from the yard that leads to the reservoir, when that door was supposedly locked.'

'That's significant. The police will have followed up on that.'

'I'm sure they will, or already have, but Charlie thinks they haven't taken his report seriously.'

'It's the man entering the mill through a supposedly locked door in the yard who is a person of interest.'

'Despite not seeing the man's face, Charlie says he could identify him.'

'And the man is?'

'We need to wait until Charlie recovers, or stand outside a church on Sunday looking for a man who holds himself upright but whose gait is slightly tilted and who swings his arms.'

'Right,' said Sykes in his eyebrow-raising voice. 'Will you report this to Inspector Mitchell?'

'Of course.'

'Did Charlie tell anyone else what he told you?'

'He told a security officer called Paul who warned him about the laws of slander.'

Sykes came a stop mid stride. 'Hang on, if there is something going on, and Charlie has wind of it, maybe his symptoms are not entirely connected with ill health.'

Sykes has a talent for playing Job's comforter. That seemed preposterous. It was bad enough that Charlie's poor health may jeopardise his employment, just when he and his family were making ends meet.

I thought of Charlie's search for his pills. What were they and where were they? I wondered. He would have kept quiet about poor health for fear of losing his job. 'The tea break was when Charlie took his last pill. He checked his pockets when we were by the river. He felt sure that he had more pills.'

We had reached the entrance to the hospital. 'I'll go inside and speak to the doctor.'

Sykes nodded. 'Do we wait to hear how Charlie progresses overnight?'

'Yes. Mrs Benson will decide what she says to Charlie's boss.'

'Agreed,' said Sykes. 'This isn't the moment to tell Arnold Whitaker that his chief sweeper-up has suspicions about Mrs Whitaker, her godson and a man with a unique gait.' He looked at his watch, clearly wanting to be off.

'Don't wait for me. I'll walk back.'

TWENTY-SEVEN

Having practised her driving close to home, with Mrs Shackleton sitting beside her, Mrs Sugden needed to hold her nerve in unfamiliar territory. She slowed to avoid mowing down two boys on bikes, riding recklessly, showing off, and then a Ringtons Tea van coming to a heedless halt.

That top road looked busy. Trams seemed an appropriate size when riding on one, but alongside tram rails, and hearing a tram behind, would make a lesser woman lose her nerve.

Having a bump in Mrs Shackleton's motor car in a strange place where people would be ready to mark her down was not a shining prospect. Shipley seemed a long way off. It took three sightings of the same motorbike for Mrs Sugden to realise she was being followed. The person on the motorbike wore a helmet and kept his head down. He passed her, turned off, passed her again a few streets further on.

Perhaps it was a person who liked to torment women drivers, or recognised a learner. Going to talk to Gwyneth's landlady had seemed a good idea. Mrs Sugden knew Shipley. She once had a job at the Norman Rae Nursing Home, but that was a long time ago and now the place no longer seemed familiar.

Mrs Sugden pulled in at the side of the road. She looked at the map. Going all the way to Shipley would miss the house where Gwyneth had lodged. There would be a turnoff on the left.

As she set off, there was that motorbike again. Was he lost as well? That must be it. Anyway, he had gone now.

Ignoring the children who stopped playing to stare, and the crowd of youths gambling for pennies on the street corner, she kept her eyes on the street names until she reached the one she wanted and slowly turned.

Immediately, she felt at home. The sun shone on clean windows with neat curtains. Doorsteps and windowsills had been scoured. Empty washing lines stretched across the street. Some of the doors were open. Children left off playing ball and taws and chalking on the pavement as they turned to stare at the car. At number 22, a woman sat on her doorstep, nursing a baby. Outside number 18 was a basketwork invalid carriage about five feet long and with four large wheels. Mrs Sugden stopped. Number 18 was her destination. She got out of the car and approached the invalid basket, looking down at the sun-kissed face of a curly-haired woman of indeterminate age who was covered with a red blanket. From the waist the woman's body bent backwards. Her legs followed the same line, creating the shape of a bow.

'Hello,' Mrs Sugden said. 'I'm sorry to bother you.'

The woman smiled, displaying four yellow-stained teeth. 'You're all right. I'm out here so folk will bother me. I don't suppose you've got a Woodbine?'

'I don't smoke but I'll get you a packet.'

'That's kind of you. You from the hospital?'

'No.'

'Oh, only they take me in every once in a while, to torment me.'

Smaller children, sensing a change taking place in their world, appeared on the doorsteps of nearby houses. They stared at the car from a safe distance.

Mrs Sugden smiled at her new acquaintance. 'I better tell you who I am and then you can tell me who you are. I'm Mrs Sugden and I'm up at the mansion near Saltaire.'

'Everybody calls me Jean because that's my name, and I'm here. Always.'

'Well, Jean, for the time being I'm taking over housekeeping at Milner Field and we've a bit of a mystery over Gwyneth who worked there and lodged with you.'

'I'm saying nowt. She's honest as the day is long.'

'No one's saying different. She was a good worker. We're starting afresh tomorrow to clean up the mansion. Might she be wanting to come to work?'

'I wish she was here. Best lass I ever had stopping. She'd see to me, wheel me in and out, pay rent.'

Mrs Sugden was curious. She wanted to know who saw to Jean now, and who wheeled her in and out, but that was not her business.

'The thing is, Jean, Gwyneth left on the night of the May Ball, without her evening's pay and no sign or sight of her since.'

Jean laughed, tossing her head back so that it seemed she was stretching back the bow of her body ready to fire an arrow. 'You've no cause to worry about Gwyn. She finds her feet.'

'Some feller?' Mrs Sugden asked.

'I'm giving nowt away. But she'll be back to see me one fine day, wearing a fur coat and a gold ring.'

Mrs Sugden made herself appear suitably impressed, at the same time glancing to her right. A woman wearing a purple turban and a red pinny stepped out from number 22, calling, 'You all right, Jean?'

'I am that. This lady from the mansion is going to fetch me five Woodbines.'

'That's all right, then,' said the neighbour and disappeared, turban first.

Jean lifted her nicotine-stained fingers to her hair and combed through it. 'If you could see your way to fetch a bottle of pop, too? It's been a parching day.'

In the corner shop, Mrs Sugden felt like the big spender. A pork pie, five Woodbines and a bottle of pop. I'm a fortunate woman, said she to herself, liking the look of the pork pies and making it two. It's a crying shame that yon poor lass is confined to an invalid basket and has lost her best lodger. Once she has a cig, she'll feel better in herself. We'll have a good natter and I'll find out what's what.

As she came out of the shop, the motorbike went by again, the rider not looking right or left but heading for the main road. He must be doing what I'm doing, Mrs Sugden thought, practising his driving.

The woman in the purple turban was at her door when Mrs Sugden came back with the pies, pop and cigs for Jean.

'Oh,' said the woman in the turban. 'I'm keeping an eye because someone went in Jean's house yesterday and opened every cupboard and drawer and left all her stuff strewn about.'

'A burglary?'

'No. What is there to steal in there, or from any of us? It was some devilment. We can't think who it was but we're all watching now.'

'What about that motorbike?'

'Well, that's just gone by once and it's another mystery because I've never seen it before.'

Mrs Sugden decided not to say that the motorbike had followed her all the way from Saltaire.

TWENTY-EIGHT

The nursing sister was wearing her cape and I guessed had been about to go off duty. As Charlie was being taken to a ward, I gave her an account of his symptoms.

'You're not new to this, are you?' she asked.

'I served with the VAD.'

'Mr Benson is in good hands, thanks to your prompt action.'

'He couldn't find his pills. All I did was give aspirins and have him brought here quickly.'

She nodded. 'We have his address from one of the young men who brought him in.'

I had a sudden sinking feeling as I thought of Stanley. I hoped this would not be the last time that Stanley's granddad took him to the park. 'May I use the telephone?'

'One of us can make a call for you.'

'It's to the police inspector. I'd sooner speak to him myself to pass on some information.'

'In that case, use Matron's office.'

Inspector Mitchell listened carefully as I told him of Charlie Benson's concerns, and the circumstances of his collapse. From the inspector's tone of voice I thought he probably remembered Charlie Benson's statement. One would, if among all the other statements here was a man who claimed to have seen a suspicious character.

The inspector asked, 'Do you really think Charlie Benson was on to something, regarding the man he saw entering the mill building from the yard? A sick man, in pain, covering up poor health and dizzy spells might easily become confused.'

'He gave a sober, straightforward account to me of who and what he saw. He also told the security officer. The officer assumed Charlie made a mistake about the door being unlocked. That is possible, and the security officer may be considered more reliable, but Charlie was in the yard, an eyewitness. He hesitated to come back to you with his added information about recognising the man by his gait, probably because it sounds far-fetched. But given Charlie's lameness and his interest in how people walk, that observation has the ring of truth for me.'

'I understand why you see it that way, Mrs Shackleton. We won't rule out that someone got hold of a spare key, or a door being accidentally on purpose left unlocked. So, the man's appearance?'

'It was his gait rather than his appearance. The man had an upright stance but with a slight preference for one side, which I suppose would indicate greater wear on the right shoe. And there is one other detail – something David Fairburn mentioned when I drove him home from the police station.'

There was a slight pause before the inspector said, 'Something he forgot to tell us?'

'Not forgot. When we stopped outside the Fairburns' house, David said he'd been trying to recall what was the faint smell he noticed as he went down the steps into the reservoir. He realised it was Brylcreem.'

'What brought on this sudden revelation?'

'PC Harrison, who completed the discharge papers, wears Brylcreem.'

'Does he indeed?' The inspector's heavy sigh tickled my eardrum. 'Thank you, Mrs Shackleton. And is David Fairburn suggesting my constable is Charlie Benson's big man who went to the reservoir and lay in wait for Ronald Creswell?'

As we ended the call, I wondered whether the inspector would find a pretext for being sniffing distance from Constable Harrison's hair and surreptitiously examining his boots for signs of uneven wear.

I thanked the hospital sister for the use of her telephone. 'What do you think are Mr Benson's chances of pulling through?'

'We'll do our best for him. If he does pull through, I hope he will be given a sitting-down job.'

'Was it a heart attack, Sister?'

'Sadly, yes, and not his first.'

TWENTY-NINE

After leaving the hospital, I set off to follow that same path to Milner Field as I had last Saturday. I felt downhearted. Instead of being able to fathom Ronnie's letter, here I was caught up in events that made no sense.

Charlie Benson's sightings and suspicions seemed like the product of a powerful imagination. As I walked the path, I was aware of the greenery around me, and the quiet as evening drew in. Overlaying the present were the scenes Charlie Benson had created for my mind's eye of Mrs Whitaker and Kevin Foxcroft going into Whitaker's office back in June, staying for more than an hour, and visiting again on the day of Ronnie's death.

These images belonged to a film rather than real life. In this silent picture, the actors playing the two figures approaching the mill sported heavy, lively eyebrows and darting eyes. As they entered the mill, a watchman snored gently, leaning back in his chair of oblivion. The unknown man with a particular style of walking wore black. As he turned and looked over his shoulder, he smoothed his villain's moustache before entering a door that led from the yard, down to the gallery of the reservoir.

I tried to banish these images and think clearly.

My hopes for clarity faded as the Creswells' Uncle Nick blundered into view, seemingly appearing from nowhere, carrying bunches of buttercups and daisies. He hailed me. 'Just the person, just the lady I want to see. You brought Nancy home.'

'Yes, I did. Hello again. I know you're Uncle Nick, but I don't know your surname.'

Not that it was a test, but I wondered how far gone he was, and whether he still knew his own name. Nobody ever used it. Perhaps his eccentricities and memory lapses hid a more serious condition.

He waved my comment away. 'I'm Nick. I'm Uncle Nick. I'm him over there on the straight-back chair. All's one. I trod the boards, you know, in the amateur dramatics. "The shepherdess is in danger, her face, dirty from crying about her sheep." That was my line.'

'I believe I've heard that story.' Once he could remember lines, now the part of King Lear might suit him.

'The schoolteacher knows how to tell it. You'll find Miss Mason along the path at Jane's Hill. She forever had us singing when I first started at that school.'

'I'll walk in that direction one day soon. Have you picked flowers for Miss Mason?'

'These are for the well. I throw flowers down the well, always have.'

'Why?'

'If you've heard the story you'll know why. Sing the right tune to Miss Mason. She'll know you come from me. That will be your recommendation.'

'What shall I sing?' I asked.

'A nursery rhyme.'

I couldn't make this man out. Was he losing his marbles, or lining them up in a different order? Perhaps this was a place of preposterous stories. Uncle Nick's shepherdess merged with the caretaker's image of a furtive Mrs Whitaker in slacks, escorting Kevin Foxcroft into the mill.

Uncle Nick began whistling a familiar tune.

He took a deep breath, rolled back his shoulders, opened and closed his mouth twice, so thoroughly that I heard his jaw crack, and then he began to sing.

> 'A-hunting we will go,
> A-hunting we will go
> Heigh-ho, the derry-o,
> A-hunting we will go.
>
> A-hunting we will go,
> A-hunting we will go
> We'll catch a fox and put him in a box
> And never let him go.'

He looked at me, waiting for comment, or praise.

'I've heard that song before, but a different version.'

He nodded. 'They change it. Nancy puts her hands over her ears. "Wrong words!" she says.'

'How should you sing it?'

'Like this, "We'll catch a fox and put him in a box, and then we'll let him go." There's no peace if I don't sing it her way. The fox must be set free, the cat must be brought from the well, Jill must mend Jack's head with vinegar and a bandage, not vinegar and brown paper. We agree that "Ten Green Bottles" needs no alteration.'

'Well, you have a fine voice. It must run in the family. How are you related to the Creswells?'

'Through great-grandparents, I think.'

We turned towards where I had seen a woman picking bilberries on Saturday. She had not entirely stripped them all. Among the shiny green leaves and the delicate pinkish-red flowers, the dark berries shone. We each picked and ate some, deliciously sweet. 'Good for your eyes,' said Uncle Nick.

By the well, he stood for a solemn moment, and then dropped his bunch of buttercups and daisies, watching them as they fell.

'Why do you do that?' I asked.

'For the shepherdess.'

'That's kind.'

Nick picked a few more bilberries. 'How did she bake such good pies over a fire?' he asked.

'The shepherdess?'

'My grandmother baked pies. I thought she died because I put the bone in the wrong place.'

What was he talking about? 'Did your grandmother break a bone, and ask you to set it?'

'Not that, but it was my fault.'

He's blaming himself, I thought. Children do. They are the centre of the world. 'Nick, whatever happened so long ago, why do you blame yourself?'

He screwed up his face, as if this question required him to name the planets according to size, but he then produced his answer.

'I buried the bone in the wrong place. By the well is

where the bone should lie. "Bury it where you found it," Grandmother said, and, "Bad luck doesn't come without a reason." I thought I made the well run dry, but the builder explained. He said when the old house was pulled down, they let the water find another way to flow. I began to put flowers in the well for the shepherdess and I've done that ever since. The clever one among the builders put his ear to the ground. "Listen," he said. I listened and I heard the water. He put a pipe in the ground and a pipe and a tap above the ground.'

An engineer could not have explained that better. Nick was a man of sense and riddles.

'I did two good things,' Nick said. 'I helped my teacher. I give flowers to the shepherdess, but that doesn't weigh out the bad.'

'What weighs for bad?'

'Moving the shepherdess's bone, and . . . '

'And what?'

'The other thing.'

I knew the stories, the story of the shepherdess, and the story of the boy who died while the house was being built. He fell down a shaft, it was said. 'Sit beside me, Nick. We won't fall down.'

'I don't sit on the well.'

'Just for a short time. I want to ask you something. You might be able to help me with a puzzle that Ronnie set for me.'

'I don't think so.'

'Ronnie wrote to me. He wanted to tell me something about long ago. I think he wanted to know about the boy who died, Billy. Ronnie shared his likeness.'

'They weren't alike, except the hair, eyes, nose.'

That seemed enough of a likeness to me. 'Only in appearance then, but two very different boys?'

'That's it.'

'Billy died when the mansion was being built, when you were a child. He was about your age, part of your family. What were you to each other?'

At first I thought he would not answer me. A raven landed on a branch, and looked at us. Nick looked away. He said quietly, 'When Billy came to the village, Miss Mason said we were cousins. She sat us side by side.'

'So you were friends?'

'A few of us palled up.'

'All the children would have been asked about what happened that day, and whether you played together. Boys do dares in twos and threes and little gangs. Who was with Billy that day?'

'I don't know.'

'I'm asking for Ronnie, because I believe that is what he wanted to know.'

The raven tilted its head.

'I was helping Miss Mason. She fell down by the river. I saw her fall. I was on my own. She'll tell you.'

'And what about Billy? Where did he fall? We brought flowers for the shepherdess, shall we take flowers to the place where Billy fell?'

'No.'

'Perhaps Ronnie would like me to give flowers to Billy.'

'Billy tore the petals from flowers. He threw stones. He never shared.'

'Billy was ten or eleven, like you. He might have grown up to be a better person.'

214

Nick stared at his hands, saying nothing.

Nick knew, I felt sure. As a child he would have shaken his head, avoiding trouble, so would other boys who faced the cane, faced disgrace. Ought I to leave well alone? I thought of the psychiatrist that I got to know, and his talking cures. Might it be a help to Nick if he was carrying a burden and could share it? 'Nick, I'm living in the mansion where Billy died. I'm in the Tower but he died so close by. I think I know where because it feels cold in that place. The shaft of the dumb waiter gives me shivers, does it you?'

'I don't go there.'

I slid off the edge of the well and held out my hand. 'I think you are the only person who can tell me what Ronnie wanted to know about your cousin Billy.'

'Fergie is in the alms house. Ask him.'

'I think you are the one who knows.' The raven flew towards the mansion. 'The raven is showing us the way.'

He took my hand, and then hesitated.

I said, 'Nick, no one need know, except you and Ronnie and Billy and me.'

'Who are you?'

'I'm Kate. I'm a stranger, here for just a short time.'

Who led whom I couldn't say, but we walked hand in hand like the babes in the wood towards the mansion.

'What flowers shall we pick?' I asked.

'Dandelions. Billy wet the bed and he sometimes wet himself.'

As we picked dandelions, I asked, 'Did you and your cousin Billy share a surname?'

'He was Billy Creswell. I am Nicholas Reeves.'

I had a sudden misgiving. What I was doing was not for

215

Ronnie, or was it? What obligation do we have to the dead? To remember them, to say their name, to know their fate? Ronnie had been curious about Billy, but it was too late for Ronnie, and I might tip Nick over the edge, or help him find some steadiness. We walked in silence towards the house. At any moment, Nick might change his mind, veer off, forget his name and his destination. If I went to the Tower to find the key to the main door of the mansion, I would be letting go of his hand. As it was, he was finding the way, walking with the Tower to our left, all along that wing of the house and round the other side to a door half at ground level and half below.

'Look away,' he said, 'while I find the key.'

I turned away.

'You can look now.' He took three steps down and then unlocked the door. It led us into a cellar that smelled of coal dust and wood. He left the door open so the light was sufficient until he found a torch. 'Children always went this way. No one told.'

I thought of the cold air I had felt by the dumb waiter. We were in the wrong part of the mansion for that. If I had expected anything from Nick, it was to have been taken to that dumb waiter. Now I realised that we were not where Billy fell from, but where he fell to.

Nick pointed to an oversize dumb waiter whose door stood open. 'Special build, special chain, to take logs and coal. The carrying part wasn't put in when Billy fell from the rafters upstairs. The shaft was there but not the innards. This is where he was found.'

'What happened?'

'He swung on the rafters. He got spells in his hands. He wanted me there so he could try, without the others seeing

216

he was scared. He was holding on and glad and scared, and then he said, "We come here every Sunday or I'll tell". He would have told. He would have told a secret. And then he was holding on with one hand and . . . '

'And?'

'He reached out to me . . . '

Tears welled in old Nick's eyes. He blinked, brushed them away with the back of his hand. The tears trickled over the deep lines on his face. He wiped his face on his sleeve.

'Afterwards people said that Billy's dad used to hit him. He had black and blue bruises. He'd scraped his knee that day.'

A rush of air turned me cold. It was the same cold rush that I had felt at the other dumb waiter, as if a wind of pain and loss blew around behind the walls of this place.

Nick suddenly reached out into the darkness of the shaft, calling, 'Billy!'

I held on to Nick, until he clasped his arms around himself.

'Listen,' he whispered. 'Can you hear him? Can you hear Billy scream?'

And yes, I could, but there can be too much truth.

'Nick, I can hear Billy saying that it's time for you to stop crying inside. You were just a child. You couldn't have held on to him, but another minute and you would have tried.'

We turned to go. Nick put the torch back in its place.

We walked back and through the door into the warmth of the evening sun. Nick blinked against the light and then turned to me. 'Some said Billy let himself fall because he didn't want to go home, but he held out his hand just before he fell.'

'And you reached for him just now.'

Nick locked the door and hid the key.

A little way off, someone whistled.

After a moment, Nick answered with the same whistle.

'Someone seeking you?' I asked as we walked back round to the front of the mansion.

'Ronald keeps an eye on me of an evening, when I'm on my walk.'

A few moments later, Ronald Creswell came into view.

He walked steadily, with a drag to his step, shoulders slumped. There was no change in his movement or manner when he saw Nick. The son he wanted to see stepping brightly into the future was gone. Now here was the old uncle who must be turned around, pointed in the opposite direction, and perhaps taken all the way to his door.

'Nah then, Uncle Nick.'

'Nah then, our Ronald.'

Mr Creswell touched his cap. 'Mrs Shackleton.'

'Mr Creswell.'

Now I felt sure that the mystery of Billy Creswell had been the reason Ronnie wrote to me. That mystery had unravelled, but no one else would ever know. The answer was for me and for Nick. Tomorrow, Nick may have forgotten the question but I hoped that passing the story to me might take a weight from him. His step as he and Ronald Creswell strode seemed a little lighter and he was talking in an animated fashion. Perhaps a talking cure could work. But I would not try it again. And in future I would take on assignments only for the living, and leave the dead to their own devices.

THIRTY

Sykes's car was parked outside the Tower. He stood back, assessing the building. I waved to him to come in, calling, 'The door's open.'

His first words were, 'I want to see this room with a noose.'

'Two floors up if you want to see the hangman's noose,' I said.

Sykes went upstairs.

Mrs Sugden excels at scratching up a quick meal when we are busy. By the time she dished out three pork pies and a hill of baked beans, Sykes was back from his inspection of the top room.

'Are you having me on? There's no noose in that room, just a punchbag hanging from a hook in the ceiling.'

'Well, there was,' said Mrs Sugden. 'We're not losing our marbles. Whoever put the rope up has let himself in, done a swap.'

Sykes raised his eyebrows. 'Someone's trying to put the wind up you.'

I thought of Nick's big bunch of keys. 'There must have

been different people over the years walking off with a key, temporary residents, visitors, staff needing to come in for one reason or another.'

As usual, Sykes had a practical solution. 'I changed a couple of locks on my last job. I have the old ones with me. One should be right for this door. Do you want me to put it on?'

'Please do,' I said.

Mrs Sugden then dropped what I thought was a bit of a bombshell, but she was matter-of-fact about it. 'I was followed by a motorbike rider on my way from Milner Field to Shipley.'

'That's worrying. But might he have just been riding in the same direction?' I asked.

'That's what I thought, or that he might be practising his driving, like me. But it was deliberate. Passing me on one street and coming back the other way, as if he wanted me to know he was there. Should we tell the police?'

'Yes,' I said. 'We'll report it.'

'Could have been someone just playing the fool,' Mrs Sugden conceded. She took out her notebook, eager to give her account of visiting Gwyneth's landlady.

Knowing Mrs Sugden's tendency to begin a story in the middle, and to prevent a cross-examination by Sykes that would annoy her, I told Sykes, 'On the night of the May Ball at Milner Field, Gwyneth Kidd was one of the cleaners who served at the supper, dressed as serving wenches. They stayed behind to clear up, all except Gwyneth, who left early, with no explanation, and hasn't been seen since. That was the night that the family silver went missing.'

'Why are we interested in a theft?' Sykes asked. 'I'm looking at shady dealings and you, Mrs Sugden, are sprucing up the mansion.'

'I'm short of a cleaner and Gwyneth is a cleaner,' Mrs Sugden said. 'Besides, she's a missing person. I'm in charge now. What or who made her leave so suddenly? Somebody else might float away tomorrow and then there'd be four.'

Sykes was right in that we were not investigating the theft of silver, which by now had probably been melted down and the insurance claim settled. If Mrs Sugden wanted to find out about Gwyneth Kidd, then that's what she should do. I backed her up. 'Gwyneth left that night in a hurry without saying why or where she was going. It would be good to know whether she saw or heard something on the night of the ball.

'Who better to listen in than one of the so-called "serving wenches", and who might she tell?'

Sykes looked at his watch. 'Not that I'm being rude, but I need to get off to meet my contact and I'll call at Shipley police station to give them this.' Like a magician about to produce a rabbit from a hat, Sykes took a cotton drawstring bag from his inside pocket. He revealed a small pillbox. 'I think this is what Charlie was looking for.'

'Where did you find it?'

'In the rubbish bag from the watchman's hut. I found out that Charlie sometimes went in the hut during his tea break, if he had something to report. Today was a warm day. I'm guessing Charlie hung up his coat and sat down to drink his tea. Either someone took the pill box from his pocket or he lost it. I just thought I'd check.'

Only Sykes would have thought of the pills as pick-pocketed, rather than mislaid. Only Sykes would have sifted through a sack of rubbish.

He clicked open the pill box, revealing four aspirins.

'Thank God I had aspirins with me to give Charlie,' I said.

'The state he was in, he might have had a total collapse before the cricketers got him to hospital.'

'Whoever took them from his pocket didn't know that you would come to his aid. Either Charlie was careless or there was a deliberate attempt to harm him because he was on to something.'

Sykes went to the mirror and combed his hair. 'I'll call at the station on my way to the Boy and Barrel. I might be a laughing stock, handing over an old pill box, but Charlie's wife will be able to say if it belongs to him.'

'And before you go to meet your contact at the Boy and Barrel, is there anything else you've come up with today that I ought to know?'

'We can rule out the estate manager as far as having anything to do with shenanigans in the mill. He has no connections with the woollen industry. Aldous Garner is purely a property man. I looked at staff files. Garner was in the army and then the War Office, and not a bad strike against him. If he was on the take, it would be from the wine cellar or skimming something off the rents.'

THIRTY-ONE

When Sykes had gone, Mrs Sugden began her account.

'I drove to Shipley and found the address easily enough.' She allowed her words to sink in. Too much praise for her driving a few miles without becoming lost would seem patronising. I simply said, 'That's good.'

'Gwyneth lodged with a woman called Jean who is confined to an invalid carriage. On the days when Gwyneth didn't work at Milner Field, she had other cleaning jobs, an evening job as a barmaid, as well as helping Jean. By Jean's account, Gwyneth is popular and attractive and had fended for herself from a young age.'

'How old is she?'

'As far as I can make out from her history and a photograph with a previous boyfriend, Gwyneth is in her late twenties or early thirties. According to Jean, she met a new man but was playing it close to her chest in case it came to nothing. The morning after the fancy-dress ball, she packed her bags, made toast and a pot of tea for herself and Jean and left, saying she'd write.'

'Where has she gone?'

'When the police came asking, Jean could truthfully say that she did not know and had no forwarding address. Not that Jean would have given out an address to the police. She's too fly for that. Similarly, when Mrs Creswell enquired.'

Mrs Sugden delved in her handbag and produced a picture postcard. The postcard featured one of those grand buildings that could be a mansion or a public library. Mrs Sugden read the message aloud. 'Landed on my feet this time, love Gwyn. PS Will be back to see you.'

Mrs Sugden handed the postcard to me. The postmark was smudged. 'It's Doncaster Town Hall,' said she. 'I know because I went to a wedding in Doncaster once. I left our address and telephone numbers with Jean and at the corner shop. Someone else is interested either in Jean or Gwyneth because drawers and cupboards had been opened and stuff gone through. The reason Jean could give me the postcard there and then was because she had it in her invalid carriage to show neighbours, along with a photo Gwyneth had sent her.'

'Did Jean have any idea what the intruder was looking for?'

'Not at all. She had nothing worth stealing.'

This had been a long day. I thought of Charlie and wanted to know how he was, but it was too soon to telephone the hospital, or Inspector Mitchell. I focused on the postcard. 'What is Doncaster known for?'

Mrs Sugden thought for a moment. 'The town hall? The minster? The Romans.'

'What else?'

'Aeroplanes, and horse racing. The Doncaster Cup.'

'Exactly. Horse racing and the Doncaster Cup. Aldous Garner couldn't resist telling us that when he leaves the estate manager's job he has the prospect of managing a racecourse. A manager of a racecourse needs a right-hand woman, organised, competent at catering and cleaning, and good-looking.'

Mrs Sugden said, 'But if Garner accused Gwyneth of stealing the silver . . . '

'Exactly. He lets her take the blame, and then persuades her – a woman who survives on part-time jobs, and has a shady past – that she will have a charmed future, and it begins now, but it's all hush-hush and she must leave immediately.'

Mrs Sugden liked this idea. She joined in what might be make-believe. 'Garner sells on the silver, it's melted down. He has ready cash to support his move to a new job and a new life, managing a racecourse.'

Our euphoria about the Doncaster connection lasted at least a minute. There was no good reason to suspect Garner of anything but cunning, dishonesty, taking a fancy to Gwyneth and falling on his feet.

Mrs Sugden put the postcard and photograph of Gwyneth on the mantelpiece. 'I'm starting in the morning and I don't even know where the mops and brushes are kept and whether we need supplies. It's what goes on below stairs that makes a house tick. A purchaser of a mansion with the sense they were born with will have someone inspecting the kitchens, reporting on the likelihood of food poisoning, the usefulness of pantries and the state of the wine cellar. It could make the difference to how much they bid.'

'I'm as curious as you are, but it's been a long day. Let's look early tomorrow morning, before you meet Julie in the Lodge. This is your opportunity to manage and delegate.'

Mrs Sugden liked this idea. 'You're right. Tomorrow it is.'

The telephone rang.

I picked up. 'Milner Field, Mrs Shackleton.'

'This is Sister Wren, calling from the hospital. I'm sorry to tell you that Mr Benson has died. It was a peaceful death. His wife was with him.'

THIRTY-TWO

Jim Sykes parked his car outside the Boy & Barrel. He first met Hector Gawthorpe eight years ago, when Mrs Shackleton investigated for her old friend from wartime days, Tabitha Braithwaite, daughter of mill owner Joshua Braithwaite. Tabitha wanted one more try to find her missing father, in the hope that he would walk her down the aisle when she and Hector married. Since then, Sykes and Hector had met occasionally. Hector, younger than his wife and unfamiliar with sitting on a company board, often had some knotty problem that talking to Jim helped him unravel.

Since marrying Tabitha, Hector had become an industry insider. He was a member of the important Bradford Wool Exchange. When Sykes contacted him, simply saying there was something shady going on in Worstedopolis and he'd like to hear Hector's views, Hector was cautiously agreeable.

Sykes liked the Boy & Barrel. It was the kind of pub where people minded their own business. Sykes chose a quiet table, situated between three men absorbed in a game of dominoes

227

and the fireplace, where an unlit log fire testified to the warmth of the evening.

They ordered pints of bitter. Hector took a drink. 'I don't get out much, or get into Bradford a great deal, apart from business.'

'That makes two of us,' Sykes said. 'Do you play dominoes?'

'I never have.'

'We'll have a go one night,' Sykes said. 'They say it's an old fellers' game but since we all get there in the end, I don't see it does any harm.'

Hector laughed at this. 'We have a set somewhere at home. I'll see if Tabitha will take a turn at it, be a change from her jigsaw puzzles.'

'I expect the mill keeps you both busy.'

'Oh, it does.' Hector went quiet, and then he raised his glass. 'Here's to Ronnie Creswell. I miss him.'

They clinked glasses. 'I never met him,' Sykes said, 'but I wish I had. He was a grand chap by all accounts and a great asset to Salts Mill.'

'He was. I know every man is a grand chap after he dies, but he really was.'

It surprised Sykes that Hector and Ronnie knew each other.

Hector did not wait to be asked how he and Ronnie met. 'First time our paths crossed we were sitting next to each other at a Mechanics' Institute lecture. We both attended all the lectures. Ronnie was a clever chap. I learned a lot from him. Obviously he was younger than me, but he'd started his apprenticeship at fourteen. I'd say we were on a level with each other in some ways. When I suddenly found myself on the board of our mill, I was Ronnie's age. I was accepted at the Wool Exchange. I think Ronnie would have got there

228

eventually, under his own steam. After the lectures, we'd go to a pub and do swaps on what we knew, what we'd learned. We didn't agree on everything.' He lowered his voice. 'He was a socialist.'

For a fleeting moment Sykes felt like confiding his own differences of opinion with Mrs Shackleton, but he refrained.

Hector sighed. 'I can't believe Ronnie's gone. Drowning is such a terrible death. I never asked if he could swim, but he could do everything else. I went to see him play cricket. He came to Bridgestead when we had our village cricket match. Tabitha said I should offer him a job, but I wouldn't do that. He was all set to rise where he was.'

This gave Sykes his opening. Whatever their differences, Hector and Ronnie believed in fair play. They had much in common, though their ideas of what constituted fair play might differ.

Sykes caught the waiter's eye. He ordered another two pints.

'Hector, you and Ronnie played by the rules. Not everyone does and, just between us, I'm looking into shady dealings. Someone has inside information and is using it against my client. When we spoke on the telephone, I had the feeling that you might have heard something.'

'Yes.' Hector looked at the fire for inspiration, and then across at the dominoes players, who had suddenly found something to laugh about. 'Things are all meant to be deadly secret at the Wool Exchange. A man who shakes hands keeps his word. But not everyone is a gentleman.'

Unsure whether to feign surprise at Hector's revelation, Sykes attempted neutrality. 'I like to think we fair-minded folk are in the majority, Hector.'

'I like to think so too, Jim. I got to know a chap quite well. I hesitate to tell you his name. He is not a proper wool man, which may account for his faults. He's carpets, but not just carpets. He has positions on boards – engineering, furniture – a fingers-in-pies man, so if something goes down or is allowed to collapse because of a spell of poor business, it's not the end of the world for him as it would be for some.'

That the man was 'carpets' told Sykes what he wanted to know, but without Charlie Benson's story of Mrs Whitaker and her godson spending so much time in the mill, Sykes would not have made the connection so quickly.

'What sort of tricks does this fellow get up to?'

'He talked to me about going in with him on something big, a consortium of small mills bidding for big contracts. It sounded a good idea to me. Obviously, I had to speak to Tabitha.'

'Of course.'

'I took him round to the house.'

'And?'

'Tabitha told me to never again bring that man to our house or the mill. She didn't like him. She didn't trust him. She took me by surprise because up to that day, I'd thought the chap was so very charming. Tabitha said that was the point, and she had met him before in a hundred guises. Tabitha can be quite mysterious sometimes.'

Sykes wanted to be sure. 'Were you and Tabitha at the Whitakers' fancy-dress ball?'

'We were.'

'On the night of the ball, would the man in question have been dressed as Napoleon?'

Hector's eyes widened. 'You have him in one!'

'Hector, either from spite, foolishness or ambition, Kevin Foxcroft has plotted against the mill where his godfather is chairman.'

Hector made a gesture of defeat. 'Who would have seen that coming?'

Sykes wanted to say, *Tabitha?* The thought must have floated across the table.

'Tabitha said he was after marrying Pamela Whitaker and that he intended to be on Salts board, because it will open doors for him.'

Sykes gave a low whistle. 'He is ruthless. Have you warned Mr Whitaker?'

'I certainly shooed Kevin away, as Tabitha said. These mysterious codes of the Wool Exchange – I almost have the hang of them now – prevented me from doing more than dropping a big hint to Mr Whitaker. I'm sure he took my hint.'

'He doesn't know. Your hint was too subtle.'

Wide-eyed, Hector shook his head. 'I must be more direct. You and Tabitha would hit it off. I tell her something, and she tells it back to me with greater meaning.'

'Then you're a lucky man. Tabitha sounds a wonderful person.'

'Oh, she is. I hope she'll think I've said the right things and not crossed the Wool Exchange confidentiality line.'

'I'm sure she will.' Sykes wanted to know which woollen mill had the good or ill fortune of Kevin Foxcroft as a board director, but too many questions would make Hector uneasy. Searching directories would take too long. Sykes did not want to ask Mr Whitaker. Sykes was the man paid to come up with answers. He brought the conversation round to Hector's children. 'I suppose your lad is in the Wolf Cubs?'

'He is indeed and loves it. They'll be off camping next week, just above Hebden Bridge.'

Sykes took a stab. Since woollen mills thrived mainly in the West Riding, he could not go far wrong by saying, 'Am I right in thinking that's not a million miles from where the man in question sits on the board of a mill?'

'East a few miles.'

'Mytholmroyd?'

'East a bit more.'

'Sowerby Bridge?'

Hector smiled. He liked games where he knew the answer. 'Close. A few points west.'

'Luddenden Foot!'

'Spot on.' Hector wagged his finger. 'I'm catching on. I'm learning from you, Jim. You deliberately didn't ask me but I told you, and before you trick me again – it's Sparks Mill.'

'You caught me out, Hector. Next time we meet, the first pint's on me.'

They stood. Sykes picked up his coat.

Hector did the same. They said goodnight to the dominoes players. Concentrating hard, the players acknowledged in an absent-minded manner. There were pennies on the table to be won or lost.

As Jim and Hector left the pub, Hector said, 'Did you notice the dominoes player with the kiss curl in his hair?'

'I did.'

'One night, when he thought no one was looking, he picked up a bar stool, put it under his coat and walked out with it.

He said to his pal, loud as you like, "This will suit our Sam. He's fed up of sitting on the fender."'

Sykes said, 'Just walked out with a bar stool? There are some shocking villains in the world, Hector.'

They walked to their cars, which were parked close to each other, and said goodnight.

Sykes waited until Hector set off. He gave him a few moments and then went back into the pub. Arnold Whitaker had given Sykes his home number. Sykes asked the publican if he could use the telephone.

Arnold answered after half a dozen rings.

'Jim here, Arnold. Do you have some time in the morning to see Mrs Shackleton and me? I have something to report.'

'Nine o'clock?'

'We'll be there.'

Sykes's car wanted to go back to Leeds, wanted to arrive at the gates of St James's Hospital, so that he could see whether there might be a new notice on the gates. But the car didn't have a brain, and Sykes did. He must be logical. There would be no notice saying that Rose Sykes was ready for discharge, and if her husband barged in now, he could take her home. Don't be foolish, he told himself. You'd earn yourself a telling-off for disrupting hospital procedure. We're on a job. Go back to Milner Field.

There will be news. There will be good news.

He must report to Mrs Shackleton. Kevin Foxcroft was a wrong 'un, a greater villain by far than the man with the kiss curl who walked out of the Boy & Barrel with a bar stool under his arm. Yet who would come out best in the long run? No one could predict. Companies and businesses rise and fall. A bar stool might remain in the kiss-curl family for generations, treasured by Sam and his descendants across the centuries. They were well-made items, bar stools. Had to be. If it came to a fight and one became a handy weapon, it must be the skull that cracked, not the bar stool. Otherwise publicans' contents insurance would be seriously high.

It was late when Sykes arrived back at the mansion. He slowed the car as he approached the Tower. If there was a light, he would ring the bell.

The Tower was in darkness.

He took a postcard and pencil from his inside pocket and wrote a note.

Boy & Barrel. Hector G. Cracked it! Have asked for us to meet with Mr W at 9 a.m.

He drove to the South Lodge and opened the door. There was a folded note on the doormat with 'J. S.' written in Mrs Shackleton's perfect script. He unfolded the paper.

Charlie Benson died peacefully at 9 p. m.

THIRTY-THREE

My bed was close to the window. I had left the curtains and the window open and so caught the glow of car lights and heard the engine. We had turned off all the lights. It must be Sykes. My clock said eleven. I could have stayed up to hear what he had to say because sleep escaped me.

After a few minutes, he drove away. When I did drop off, it was not for long. A piercing scream made me sit bolt upright. I looked out of the window. In the moonlight, I saw something was moving near the shrubbery. A creature came from the bushes, and then another appeared. It was a pair of foxes. One screeched again.

Shut your eyes, I told myself. We have an early start. Go to sleep. Recite Portia's speech in your head, or 'The Charge of the Light Brigade'. Count backwards in sevens.

I must have slept again, because I woke in a panic, sweating, quite sure I would have a heart attack and be unable to call for help. It was from a dream, of carrying a stretcher, with someone at the other end I couldn't see but that person was slowly letting go. Our patient would fall.

There was a hollow sound, and then a creak. At first I could not tell whether the sound was in my dream or in the room, or whether I was in the dream or in the room. Whatever the sound was, it was close enough to touch me, to strike terror. I froze.

When I looked at my clock, it was 3 a.m.

I was not meant to sleep this night. After a few deep breaths, I sat up and reached for my glass of water. Outside, someone was walking by. Footsteps passed under my window, not heavy but distinct, nothing ghostly or dreamlike about them. I made myself look out.

It was a man, walking slowly, going nowhere by the looks of him, just walking. By his walk, I thought it might be Mr Creswell. That would not surprise me. I believed that since Ronnie died he had slept in his hut. If I could not sleep, how could he who had lost his son? Walking was better than lying awake, with the weight of sorrow and regret. I felt a powerful grief for a man I barely knew, and a sense of guilt for not being able to do more for Charlie Benson.

A post-mortem would give answers. All the answers in the world would count for little.

Sometimes giving up on sleep helps. Feeling cheated, sleep comes.

I woke to the dawn chorus. A bright white cloud slid across clear blue sky.

My first thought on waking was of Charlie Benson. I told myself, had we not got him to hospital, he might have died in the park in front of his grandson.

Mrs Sugden was already up. I could hear her moving about downstairs.

I put on my robe and went down. She was in the scullery. There was a pot of tea on the table and two slices of bread and butter spread with jam. Next to the teapot was a pencilled note from Sykes.

Boy & Barrel. Hector G. Cracked it! Have asked for us to meet with Mr W at 9 a. m.

Mrs Sugden looked pleased with herself. She was dressed and ready to go out. Her housekeeping file was on the table. 'Sykes's note bodes well. Not that I know what he's talking about but it's sufficient for him to have put an exclamation point. And we're in good time to find out all the necessaries for today's big cleaning job.'

I read Sykes's note again.

'What does he mean?' Mrs Sugden asked.

'Search me.' It was not until I'd had two cups of tea that I interpreted Sykes's cryptic note. 'He went to meet one of his contacts at the Boy and Barrel in Bradford. The only Hector G. who comes to mind is Hector Gawthorpe who married Tabitha Braithwaite. She inherited her father and uncle's mill, so Hector must be on the board and be a member of the Wool Exchange. We'll be meeting Mr Whitaker this morning. I'll find out more then.'

I would park in the back yard, to take a look at the doors that led from the yard into the mill, as Charlie had described, one giving access to the reservoir, and giving the man with the distinctive gait the opportunity to take Ronnie by surprise, perhaps with the help of Kevin Foxcroft, if Kevin had indeed taken a look at the timesheet to find out what time Ronnie might check the reservoir.

I must also find a way to speak to Dorrie Fairburn, David Fairburn's sister, as per Mr Cohen's request. It was Dorrie that David and Ronnie argued about on the night they came to blows. Dorrie also worked as a waitress on the night of the May Ball. Now I knew from Nancy that for a good part of that evening Dorrie had gone missing. Where was she, and what was she up to? I kept these thoughts to myself for now. Mrs Sugden had enough to think about. She had pored over her mansion-cleaning plans with the concentration of a general preparing for battle.

It was a little before 6 a.m. when I put sets of keys and a flashlight in my satchel. We did not know how the basement area of the mill would be lit. Mrs Sugden brought her lantern, just in case. She put on her big coat. 'I don't want to catch my death.'

The Tower being self-contained, we needed to go outside and walk to the nearest entrance that would take us into the mansion proper. We went through the orangery, simply because I liked that way. Walking through the greenery gave me the feeling that I might be entering a tropical forest.

We went to the lower-ground floor. Mrs Sugden was not impressed by the cobwebs in the kitchens. 'We'll get cracking in here. Cleanliness starts from the bottom up.'

With each stone step on the way into the basement area, the air grew colder.

Something with a tail scurried across the floor. Before Mrs Sugden began noting down tasks to be done, I led her away. 'You know what's to be done. Just write, "Good clean". Let's do a quick move through. It won't be so cold later on.'

Mrs Sugden was in disapproving mood. As we walked

238

along the corridor, opening doors, finding the right key, she grumbled at the lack of thought for those who worked below stairs. 'With the kind of money spent here, they could've put pegs all the way along this corridor with a fox fur coat on every one.'

We explored a room of buckets and mops, cleaning stuff, pantries, a cold store and a depleted wine cellar.

One cellar room contained locked trunks and tea chests that somebody must intend to come back for, or that were surplus to requirements. We shone the flashlight and the lamp, lifted lids.

'A sweep and a mop will do for this area,' Mrs Sugden said. 'No one will linger here.'

When we reached a cellar to which she could not find a key, I suggested we move on, telling Mrs Sugden that Julie the cleaning oracle would know which key would work.

'What about your keys, from the old uncle?'

'Go on, then.' I handed her the keys. 'I'll shine the torch.'

I went on shining the torch after Mrs Sugden turned the key and opened the door.

We stared at the figure on the cold stone floor. She lay still, too still. Her head was on a cushion, her face covered with a white linen napkin. I lifted the napkin. Her eyes were closed.

I knew she was dead. All the same, I must be sure.

I felt for a pulse. There was no pulse on her wrist, or her throat.

I turned to Mrs Sugden and shook my head.

'It's Gwyneth,' she said.

'How do you know?'

'Her photograph, and her hair. Blonde out of a bottle, according to her landlady.' Mrs Sugden shivered. She pulled her sleeves down over her hands. 'Was she accidentally locked in here and froze to death? Has she been here all these months, since May, and no decay? She'd smell.'

'I think she may have been suffocated, with the cushion.' From the doorway, I looked back at Gwyneth, with the sort of mad hope that I was wrong. I nudged Mrs Sugden. 'We need to go, now, quickly, quietly, locking the door behind us, and we must be out of here fast.'

There was no decay because Gwyneth's body was still warm. I thought she may have been suffocated because who-ever did that had not been gone long.

Out of habit, I had brought my satchel and so had car keys with me. Once outside, I said, 'Come on. We're going.'

'Where to? Shouldn't we telephone?'

'I'm going to drop you at the Lodge. I'll wait until Sykes has let you in. Tell him what's happened and that I'm not using the telephone here because of it being a party line and connected with the mill. I'll call the police from the hospital and see Sykes at the mill as arranged. Stay clear of here.'

'What about the cleaners coming?'

'I'll talk to Julie and put them off.'

After being allowed to use the hospital telephone, I sat in the entranceway and waited. Two local bobbies arrived within ten minutes: PC Beale, who had come to the Lodge on Saturday to break the news of Ronnie's death to Mrs Creswell and PC Harrison, the son of Mr Whitaker's secretary. After warning me not to share information of the death with anyone until told I could do so, PC Beale went to use the hospital telephone, leaving me to give a more detailed account to his young colleague.

PC Harrison asked me how we identified the deceased, and

why we thought the perpetrator must be on or close to the premises. 'We have a photograph of Miss Kidd. She was still warm when we found her.'

'Where is Mrs Sugden now, Mrs Shackleton?' PC Harrison asked.

'I dropped her off at the South Lodge.' If it had not been for Inspector Mitchell asking me did I suspect his officer because he used Brylcreem, it would never have occurred to me to be cautious in my replies. Suddenly, I dare not take a chance on trusting him. 'Mr Sykes has taken Mrs Sugden somewhere safe,' I said. 'Now I must go to Ada Street and give a plausible explanation to Julie as to why the cleaners can't start work in the mansion today.'

'And after that?'

'I'll go to the mill. As I'm not to share information, would you please ensure that Mr Whitaker knows about Gwyneth's death?'

He nodded. 'Of course. Did you inform the estate manager?'

'No. We left immediately. I don't even know whether he is on the premises. I didn't see him.'

PC Harrison was doing his job, yet I was beginning to feel uncomfortable. Was Garner still there? He must know every inch of that place, the mansion, the grounds and the area.

'Do you happen to know Gwyneth Kidd's last known address?' he asked.

'Somewhere in Doncaster, I believe. She sent a postcard to her former landlady saying she had fallen on her feet but giving no address. The landlady's address is in the Milner Field housekeeping file.'

'Well, thank you, Mrs Shackleton. That will be all for now. I'll see you out.'

PC Harrison seemed not weighty enough and too tall to answer Charlie Benson's description of the man with the slightly lopsided walk, but he did swing his arms as he walked me off the premises.

THIRTY-FOUR

I met Sykes at the entrance to the mill. He tipped his hat. 'I left Mrs Sugden in the buffet at the railway station, with a morning paper and a cup of coffee. She's safe in a public place. There's a plain-clothes man talking to her now. I'm sorry you had such a shock.'

'And I'm sorry about Gwyneth.'

It would not suit Mrs Sugden to sit still for long. I hoped she would stay put. 'I got your note, about the meeting with Hector Gawthorpe. Have you told Mr Whitaker?'

'Not any details, just that I had news and to arrange for us to meet him. I'm so sorry to hear about Charlie Benson. Poor fellow.'

Sometimes words seem so inadequate. I thought of Mrs Benson, and of the little boy who would not see his granddad again. 'We're a little early but let's go in. Mr Whitaker will know about Gwyneth's death by now. I asked PC Harrison to be sure to tell him, since they put a prohibition on me.'

Mr Whitaker very clearly knew about the deaths. He sat at

his desk looking dazed. Mrs Harrison was beside him, stirring sugar into his tea.

He nodded a good morning. 'Mrs Harrison will join us,' he said.

Mrs Harrison took her seat at the side of Whitaker's desk. Sykes and I sat opposite.

'Where was the estate manager?' Whitaker asked.

'I don't know,' I said truthfully. 'Mrs Sugden and I locked up and left. The police may find Mr Garner fast asleep in bed, or he may be in Doncaster.'

'How did Miss Kidd get in, and who was with her?'

'I expect all that will become clear.'

'Mrs Shackleton, Jim, I'm trying to think where to start. Two deaths within hours. I can't recall Gwyneth, but I'm seeing Charlie in my mind's eye. The kind of person you don't notice unless he's in front of you. He was lame. Why didn't we give him a different job?'

Mrs Harrison said gently, 'It was the job Mr Benson had done before and wanted to do again. He liked walking about the place, watching what was going on. I spoke to his wife this morning. He insisted on making light of his heart condition. I'm sure we can do something for Mrs Benson.'

I owed it to Charlie to give a full account of what he had told me yesterday evening. It was an uncomfortable thing to do, telling tales of Mrs Whitaker's visits to the mill with her godson Kevin Foxcroft, Kevin's attention to the time card slot by the entrance to the reservoir. The mystery man, seen from the back, with his particular gait. All this may have counted for little were it not for Sykes's information about Foxcroft from Hector Gawthorpe of Braithwaite's Mill.

We listened while Sykes told us what he had learned from

Hector. He kept his voice neutral, though this did not hide his opinion of Kevin Foxcroft. 'There is nothing in any rules against smaller companies forming a consortium to compete with a larger company,' Sykes concluded, 'but there's a different slant on the matter when set alongside the possibility of Kevin having illicitly obtained insider information about your Montague Burton contract.'

Mr Whitaker turned to his secretary. 'Was my wife here alone with Kevin on any of her visits?'

'Perhaps four times during the past six months.' She looked at me and Sykes. 'I have one Saturday morning a month off and usually take it when Mr Whitaker is away.' She opened her diary.

'Mrs Whitaker occasionally leaves plants, and any special instructions about watering. When we miss each other, because it's my Saturday morning off, I ring on the Monday to thank her for the plants and have a chat. There was a day, here we are, six weeks ago, when Mrs Whitaker had matters to discuss with the social committee, connected with the catering for the big cricket match, the children's outing and transport for a netball match. She also likes to have a chat with the older members of staff. Usually she'd mention if Kevin was with her. She's immensely fond of him. I remember saying that Kevin must have been bored. She said not. While she did her rounds, he was content to sit in the office reading the *Wool Gazette* and looking at our samples and brochures.'

'You didn't smell a rat?' Whitaker asked.

'Not at all. Kevin is devoted to his godmother. I thought he was waiting patiently to take her out.'

Frowning, her mouth a tight line, Mrs Harrison turned back pages of the diary. I could tell that she did not like doing this. 'When I was helping to plan the May Ball, Mrs Whitaker came in and looked at our contacts list, so as to draw up the invitation list.'

'And was Kevin with her?'

'Yes. I can cross-check the other dates with the visitors' book.'

'Thank you.'

'I'll do that now.'

Mrs Harrison left.

Sykes went across to the safe. 'It's a very good old safe, built to last. The trouble with old safes is that crooks get to know them well. It wouldn't be hard to find out the easiest way to get in. If Mr Foxcroft has been up to tricks, he may have left fingerprints. I'll follow this up, talk to an ex-con, bring our own fingerprint kit back with me.'

Fingerprints. Sykes's words set me thinking. 'Mr Whitaker, has Kevin Foxcroft been interviewed by the police?'

'No. I would have heard. What are you thinking?'

'Mr Sykes is right. We need more information about what he was up to here in your office. Also, according to Charlie he was hovering near the time cards by the ground floor door that leads to the reservoir on the day Ronnie died. Inspector Mitchell told me that there were two sets of unidentified prints found in the area of the reservoir. One set belonging to a woman or a man with small hands.'

Whitaker leaned forward. 'Kevin wouldn't have it in him to murder Ronnie, and wouldn't have got the better of him. He was probably wandering about gormlessly, imagining himself as chief of Salts.'

'You could be right. But if you invite Kevin in, and also let the police know he is here and willing to answer questions, he could be sufficiently softened up to admit to his dirty tricks, including deceiving Mrs Whitaker.'

Whitaker thought for a moment. 'You're right. It will hit Josie hard, but I'll do it.'

We talked in circles for several minutes, agreeing the deaths were more important but that there was nothing we could do for Charlie, or for Gwyneth.

'I'm not overegging,' said Whitaker, 'but if I lose the contract, Salts goes to the wall. Can I trust information from Hector Gawthorpe?'

'Yes, you can,' I said. 'We ought to ensure the Gawthorpes won't object to our using the information. May I make a telephone call to Mrs Gawthorpe from Mrs Harrison's office?'

Mr Whitaker gave a wave of his arm. 'Please do.'

The best way to take Kevin Foxcroft down would be through the people who knew what he was up to. I sat in Mrs Harrison's chair, waiting to be connected, bracing myself for what might be a difficult call. Sykes's contact, Hector Gawthorpe, would be obliging, and delighted to hear from me. It was Tabitha Gawthorpe I needed to speak to.

An operator answered, 'Braithwaite's Mill.'

'Hello. My name is Kate Shackleton, I should like to speak to Mrs Gawthorpe, please.'

'Just a moment, I'll see if Mrs Gawthorpe is available.'

Mrs Gawthorpe was available. 'Kate?'

'Hello, Tabitha.'

'Hello. Long time.'

'Too long.'

'I know why you're telephoning.'

'I thought you might. Jim Sykes had a good chat with Hector. We're working for Mr Whitaker at Salts. He asked us to look into the legitimacy of a rival bid sent to a Salts regular customer by – we think – Kevin Foxcroft, containing information that must have been stolen. Do you have any objection to your company being named as the source of Mr Sykes's information that Kevin Foxcroft has plans for a consortium?'

'Named to whom?'

'The Salts board, the Wool Exchange, and the customer if appropriate?'

'No objection whatsoever. Not that there's anything wrong with a consortium in principal, but it's never going to happen. I held my dainty nose and talked to Foxcroft. He was trying to find out too much about our business. We can't compete with Salts. Foxcroft is a fool to try. I want that worm thrown out of the Wool Exchange.'

'That bad?'

'He wheedled his way into our home and our mill through being sweet as pie to Hector.'

'And that got up your nose?'

'He's a carpet man that I wouldn't buy a coconut matting doormat from. He gains entry to the Wool Exchange when I am not allowed through the door. It is infuriating and demeaning. I want to see a rule change. I want to be nominated for membership to the Exchange in my own right. Pass that on to Mr Whitaker. He seems a reasonable man, and the Whitakers threw a decent party in May.'

'I certainly will pass it on, and thank you.'

'I'll gladly dish the dirt on Foxcroft. I'll send across everything I know. Who to?'

'To Mr Whitaker.'

'With my compliments.' I heard a voice in the background. 'Sorry, Kate, must go. Come and visit.'

'I will.'

I went back into Whitaker's office. 'Tabitha Gawthorpe will send over what she knows about Kevin Foxcroft's shenanigans. It should make interesting reading.'

'That's very good of her. I hope we'll have enough to eject Kevin from the Wool Exchange.'

'Talking of that, Tabitha wants to be nominated to the Wool Exchange, after you've proposed and passed a rule change.'

The surprise of Tabitha's request momentarily sent Mr Whitaker's troubles out of the window. He smiled, raised his eyebrows and shook his head at such a shocker of a suggestion. 'I admire Mrs Gawthorpe. Of course, she's pushing at a locked door, but if that's her price, I'll make the proposal. I might even find a seconder other than her husband.'

THIRTY-FIVE

Sykes had sung the praises of his tour of the mill, its size, grandeur, ingenious design and efficiency. He described the building as a cathedral of industry. It was also Dorrie Fairburn's workplace, and Mr Cohen had asked me to talk to her. David Fairburn had kept me from seeing his sister. Might she and Ronnie Creswell have been more than dancing partners? David was not yet officially in the clear. What Dorrie had to say might impact on her brother's defence, one way or another.

Breathing in the smell of lanolin from the wool, Mrs Harrison and I climbed the steps towards the room on the top floor, where burlers and menders worked. This was what I wanted to see. This was where I would find Dorrie Fairburn. I had confided in Mrs Harrison.

Sykes was right. This mill was Sir Titus Salt's answer to the glorious cathedrals and abbeys of the Middle Ages.

The old handloom weavers saw textile mills as the work of the devil, monstrous places of noise and horror, with devilish machinery that made their skills count for nought.

We stopped by the door. Mrs Harrison said, 'I'll bring you in and introduce you. Dorrie is the youngest burler and mender.'

'What age is she?'

'Eighteen. She has auburn hair in short ringlets.' Mrs Harrison glanced about. We were alone. She went on, 'I have a suggestion. The dinner break is at noon. You might take a look around and then nab Dorrie during her dinner break for a private word.'

'That's a good idea. Thank you.'

'Not everyone stays in the canteen. The Fairburns live close by. She may go home for her bite to eat.'

We stepped inside. By comparison with the rest of the building, the top room of Salts was quiet and peaceful. It ran the length of the building, and was bathed in natural light from the huge windows.

Mrs Harrison introduced me to a middle-aged man who stood close to the door by something resembling a giant easel, with cloth draped over it. He was looking and touching, running his fingers over the material. He stopped, and pointed out a knot in the fabric before giving a nod of permission for me to look round. He made a short announcement to the other workers, who took no notice whatsoever. There was a hush of concentration as employees examined cloth, looking, touching. One had a needle and was mending. One or two women looked at me, without breaking off their work. I was glad not to be an object of interest. The burlers and menders could not afford a lapse in concentration. Given the fame of this mill, they would be used to the occasional visitor.

Mrs Harrison accompanied me. We walked slowly round the room. Suddenly, being here seemed not my best idea.

What would I do, stare at Dorrie's middle? Offer congratulations? Ask when is the happy event and what do you know about Ronnie's death?

There she was, looking younger than eighteen, with auburn ringlets, wearing a printed cotton smock dress patterned with clusters of bluebells.

Mrs Harrison helped. 'This is Dorrie, eighteen years old and our youngest burler and mender. Dorrie, this is Mrs Shackleton.'

'Hello, Mrs Shackleton.'

Mrs Harrison turned to look out of the window.

Dorrie moved the fabric she was working on so that it shielded her body from scrutiny. I wondered how much concealing she would do over the coming weeks and months.

'Intricate work,' I said.

She held her needle tightly, and close to her, like a talisman. 'I'm undoing a knot,' she said, without looking at me. She lowered her voice to a whisper. 'You brought my brother home in your car.'

Matching her whisper, I said, 'I trust all will be well.'

'He didn't do it.'

I leaned close to Dorrie, as if to examine her work. 'Then talk to me, during your dinner break?'

Dorrie kept her head down. 'Come to our house when the twelve o'clock hooter sounds.' Looking up, she said, 'It is intricate. You have the knack or you don't.'

I smiled at Dorrie and followed Mrs Harrison, who I felt sure must have primed Dorrie about the likelihood of my visit. Small wonder Mrs Harrison's son had joined the police force. Perhaps she put his name down at birth.

THIRTY-SIX

Mrs Harrison was waiting for me at the lift. 'What did you think to the top room?'

'It's a magnificent room, and such skills, and I'll be seeing Dorrie. Thank you for that.'

A lift attendant opened the door and we stepped in, staying silent on the journey down.

Mrs Harrison came to the door with me. 'Your Mr Sykes wants a word. He's across the road, by the canteen door.'

There was something else she was reluctant to say. I waited, and then asked, 'What is it?'

'I don't usually interfere with family matters, but Pamela needs to come home. She has a good head on her shoulders. I know she's in mourning, but with things as they are . . . And it might help her, too.' She did not wait for an answer.

The roar of machinery abated as I climbed the steps from the yard and crossed Victoria Road. The mill hooter had not yet sounded the midday break. Sykes was in the canteen doorway, looking a little anxious, which was unusual for him.

'I'll get off then and come back with the fingerprinting kit.'

Something was wrong. Suddenly deciding to take finger-prints from what must be a well-used safe weeks after Kevin Foxcroft may or may not have got in there did not make sense.

'I'll walk to the car with you.'

He nodded.

I fell into step with him, not easy as he was taking long strides and looking straight ahead. I would not let him drive off without telling me.

'What's up?' I asked.

Silence, followed by a grunt. 'The hospital. That's what's up. I'm glad of an excuse to go back to Leeds.'

'The fingerprint kit?'

'I'll have to bring it now.'

'What have you heard?'

'I telephoned Miss Merton earlier. She had a message for me from the hospital. I'm to present myself at the porter's desk. I'm being allowed to see Rosie.'

'That's good, isn't it?'

'It would be if they were saying, "Come and take her home." They're not saying anything.'

'They will when you get there.'

'They're not even saying Rosie is "comfortable".'

He increased his pace. I put my hand on his arm. 'Slow down! Hospital staff won't give out information, not over the telephone, and certainly not to someone who isn't a relative. Miss Merton was simply taking the message.'

We reached his car. I ordered him to get in and sat in the passenger seat beside him. 'Now, before you drive steadily to St James's, answer me this. Have you had any word from the hospital other than "comfortable"?'

'No.'

'Then Rosie is comfortable.'

This did not satisfy him.

'Why call me in all of a sudden, when she's been there five days—'

'Four days and a bit. Be glad she's being looked after and don't worry. Give Rosie my love. Everything is going to be all right.'

Sykes started the car as the mill hooter sounded for noon. I stayed just long enough to wave him off.

Time for me to talk to Dorrie Fairburn.

THIRTY-SEVEN

I negotiated my way around the crowd of people leaving the mill for their dinner break, some on their way home, others flooding Victoria Road as they crossed to the canteen. There would have been a greater swell were it not for an underground passageway that provided an alternative route.

Heading for Titus Street, where the Fairburns lived, I looked out for Dorrie's auburn curls. I spotted her coming out of a bakery and kept my distance in case she did not want to be seen with me.

I slowed my steps, unsure whether she might want to alert whoever was at home to my visit. As it turned out, she was alone, and opened the door quickly, shutting it just as quickly behind me.

We stepped into a neat, all-purpose room with kitchen table and chairs as well as a rocking chair and stools. Through an open door, I saw into a small scullery that opened onto a yard.

'Sit down, Mrs Shackleton. Beryl, that's my sister-in-law, left me two sandwiches. Not that she expected me to have company.'

'That's David's wife?'

'Yes. I've only one sister-in-law. She and Mam have taken the children on the funicular railway. And before you ask, Dad's at work and David is out doing repairs, else I wouldn't have asked you here. You probably know David has been put on alternative work until . . .'

When she didn't finish her sentence, I said, 'I didn't know. Until when?'

'He'll go back to his millwright work, but he won't go near the reservoir. He's waiting for the police to say, "We know it wasn't you".'

'Their way of saying that will be to arrest and charge the guilty person.'

'The sooner the better.' She sat down, pushing a plate with a sausage sandwich to me, saying, 'There's pickles in the jar.' She spooned a pickled onion onto her plate and passed me the jar.

'I'm all right, thank you.' I took a bite of the sandwich.

She put the lid on the jar of pickles. 'I thought you must have heard something, like the police saying they're sorry to Ronnie.'

'They were investigating, and still are. They won't apologise. But I'm sorry that you lost your friend and that you had such a terrible time of it and David is so badly affected.'

'Beryl and me are the ones who want to know. Mam and Dad and David have their heads in the sand, pretending no news is good news. But that's because they know how ridiculous it is to think David would have harmed Ronnie. Ronnie was part of our family, and us part of his.' She went into the scullery, to watch the kettle boil, leaving the door open.

'You've known each other a long time.'

257

She poured water into the teapot and swished it about to warm the pot, before tipping it out, spooning in tea and pouring on water. 'I was in the same infant class as Ronnie's brother Stephen. Their little sister Nancy, when she was two or three, all the way to starting school, it had to be me that washed her hair or she'd scream. She was a funny little thing, had it in her head that if anyone but me did her hair she wouldn't grow ringlets.'

'You've known each other all your lives.'

'Our mams are friends. They were right proud when me and Ronnie won prizes for dancing.'

'Tell me about it.'

'A few of us took lessons. The dancing teacher paired us up, said Ronnie and me were naturals. We've won prizes for the waltz, quickstep, foxtrot. We were hoping to win the tango at the Tower Ballroom this Tides week. There's a cash prize, a shield and your photograph in a frame. Ronnie said it would probably be our last time because he would marry Pamela, and she would expect him to be dancing with her.' Dorrie poured tea. 'When I told Ronnie I wouldn't dance this year, I couldn't take part, he wouldn't believe me. He asked why. Only Beryl knew. She'd guessed before I knew myself. I told Ronnie the truth because he was looking forward to Blackpool, and we would have won. He'd been coming with us for years. Mr and Mrs Creswell always went to Morecambe. Ronnie was bored with Morecambe. When he was David's apprentice, he came with us to Blackpool and he's come with us ever since.'

'I'm so sorry. It must feel as if everything has come to a stop for you.'

'Doesn't come to a stop, though, does it?' She tore open

a small brown paper bag. Two vanilla slices were stuck together. She divided them and pushed the one on the paper bag across to me.

'Thank you.'

'Beryl said we could have danced the tango. She said I wouldn't have shown if I'd worn her red frock, and that a bit of fancy dancing might have put an end to my troubles and to be sure to take part in the netball on Saturday afternoon, jump high and land heavy.'

'And what do you think?'

'I've no idea. My brain's come to a stop.' Dorrie picked up her vanilla slice. 'They're a bit messy.' She sucked custard from her finger. 'I'll need to wash my hands well and dust myself off before I go back to work.'

'Am I allowed to ask if you have any plans for when the baby comes?'

'You can ask. I can't answer. I've messed up. Tom Harrison took me out twice, once to the theatre and for supper, and then to the pictures.'

'Is that Tom Harrison the police officer?'

'Yes. He was so respectful, such a gentleman. He even took dancing lessons so that he wouldn't step on my toes, but . . .'

'But?'

'It's too late.'

'He's not the father?'

'No, not Tom. He never touched me. We only went out together those few times and saw each other at the dancing. And he's in the police force. He won't marry someone with a bun in the oven.'

'Don't give up on yourself. You're too young.'

'Beryl says that if David agrees, they'll say the baby is theirs.'

'Have you told Beryl who the father is?'

She nodded. 'I'm only telling you so that you can pass on to Mr Cohen that it wasn't Ronnie. I don't want the police thinking that David had a reason to hit out at Ronnie.'

'Then I ought to tell Mr Cohen the man's name.'

'What if he says I'm lying? I was that sick the next day I couldn't move. I never knew what a hangover was.' She picked up the plates and took them into the scullery. 'What if he doesn't even remember me?'

I followed her into the scullery, bringing the jar of pickles. She turned on the tap and began to wash her hands. 'What if he does that all the time?'

'When was this?'

'The night of the May Ball. Mrs Creswell and Julie gave me a serving-on job; they gave us all black skirts and puffed-sleeve white blouses. When he took a glass of wine from my tray, he said I shouldn't be carrying a tray, I should be enjoying myself. We each had a glass. It was sparkly, tickled my nose and made me laugh. We got talking, in a corner. I'm so stupid. I thought I was special and he was the one I'd been waiting for, love at first sight. He carried the tray of drinks and cheesy bits. There are places to hide away in Milner Field. He told daft jokes and made me laugh. We finished every glass on the tray. I think I had the most. Afterwards, I thought he might try and find out who I am, like Prince Charming with the glass slipper. Search Saltaire for the girl with curls.'

'You didn't tell him your name?'

'I can't even remember. I don't think so, because I wanted to be mysterious, so he'd come looking.'

'You were a daredevil.'

'I was an idiot.'

Dorrie picked up her coat.

'We can track him down,' I said. 'Tell me his name. He has a responsibility.'

'Does he? He hasn't come looking for me.' She went to the coal bucket by the fireplace and swiped off crumbs from her dress. 'With Ronnie gone, he'll be after marrying Pamela Whitaker.'

It took a moment for me to make the connection. 'Are you talking about Kevin Foxcroft?'

'Yes.'

Salts' hooter sounded the end of the dinner break. We set off for the mill, where I had left my car. Dorrie hurried ahead of me. I felt uneasy about what she had told me, and surprised that she had confided in me. It was almost as if she expected me to do something, but what? Perhaps she saw me as the safe outsider, beyond Saltaire circles of gossip.

As I walked, I thought of Sykes, driving back to Leeds, anxious about Rosie. His plan to check Mr Whitaker's office safe for fingerprints, so long after Mrs Whitaker and Kevin had been in the office, was not his finest idea, but a good spur-of-the-moment excuse for departure to the hospital and Rosie. Charlie's account of seeing Kevin near the time cards by the reservoir entrance was now on record twice: in his statements to the police and to me. Kevin had got Dorrie drunk and might well wriggle out of any responsibility for her and the baby, but I would make sure Mr Cohen had the full story.

I had several ideas of my own, but first I wanted to talk to Inspector Mitchell at Shipley police station. Charlie Benson had used his last breath to give what he thought of as vital evidence. I hoped that would not be in vain. I had spent one of last night's sleepless hours with my writing pad, committing to paper what Charlie had told me.

THIRTY-EIGHT

Fortunately, Inspector Mitchell was at his desk. He came to meet me, looking at his watch. 'Come through, Mrs Shackleton. I'm due in a meeting shortly, but I heard the shocking news about Gwyneth Kidd. Is there anything you'd like to add?'

'Yes, there is, about meeting Charlie Benson, and about last night. You know that I talked to Charlie in the park and saw him into hospital?'

'Yes.'

'I've written down everything that he told me, including his search for his pills.' I put my writing sheets on the desk.

He took them. 'Thank you. I'm very sorry that your efforts on Mr Benson's behalf were to no avail.'

'So am I, Inspector.'

'And the distress of finding Gwyneth Kidd's body. A lesser woman would have gone to pieces. Is there anything I can do for you?'

'Mr Benson made a point of wanting to talk to me, because he worried that his statement may not have been thought of as important.'

'You can rest assured that we will take it into account. He seemed to have kept an eye on Mrs Whitaker and her godson.'

'There is that. Also, on the day Ronnie was murdered, Charlie saw a man entering the mill by a door from the yard. He described him to me. Your officers may have this already, but I have written his description.'

'Thank you. This will be a matter for CID. And it was good of Mr Sykes to hunt the missing pill box. Since you gave Mr Benson aspirins it seems that the lack of them would not have contributed to his death.'

'Someone had dropped the pill box in the waste sack used by gate security. That seems an odd thing to have done. Mr Benson also expressed his suspicions about the man in the yard to Paul in the security office.'

'Mrs Shackleton, I realise you are upset by Mr Benson's death. So am I. I remember Charlie from years ago in Bridgestead. A family man who deserved a better job, in my opinion. We'll inquire as to how his pill box ended up in the waste. It may have fallen through the lining of his jacket pocket—'

'The lining of his jacket pocket wasn't torn. When he took off his jacket, I helped him look.'

'We're keeping an open mind. I haven't had the opportunity to catch up with the CID officer regarding Mr Benson's death. I will be surprised if the coroner finds anything other than natural causes.'

I would be banging my head against a brick wall to continue. He was right that aspirin-snatching was not an efficient way of ensuring the silence that comes with death, and would be impossible to prove.

'And Ronnie Creswell?'

'The preliminary post-mortem report noted wounds from a blunt instrument to Ronnie's left jaw and left temple, a fresh bruise to his right jaw, marks on his throat.'

'Which of the blows caused Ronnie's death?'

'It will be public soon enough, after the inquest. Ronald Creswell died from a blood clot on the brain, subsequent to the trauma to his temple, caused by the blunt instrument. A knuckleduster.'

For a few fleeting seconds, I wished I hadn't asked, but at the same time I was processing this information. 'Then whoever killed him is right-handed, has a strong punch and a great deal of pent-up rage.'

The inspector nodded. He leaned back in his chair. 'As long as this is for your ears only . . .'

'Yes.'

'CID are pursuing a line of inquiry. Someone may have been hired to murder Ronnie. That suggests Creswell was up to something, that he'd crossed the wrong people, or found out information he wasn't meant to know. He'd visited pubs in Bradford and Leeds that are known for illegal gambling, debt collectors skimming off what they collect, contraband liquor coming from Hull, loan sharks, dealings with people who would not take kindly to interference or muscling in.'

I tried not to let my surprise show, or to voice the questions that spun into my head. Had CID created an alternative Ronnie? Why wouldn't someone from a village without a public house decide to go a little distance to try a new pub in a different place? Did CID want to brighten their lives by pretending to be in Birmingham, Glasgow, Chicago?

There was no point in arguing. Find out the truth, Mr Whitaker had said. That was what I must do.

THIRTY-NINE

Pamela's grandmother directed me to Peel Park. I would find Pamela by the lake, feeding the ducks.

I saw her before she saw me. She was standing by the edge of the lake, her hands in her pockets. Ducks pecked the ground around her, widening their circle. A couple of them waddled back into the water.

Now that I knew too much, my task seemed suddenly harder. There was nothing I could say that would soften the blow. If I were in her shoes, knowing that her father had his back to the wall and that her mother was about to hear news of her godson that would upset her to the core would be simply another but smaller blow. Ronnie was gone. Pamela's life was suddenly empty.

'Hello, Pamela. Your grandmother said I would find you here.'

I had startled her. 'Is something wrong?' She realised the absurdity of her question. 'Something new, I mean.'

'I saw your father this morning. Do you want to walk, or find a bench?'

She shrugged.

'Then let's walk. A bench will appear if we need one.'

'Have you come to tell me about Ronnie's funeral?'

'It's a little soon. I'll find out for you from the Creswells.'

She put her hand to her mouth. 'Of course. I should have gone to see them.'

'Pamela, how strong are you feeling today?'

'I can't cry any more. I've turned to stone, if you must know.'

We walked on in silence, leaving a sufficient pause for me to ask, 'What were your own plans, before you and Ronnie got together?'

'Teacher training. I'd completed a year. I wanted to do something useful. There was a time when Dad took me into the office every weekend. I was to be his right-hand woman, he said. I was about fifteen or sixteen when I saw that I wouldn't fit in.'

'You might fit in now.'

'Possibly. Ronnie and I talked about it. He said it would be a hoot if in a few years' time he and I were on the board.'

'Let's find a bench. I have things to tell you. Will you let me speak, and let me finish, and then tell me to get lost, or to give you a lift home?'

'What is there to tell?'

We sat on either end of a bench. The few birds that alighted soon gave up on us as a lost cause as far as crumbs were concerned. She listened as I told her what Sykes and I had found out about the mill, her father being undermined, his fears about the loss of a big contract, and the likely involvement of Kevin Foxcroft.

'That will kill my mother. Dad always saw through Kevin. I know Dad would have come round to appreciating Ronnie.'

'He already had. He was being cautious, that's all. Is it all right if I talk about Ronnie now?'

'Yes. He's all I think about. No one will replace him. Ever.'

We talked about hearts breaking. It was never that simple, never just one crack. What I had to tell her would do the shattering.

'Pamela, I'm sorry to be blunt. Here's the hard part of what I must tell you.'

She turned her head away. 'I can't listen.'

'Then you don't have to. It can wait. There'll be a coroner's inquest.'

We sat so quietly that I noticed every sound, the breeze through the trees, the call of a collared dove, a man shouting for his dog.

At last she said, 'You'd better tell me.'

'The likely verdict at the coroner's inquest will be unlawful killing by a person or persons unknown. The police are investigating. Eventually they will make an arrest.'

She let out a scream and began to cry. 'No! No!' After a long time she said, 'Who would want to hurt Ronnie? He shone. He was the light in my life.'

'I wish I'd known him.'

'And if I'd never known him, I wouldn't be feeling like this, but I'm glad I did. When we went for a walk on a winter's day, I took my gloves off, to hold hands.'

'Here's the truth from your dad: Ronnie would have been your father's right-hand man, just as you were once going to be the right-hand woman.'

'What are people doing and saying in Saltaire? I think life must have stopped.'

'Mrs Creswell may be arranging the funeral. She and Nancy have moved in with Uncle Nick.'

'And Mr Creswell, and the brothers?'

'As far as I know, Mr Creswell is living in his Milner Field garden hut. I don't know about the brothers.'

A flock of starlings flew from an elm tree, rustling the leaves.

We stood and walked towards the park gates.

'If you're going back to Saltaire, you might give me a lift. I want to go to the mill, talk to my dad. I think I knew he liked Ronnie. He wouldn't say it. He tried not to let it show.'

When we reached Victoria Road, I saw a boy, dressed in black, sitting on a stool outside the tall house. I stopped the car and we got out.

Pamela said, 'I must pay my respects to Mrs Creswell. The one bright spot for her will be not having me as a daughter-in-law.'

It was as if Pamela had donned an invisible suit of armour, a tough, brittle edge of protection.

The boy stood as we approached. 'That must be Mark,' Pamela said.

'The stable lad?'

'I think so. I don't really know the brothers.'

The boy was thin and not very tall. He had an awkwardness about him, perhaps because of being on sentry duty.

Pamela said, 'Hello. Is your mother in?'

'Mam had to go out. I've to tell her who called.'

'Are you Mark? You work with horses.'

'Yes, at the racecourse stables.'

Pamela took a deep breath. Her words came out clipped and controlled. 'Please give your mother my condolences, and to you, Mark, and the family. I'm Pamela Whitaker, of Salts Mill.'

'Oh, thank you, Miss Whitaker. Mam appreciates that you'll close the mill on the funeral day.'

Pamela took a breath. 'It's the least we can do, Mark. I'm very sorry for your loss. We all are.'

She turned away but seemed suddenly unaware of which direction to walk. She turned back to Mark. 'I'd rather the mill had been razed to the ground than that Ronnie died there. We planned to marry.'

I linked her arm. We crossed to the mill side of the street. She was a little shaky, but determined not to let it show. 'Do you smoke?' she asked.

'No.'

'Nor do I. I thought it might be worth a try.'

'I can drive you home to Bingley if you like.'

She shook her head. 'I've spent days lying down in a dark room and walking in the park. If the mill has got into one of its messes, I'll see if Dad needs my help, even if we only bend each other's ears.'

We were by the security hut. She put her head round the door. 'Is Mr Whitaker in his office?'

'He is, Miss Whitaker.'

'Will you please tell him I'm on my way up?'

Pamela entered the building just as Kevin Foxcroft was coming out, under escort. I stepped aside to make way. Foxcroft was walked to a car by a uniformed and a plain-clothes officer. Whatever Mr Whitaker had told the police, it had certainly put the frighteners on Kevin.

I crossed back to speak to Mark, who was watching the police car turn left onto the main road.

'Is that him?' Mark asked, his face flushed, his mouth tight. He stood at the kerb, bouncing as if he might break into a run and chase after the vehicle. 'Did he do for Ronnie?'

I didn't know, but thought it best not to help a rumour start. 'No. If it was that, he would have been taken out in handcuffs.'

An elderly man, leaning on a walking stick, came to express his condolences.

When he had gone, I said, 'It's good that you have time off from your work, Mark. It will be a help to your mam and dad to have you here.'

'I would've walked out if my boss had refused. Mam's gone to arrange Ronnie's funeral. She told me to be here as early as I could.' He suddenly turned away, too upset to go on. I waited until he gained the composure to speak again, which he did with a kind of fury. 'I could have been home yesterday if Mr High and Mighty had given me a lift. I heard he and Gwyneth were leaving. "Car is full," he said. Liar. My hands might have been dirty when I asked him, but I'd had a wash, my clothes were clean. I don't smell.'

'That was mean of Garner,' I said.

Mark managed a grim smile. 'He got his comeuppance. He's gone. Turfed out of his cottage.'

I tried to make sense of the timing. Mrs Sugden and I had found Gwyneth's body early this morning, so she and Garner must have left Doncaster late last night or in the early hours this morning.

'I'm sorry you didn't get a lift, Mark.'

'I would've rode with the devil to be here sooner. Well, he'll get his comeuppance. It'll be a slap in the eye if he's still free to go to Morecambe to watch his horse training on the sands.'

'Why is that?'

'Sparky Lass is a lovely natured creature, perfect for a young person, a learner. But she's a no-hoper. There's always going to be a horse that comes in last. Sparky was born to be that horse, but I wish she was mine. Of course, he might be locked up before he finds out no one will buy her. I don't know why he isn't behind bars now.'

'You're talking about Mr Garner?'

His eyes widened as he stared at me. 'You know him, the estate manager?'

'I met him at Milner Field, after your mother vacated the Lodge. My housekeeper has stepped in, just until the auction.'

'Are you the lady Ronnie wrote to?'

'Yes. I'm Kate Shackleton.'

For what seemed a long moment, we stood in silence. Here was the first person who knew of Ronnie's letter.

A loud clearing of the throat interrupted our silence. The man in the long black coat and tall top hat came upon us so quietly that neither of us heard him approach. He raised his hat. 'Good afternoon, young sir.'

Mark was keeper of the door. I took a step back.

'Good afternoon, sir,' said Mark.

'I am Philip Danby, of Sloper and Danby, Undertakers. I am here for Mr Nicholas Reeves.'

Mark stared. 'Oh, you mean Uncle Nick?'

'Yes, I suppose I do, and you have my deepest condolences.'

'Uncle Nick's not dead. He's gone out on one of his walks.'

'My condolences are for the loss of Ronald Creswell Junior.

272

We are much obliged to be of service. As we speak, my sons are attending on your dear mother. Mr Nicholas Reeves is, I trust, in good health.'

'Not very.'

'Then I'm sorry to hear that. I simply wish to speak to your Uncle Nick in connection with the last wishes of a lately deceased friend or acquaintance of his.'

'Who?'

'His former schoolteacher, Miss Mason – she passed away peacefully in her sleep.'

'I'll tell him.'

'Thank you, young man.' With studied care, he dipped into the top pocket of his jacket and with the tips of forefinger and thumb, took out a business card and handed it to Mark. 'Please ask your Uncle Nick to contact me. You might mention the words, "Where the daffodils grow."'

'Where the daffodils grow? They don't grow anywhere in August.'

'But that is the message.' The undertaker nodded graciously. 'Thank you, young Mr Creswell.' Mr Danby bowed to me and departed as silently as he had appeared.

Mark watched him go. 'Mrs Shackleton, do you ever think the world has gone mad?'

'Evidence mounts in that direction. Perhaps it began so long ago that we never noticed.'

We smiled. 'Mark, we'll talk another time about Ronnie's letter?'

His eyes widened. 'You didn't meet Ronnie?'

'Sadly no. I came on Saturday, too late to see him.'

'Ronnie didn't tell you in his letter?'

'Tell me what?'

'Garner's a crook. Takes bets and doesn't put them on. Sells hundreds of dodgy sweepstake tickets.'

'How are they dodgy?' I asked.

'The sweepstake tickets package includes five separate ones in a rubber band with a note that says, "These are your winning tickets." Garner might let someone win, he might not.'

'How do you know all this?'

'He picked one of my pals as his delivery boy. Still he manages to be in debt. Sells on stolen stuff. He's not even who he says he is. He has the gift of the gab and forged papers. One of the racecourse directors recognised him. I heard them talking. They were deciding what to do and didn't want a scandal. He's been turfed out of his cottage and he's put Sparky up for sale.'

'Ronnie knew all this?'

'I told him when I was here for Mam's birthday. You're invisible when you're a stable lad; you hear all sorts, but what was I supposed to do? I told Ronnie what I knew. He said he'd go to some of the pubs where Garner went, and see what he could pick up.'

Inspector Mitchell's account of CID going to seedy pubs to find out what Ronnie had been up to now made sense.

'You didn't think to tell the police about Garner?'

'The police? Who do you think gets the sweepstake tickets from the "These are your winning tickets" batch? And who'd listen to me, telling tales from work? I told Ronnie it needed to be someone who would investigate, have proof. He'd found out which pubs Garner went to.'

So CID were right in telling Inspector Mitchell that Ronnie had been out and about to pubs where he would have stuck out as someone who didn't fit. Correct information.

Incorrect interpretation. This also explained why Ronnie had not confided in Pamela or Whitaker. He wanted to be sure of his facts.

'Mark, promise me that you will go to Shipley police station and tell Inspector Mitchell or a CID officer what you've just told me. They have completely the wrong idea about why Ronnie was going to those pubs.'

Mark groaned. 'I messed up. I was too slow. I made Ronnie a target.'

'You're not the one to blame. What we have to do is find justice for Ronnie.'

Mark's face was a picture of misery. He turned his head away. 'That won't bring him back.'

'But it's what we can do.'

We were silent for a while. Mark looked as if he might have to run away and hide. He took a deep breath and lit a cigarette.

'Mark, Ronnie told me he wanted to talk to me about something that happened in the past.'

'Maybe Garner's past. He's been up to stuff for a long time. I know Ronnie planned to talk to you. He got your name from a friend of his he goes to lectures with.'

'What made you decide Garner should be reported?'

'Sparky Lass.'

'The horse?'

'Garner has a vicious streak. He oughtn't to have been riding her. He's a useless rider. When she wouldn't do what he wanted, he thumped her. I told him that if he wanted her to win she had to be treated properly. He knew I was right, but he thumped me. He's desperate for a win and it's not going to happen. When it dawns on him she'll come last . . .'

This was all in the present. 'Mark, in his letter, Ronnie definitely said there was something that happened in the past that would interest me. What was that?'

He looked blank and shook his head. 'Only what I said, about Garner's past. We think Garner isn't his real name. It makes me feel sick that you would have been on to him by now, if there hadn't been that terrible accident.'

Accident? I hoped that Mark would never find out that his brother was murdered.

A forlorn hope.

'We must tell the police about Garner.'

Mark was now looking past me. 'Aye, aye, who's set fire to Freddie's backside?'

A young boy with a basin haircut came running up the hill. He stopped suddenly by the kerb, doubled over and held his middle, groaning. 'Got a stitch!'

Mark lifted him and sat him on the stool. 'Catch your breath.' He turned to me. 'Mrs Shackleton, this is Nancy's friend Freddie.'

When he could speak, Freddie said, 'Is Nancy here?'

'I thought she was with you? You're supposed to be at the farm.'

'I waited for the cart, but Nancy didn't turn up so I went to look for her. Uncle Nick's looking for her too.'

Mark said, 'Oh, so that's where he's gone.'

'Only we don't know where else to look. Your dad sent me back here. We can't find her.'

FORTY

Freddie's story came out in bursts.

'I asked Susan and Tony's mother, she said they went on the tram to the farm to be early, to be first. She said maybe Nancy went with them. I'll be mad if she did because I've been all over looking. She's not at Milner Field, or the gardens or the park. But she wouldn't have gone to the farm without me, would she? By the time I got back to the meeting point the farmer had been and gone.'

'The kids are potato picking,' Mark explained. 'Nancy didn't have the fare for the tram. She was going to Milner Field to take Dad his breakfast, then she was going to get the cart.' He gulped and ran his tongue around his lips. 'Nancy never knows when to keep her mouth shut. I didn't know she was earwigging when I told Mam about you-know-who. Nancy said, "Is Mr Garner a very bad man?"'

'I don't think you've anything to worry about,' I said. 'Perhaps Freddie missed her, or your dad gave her the tram fare. If she's not at Milner Field, she's joined the potato pickers.'

'You're right,' Mark said. 'I'm just on edge. Only she has

no notion that sometimes you need to keep your trap shut. She might say something in front of Garner.'

Freddie wailed. 'We pick together. Nancy wouldn't have gone without me.'

'How far is this farm?' I asked.

Freddie climbed in the car beside me, shouting over the noise of the engine and using his hands like car signals to give me directions. We approached the farm up a narrow, bumpy lane. On either side, beyond the hedgerows, children were potato picking.

Freddie climbed out of the car, calling back, 'I can't see her.'

The farmer appeared from beyond the hedge. I got out, ready to explain why we were here. Freddie burst out: 'Sorry I'm late, Mr Hayes. When Nancy wasn't waiting for the cart, I went to fetch her but I couldn't find her and I missed the cart and I think she might have come on the tram.'

'Who's Nancy?'

'My friend. She wears a blue and white check frock and a white sunhat.'

Mr Hayes glanced across the fields in either direction. 'Well, I don't see no white sunhat, so she's not here, is she? And I don't set on latecomers who turn up telling a tale, so you can hop it, lad. Be on time tomorrow.'

I was about to give Mr Hayes my opinion of his rudeness, but that may have cancelled Freddie's future prospects. 'She's ten years old and we need to find her.'

'She's a regular,' Freddie piped up.

I turned to Freddie. 'Is there anyone you know in either field?'

He nodded.

'Go enquire.'

He ran through a gap in the hedge.

'I'm not hiding no child!'

'No one is accusing you, Mr Hayes. But if she does turn up, please ensure her safe return to Victoria Road, Saltaire.'

'I'm not running a taxi service.'

'Then telephone the police or Milner Field mansion.'

We waited, looking across to the field where Freddie was moving from one child to another.

'Some kids are more trouble than they're worth,' Mr Hayes grumbled.

Freddie came back, shaking his head. 'Susan and Tony haven't seen her. No one from Saltaire has seen her.'

We got back in the car and I reversed steadily. 'Don't worry, Freddie. We'll find her. I was laying it on thick for Horrible Hayes.'

He managed a laugh. 'What will we do?'

'We'll talk to Mr Creswell.'

I took a wrong turn and drove for half a mile before recognising the coach road. From here, I could go into Milner Field passing the North Lodge.

I shouted over the noise of the engine, 'Freddie, would Nancy have called at one of the other lodges?'

'Only to knock for a drink of water if she was thirsty.'

'We'll ask.'

As we came closer to the north entrance, Freddie let out a yelp. A car, its bonnet smashed in, had damaged a brick wall. A trailer was parked next to it. Two men were swinging a hook into the car to hoist it. I stopped and got out.

'What happened?' I asked the men.

'Dunno, miss. We're just here to shift it.'

His mate was more helpful. 'Neighbours heard a bang. By the time they come out, driver had gone.'

'Was anyone hurt?'

'Don't see no blood on the road. Like Mike said, we're just here to shift it.'

'What time was the crash?'

'Call came from the police in the middle of the night. We don't start until eight. And if you're thinking of going in by this entrance, don't. The police are there, not letting anyone through.'

Freddie had come to look.

'I know that car. It belongs to Mr Garner.'

I took his hand. 'Come on. Let's go.'

A police car was parked outside the South Lodge. The constable on duty waved me down. I told Freddie to wait in the car while I got out and went to speak with the constable.

'Hello, Officer. I'm looking for Nancy Creswell, the head gardener's young daughter. She set off to bring her dad his breakfast early this morning and hasn't been seen since. I saw there's been a car crash. Was anyone injured?'

'I wasn't in attendance. We got the report of a crash. I know that there was no one in or by the car when the officers arrived.'

'Do you know whose car it is?'

'Wouldn't be able to tell you if I did, madam.'

'I believe that it's Aldous Garner's car.'

'Thank you, madam. Would you please turn around and leave? There's been a major incident.'

'I reported that major incident this morning, Officer. My name is Mrs Shackleton. I'm a guest of Mr Whitaker of Salts, and staying in the Tower. Freddie here has been helping me search for his friend Nancy Creswell, who may have been in the vicinity at the time of Gwyneth Kidd's death. Freddie identified the car that crashed as belonging to the estate manager, Aldous Garner. I'm assuming that is who the police are looking for.'

The policeman's manner changed. He nodded towards Freddie. 'That lad was here earlier, sneaked past us and talked to the girl's dad. She's not turned up, then?'

'No.'

'The premises have been searched, the grounds searched. I think you need to try her friends' houses.'

'Nancy was here with her father's breakfast early on and should have gone back to Saltaire to catch the cart to the farm for potato picking. She missed the cart and isn't at the farm, or at home. I need to talk to the officer in charge.'

'Can you describe Nancy?'

'She's ten years old, about three foot six tall, blue eyes, wearing a cotton frock, probably blue and white check, and a white sunhat.'

'Wait here. I'll make a call.'

He went to the Lodge. I followed him. 'She has short straight blonde hair with a fringe.'

Nancy's intention to have wavy hair by having curly-haired Dorrie Fairburn wash it for her had been to no avail.

Dogs, I thought. We needed police dogs and some item of clothing belonging to Nancy. Why had no one thought of that? The answer was simple. Nick had been searching for Nancy, but he might search for his own shadow. The police were looking for Garner. Since this morning, Nancy's mother was out. Her dad and brother thought she had gone potato

281

picking. If it wasn't for Freddie, they would have gone on thinking that.

When the constable picked up the phone, I said, 'Please request a sniffer dog.'

He glared at me. I went upstairs, looking in the bedrooms, looking for something Nancy had left behind. I found a sock under the bed.

I went downstairs, holding it between two fingers, waving it at the constable, saying, 'Sniffer dog.'

Freddie was at the open door. 'Do you know the Creswells' whistle?' I asked.

He nodded. We went outside. Freddie pursed his lips and whistled. So did I.

I had hoped to see Ronald Creswell, but it was Uncle Nick who lumbered into view. He looked from me to Freddie. 'The police turned me out. I told them, "You can't turn me out. This is where I was born."'

'Nick, have you looked in the orangery?'

'I looked there after I went to the school. The school is closed. Holidays. Miss Lee came out. She told me Miss Mason is dead. An undertaker telephoned the school. He wants me.' He leaned close, his mouth against my ear. 'It has come to pass,' he said, with the solemnity of an Old Testament prophet. 'Miss Mason is dead. Ronnie is dead. Now my little sweetheart, our bonnie babe, has paid the price for my folly. An undertaker is looking for me, and asking questions.'

'Nick, Nancy is a wanderer. We will wander after her and find her,' I said.

Freddie got back in the car, sat in the driving seat and put his hands on the steering wheel. 'I could drive about and look for Nancy. How do you work this?'

'Ask me in ten years. If you missed the cart, where would you go?'

'Home or the park, or I'd see who would come out to play. But I've been round the park. I've seen who's playing out. Nancy isn't there.'

'Whistle again for Mr Creswell. He'll want to talk to the police'

We both whistled and then I went into the Lodge.

The constable was just replacing the telephone receiver. 'Nancy's description is being circulated to all stations and beat bobbies.'

'Will you send for sniffer dogs?'

His mouth fell open. 'Missis, we're hunting for a . . . ' He came close, so that Freddie would not see his lips and mouthed *murderer*. 'No, I can't send for dogs. Nearest dogs are in Bradford and spoken for, if you catch my meaning. You've two local men coming, PC Beale and PC Harrison, to relieve me. Us lot are called off, being allocated to a wider search.'

By the time I came out of the Lodge, Mr Creswell was hurrying in our direction. He nodded to me and asked Freddie, 'Have you found her?'

'No, Mr Creswell.' Freddie lit up with a sudden idea. 'Miss Lee is taking her class on a picnic to Shipley Glen for the end of term. Me and Nancy didn't put us names down because of going to the farm. They were to meet at the funicular railway at two o'clock. All you have to take is a cup.'

Mr Creswell waved Uncle Nick over. 'Freddie says the teacher is taking her class to Shipley Glen on the funicular for a picnic. Go there.' He gave Nick a coin. 'If Nancy is there, leave her and Freddie but come straight back and tell us.'

Mr Creswell put his fingers to his lips and gave his whistle, but with three little notes at the end.

One by one, gardeners appeared, three of them. A young man, tall and thin with red hair and freckles, arrived first. He waited for Creswell's instructions. 'Pete, go to Shipley Glen with Nick and the little lad. Look out for the teacher and children having a picnic.'

Pete nodded. He, Nick and Freddie set off.

To a solemn fellow, still holding his shovel, Mr Creswell said, 'Go to the village. Tell neighbours. See if Nancy is in someone's house or yard.'

Nick came back, followed by the gardener meant to be minding him. 'What if she is down the well,' he said, 'with the shepherdess?'

Ronald Creswell looked ready to explode. He took a step towards Nick but then just stared at him. 'Go look for her!'

The young gardener beside Nick said, 'If Garner harmed Nancy, he'll be desperate.'

'Pete, what are you getting at?' Creswell asked.

Pete said quietly, 'Garner ordered a cap for the well and said he'd see to it himself. It came yesterday afternoon. This morning, it's on and padlocked. Well, none of us put the cap in place. He'd said we needed to make it safe, to stop people chucking stuff down there; but think what he always said to any kid touching his car. He said he'd chuck them down the well.'

That was one of those threats no one thinks twice about, until a moment like this. I felt suddenly cold. Was that where Garner would have disposed of Gwyneth's body had we not found her first? This was all the more reason to have Nick and Freddie out of the way.

Ronald Creswell realised this. He stood very still. 'Just go, see if she's at the picnic.'

The police officer I had spoken to was driving away. He stopped by the gate and exchanged words with two officers arriving on bikes.

The cycling officers came closer and I saw they were PC Beale and PC Harrison, with a cocker spaniel trotting behind.

I talked to PC Harrison, offering him Nancy's sock. Solemnly, he took an evidence bag from his inside pocket and opened it for me to drop in the sock.

'He's not a sniffer dog,' PC Harrison said. 'He's trained to sit, stay, find his ball and come back on a whistle or a call.'

We were becoming a crowd, added to by Mrs Sugden and a woman with broad shoulders and an angular, determined face. She wore an overall and a turban and carried a shopping bag.

'This is Julie,' Mrs Sugden said. 'The police have given us the all-clear for cleaning the top floors. We've three more cleaners on their way.'

I went to Nick and took his arm. I spoke quietly. 'Nick, you trusted me with the keys. You trusted me with your history. Now take Freddie from here. Keep him safe. Take him up the funicular railway, to the picnic. Everything is under control.'

'But Miss Mason is dead,' said Nick.

'The teacher is Miss Lee, she will be at Shipley Glen. She'll want to meet you, and will be glad to see Freddie.'

'I need a cup,' Freddie said.

Julie went into the Lodge and emerged with two cups. 'Here you are, Freddie, and Uncle Nick.'

The pair went off, hand in hand, each carrying a cup, the young gardener alongside them.

PC Beale gave a pep talk, saying that a big search was on for Aldous Garner, in the towns and on the moors. 'Every man has Nancy's description, too.'

'You think he's got her?' Mr Creswell said. His eyes widened. He bounced on the balls of his feet, ready to leap at someone.

'I didn't say that,' said PC Beale. 'I'm as wise as you are on this.'

I drew PC Beale aside. 'Constable Beale, yesterday Nancy told me that she saw Gwyneth Kidd near the North Lodge. I have good reason to believe Gwyneth went to Doncaster with Aldous Garner in May and has been living with him since then. In the early hours Gwyneth was murdered. Her body was still warm first thing this morning. The well could have been the place where Garner would have disposed of the body. He ordered the cap for the well and said he would see to it himself. He didn't have time to dispose of Gwyneth's body because we found her. The cap is on the well. Nancy is a curious child. If she was snooping and Garner saw her, I dread to think it but she could be down that well.'

PC Beale turned to PC Harrison. 'Use the Lodge telephone. Get the mill fire brigade over here fast.'

FORTY-ONE

The well was at the bottom of the slope that led to the farm. The bilberry bush grew close by it. None of us knew whether we were right or wrong in paying attention to the well. It was a combination of Garner's sudden decision to 'make it safe' by having it capped, Garner's threat, according to Pete the gardener, that he would throw a child down there if any of them touched his car again, and the unlikelihood that Garner would have taken Nancy with him. In addition to that, the cocker spaniel, having smelled Nancy's sock, showed interest in the flattened vegetation around the well that included the spoiling of much of the bilberry bush. But the cocker spaniel also showed interest in the bark of trees, rabbit holes and my shoes.

In a village steeped in stories of human bones in a well, the thought of a child being down there held greater sway than it would elsewhere.

No one was sure how deep the well was. The new lid that capped the opening was of oak, secured by metal strips.

'The fire brigade is on its way,' said PC Harrison.

The crowd continued to grow. Miss Lee and the children arrived, Nick and the young gardener with them. Miss Lee said, 'We heard the news about Nancy and came back down, meeting Uncle Nick and Freddie on the way. No one has seen Nancy in the Glen. People are looking, but I don't want to lose more children.'

Ronald Creswell was trying to raise the lid from the well. He couldn't do it. It was fastened down and padlocked.

PC Harrison put a hand on Creswell's shoulder. 'Leave it to the fire brigade. They said not to do anything foolhardy.'

PC Beale ordered everyone to stay back in an orderly fashion. Nobody moved.

Uncle Nick said to the children, 'Spread out and sing. Nancy will hear you if you sing!'

Miss Lee said, 'Stay together! That's an order.'

Uncle Nick began to lead the children in a song, 'A-hunting We Will Go'. A small girl started crying. Freddie said, 'Uncle Nick, you're singing the wrong words. You have to let the fox out of the box.'

The teacher drew herself up to her full height. 'Uncle Nick, Nancy may hear the children, but if we are singing our heads off, we will not hear Nancy. Children, you have done your best, but we are in the way of the men searching. They do not need a chorus. When Nancy is found, I will be told. I will ring the school bell and then the church bell will ring. Now, unless you want to be crossed off my picnic list and sent to the headmaster, back to the village.'

'Miss Lee, wait a moment!' The mill fire brigade arrived without sirens or ceremony. It was made up of David Fairburn and two other men who heard Miss Lee's order. The two other men, carrying crowbars and ropes, walked on towards the well. David had ropes looped around him and carried a first-aid kit.

David said, 'We'll get the cap off the well. Let the children stay at a distance. If Nancy's down there, she'll want to know her friends are here. What better way than to sing?'

I was glad. The children wanted to be here. The alternative was for them to creep away, silently and helplessly, back to the village to listen for a bell. If this wild search failed, they would hope to go on looking.

David walked towards the now trampled bilberry bush. The gardeners stepped back to let him near. David on one side, and a fellow worker on the other side, soon had the padlocks snapped, the steel strip removed and the well uncapped. A large circle of wood, cut to fit as neat as a lid on a pan, stood against a tree.

David spoke to the children. 'It's dark and silent at the bottom of the well. Sing. Let Nancy know you are here.'

The children began to sing, but Nick's booming voice drowned them out. He sang his own version of the rhyme.

'Ding dong bell, ding dong bell,
Is Nancy in the well?
Let us ring now for her knell,
Ding dong bell, ding dong bell.'

Suddenly, Mrs Creswell was there, pushing her way in, pulling Nick away. She screamed at him: 'I go out for one day – one day! – to try to do my best by Ronnie, by all of you, and you lose Nancy.' Mrs Creswell shook Nick. 'Have you gone mad? Ring for her knell? That's tolling the bell?' She called into the well. 'Nancy, your mammy's here. If you're down there, we're coming for you. Can you hear me?'

Her words came back in a distorted echo.

Mr Creswell put his arm around his wife. She shook him off.

David spoke gently. 'Everyone, step back, please. If Nancy is there, we'll reach her. Quiet now. We need to know that when we go down, we will find Nancy. Otherwise, we may waste time trying to rescue our own echo.'

Freddie stood beside David and tugged at his sleeve, so that David had to bob down to hear what the little boy said. David nodded. 'Quiet, everyone.' He lifted Freddie, tilting him, holding him tightly just above the well.

Freddie, his voice a high and clear sing-song, repeated Nancy's name. 'Nancy, Nancy, it's Freddie. If you're there, call to me, call to me, Nancy. Call to me. It's Freddie. Call my name.'

There was a long silence, and then came a sound from deep in the well. The wordless sound followed the lilt and high notes of Freddie's words. I could fill in the words behind the sounds. 'Freddie, Freddie, Freddie.'

'Nancy's gagged!' I said. 'That's why she can only make sounds.'

Mr Creswell said, 'Freddie, sing to her that I'm coming to fetch her.'

Freddie sang, 'Nancy, don't be scared. Your daddy is coming down on a rope. Don't be scared of a big adventure. He will come and get you.'

Proceedings were suddenly interrupted by a sharp voice.

The bilberry picker I had met on my walk from the station on Saturday came marching with her basket. 'Hey! What do you lot think you're doing? These are my bilberries.'

290

Someone had a quiet word in her ear.

Absolute silence followed. Birds stopped singing. Watchers stopped breathing.

David Fairburn and one of his companions formed nooses with their heavy ropes. Both were placed around Mr Creswell, one under his arms and the other around his waist. He was helped onto the edge of the well, where he sat for a minute while the ropes were checked and checked again. Mr Creswell nodded that he was ready.

Someone ordered, 'Stand back! Make room.'

David and PC Beale, the heaviest man present, stood so close to each other that they might be one. They leaned forwards, holding the rope. Mr Creswell's descent began. Slowly, he disappeared from view.

Behind David and the other mill brigade volunteer stood two more gardeners, ready to help if needed.

A breeze disturbed the branches. The watchers were silent enough to hear Mrs Creswell's suddenly rapid breath. The men holding the rope had their sleeves rolled up. The muscle in David Fairburn's upper arm strained as if it might tear open. The slightest slip could mean a loss of grip.

All was quiet. Only the breeze, pestering trees and rattling leaves, ignored proceedings.

After a long silence, David and his companion exchanged looks. David nodded.

They waited. Miss Lee shushed a child that had begun to cry. After an age, we heard a faint sing-song. Nancy again copied Freddie's melody, her words echoing up the well: 'Dad's here. He's got me.'

Mrs Creswell let out a cry of relief.

The men with the ropes exchanged glances once more.

They had felt a tug. A few seconds later, the Creswell whistle echoed up to us.

Slowly and carefully began the raising of the pair, the men with ropes now leaning slightly back, each supported by the man behind him.

We watched, listened and waited.

Mr Creswell appeared, first his sandy hair, then his head and the back of his neck, covered in white dust.

At last, there was Nancy, in her father's arms, one arm dangling. Two men grabbed David Fairburn's rope as David reached out and lifted Nancy out.

Mrs Creswell took her daughter and kissed her head, saying, 'How on earth did you get down there?'

Nancy closed her eyes.

I whispered to Mrs Creswell, 'Keep her awake.'

Mrs Creswell said, 'Nancy, look at me, tell me if your arm hurts.'

'It hurts.'

'It'll mend. I've got you now. We're going to hospital.'

I went closer, wanting to be sure Nancy stayed awake. 'What was it like down there?'

'Dark.'

'What else? Was it bumpy? Did it hurt your back?'

'Stinky. Soft, like a heap of compost.'

Nick came alongside. 'A soft landing. I've thrown flowers down there, for the shepherdess.'

'I know.' Nancy opened her hand. 'I think this belongs to her.' It was a small bone.

Nick said, 'That bone is a match for the one I found. She was looking out for you.'

'Shush,' said Mrs Creswell. 'None of that.'

Nick took the bone. He knew just where he would bury it.

David Fairburn helped Mr Creswell to his feet. The mill fire brigade unfolded a stretcher. Nancy was made as comfortable as possible to be carried to the hospital. The bilberry picker clapped her hands. 'You poor little lass. From this day, I grant you equal rights with me over the bilberries.' They gathered up their equipment and two of them carried Nancy on the stretcher to the hospital, Mr and Mrs Creswell beside them.

Some of us could not think of anything to say. Mrs Sugden appeared and filled the breech. 'I've baked. Everyone who wants to can come back to the Tower and tuck in. Look sharp. I'll have the kettle on.'

If Mrs Sugden was disappointed at the response, she did not let it show.

Miss Lee raised her picnic basket and announced, 'Thank you very much, but for us it is time for a run around the park!' She added quietly to me, 'Not that I'm superstitious myself, but I can't shoulder responsibility for taking children into the mansion.'

As the children formed a line, Miss Lee stepped closer to me. She whispered, 'How did Uncle Nick know that Nancy was down the well, unless he put her there?'

'I believe he knew by instinct, not logic or special knowledge. And he couldn't have lifted that lid from the well.'

The watchers dispersed. Mrs Sugden and I went back to the Tower. In the afternoon, Ronald Creswell came to give us a report on Nancy. She was being kept in hospital. Her mother had persuaded her that what had happened was a big adventure, part dream, part real. It was like *Alice in Wonderland* coming to life. Unlike Alice, Nancy had injuries to show for her adventure, but they would come right.

Being indoors seemed oppressive. Mrs Sugden and I went to sit in the garden. The day was bright and clear. We sat in sunshine under a blue sky. It made what had just happened seem like a bad dream.

'How could Garner do such a thing to an innocent child?' Mrs Sugden said. 'Do you think it was him?'

'I'm certain it was. We were too late to save Gwyneth but we found Nancy in time to thwart Garner. I think he must have come back to the cellar almost immediately, probably with a sack or something. The well is where he would have disposed of Gwyneth's body. But then he heard us, or the police.'

'But Nancy? Why her?'

'Nancy saw Gwyneth by the North Lodge yesterday. Being Nancy, she probably wanted to see if she was staying at the mansion. Perhaps she knocked, or looked through a window. Garner couldn't risk Nancy nosying around.'

For a while we sat in silence. I thought that Garner must have felt trapped, cornered. It horrified me to think that he would have dropped Gwyneth's body into the well with Nancy, and Nancy still alive. I was glad when Mrs Sugden suddenly said, 'Where has Jim got to? Do you think he decided to spend the night in Leeds? I hope Rosie's all right.'

FORTY-TWO

Later that evening, a heavy knock on the door startled us. Mrs Sugden, ever cautious, went to look out of the window, calling, 'Wait on!' as I went to the door. 'It's a policeman.'

I opened the door to PC Harrison, who looked serious, and very young. Part of me wished I didn't know that he was in love with Dorrie Fairburn, and that the situation must be hopeless.

The constable cleared his throat. 'May I come in, Mrs Shackleton? I have been asked to talk to you and your friend.'

'Of course.'

He stepped inside. When I invited him to sit down, he squeezed himself into a corner of the sofa, in that way that some large, insecure but polite young men try to make themselves a little smaller in the presence of the opposite sex.

PC Harrison spoke quietly. 'Aldous Garner's car was taken away this morning. We have searched the mansion, the lodges, grounds and surrounding area. A wider search is underway. We are not seeking anyone else in connection with the murder of Gwyneth Kidd.'

As he spoke, I saw Gwyneth's body in my mind's eye, and felt the touch of her skin as I checked for a pulse. If Mrs Sugden and I had gone earlier to the mansion, we might have been in time to save her. 'She died in that cellar where we found her?'

'That appears to be the case.' He could not have been a policeman long, but he already spoke the language. 'We have reason to believe Garner left the area but we need to take precautions. I have orders to search the Tower, and then to stay on duty here overnight, to keep watch and to ensure your safety. A fellow officer will be on outside patrol. I am sorry for the inconvenience.'

'Don't be.' We did not mind in the least. 'You have a job to do,' I said.

He went upstairs.

Mrs Sugden put on the kettle. 'He seems a nice enough young fellow, smartly turned out.'

'He's the son of Mr Whitaker's secretary,' I said.

'She's done a good job bringing him up. I expect she's proud of him.'

I thought of David Fairburn's comment, that he smelled Brylcreem as he went down the steps at the reservoir, and then remembered the scent when PC Harrison, who also wears Brylcreem, discharged him from custody.

One of the gaps in my knowledge is what Brylcreem smells like. Perhaps Mrs Sugden would know. 'He's smoothed oil into his hair,' I said.

'Aye, I noticed.'

'What is it, do you know?'

'It's Brylcreem, same as Aldous Garner's. Professor Merton took to wearing it. Miss Merton can't stand the smell. She took the lid off the tin and told me to take a whiff. Why men want to smell like a polished table beats me.'

'PC Harrison will want to look in the cellar. Take him down and have a look yourself. Keep him talking while I call the inspector.'

She was on the point of asking why, but heard the constable's heavy tread on the stairs.

Mrs Sugden went into the hall and said she would show him the cellar and go down with him because she wanted butter.

I picked up the telephone. 'Mrs Shackleton speaking. Please connect me to Inspector Mitchell at Shipley police station.'

He answered quickly. 'Mrs Shackleton.'

'Inspector, regarding the Brylcreem we talked about.'

He was silent for a few seconds, and then said, 'Ah, yes. What about it?'

'My housekeeper Mrs Sugden tells me that Aldous Garner wears Brylcreem.'

'Thank you, Mrs Shackleton.'

The evening had grown dark when Jim Sykes drove the last couple of miles to Milner Field. As he drove, he thought back over the events of this strange and unsettling day.

After visiting the hospital, words had deserted him. He couldn't think straight. Saltaire and Milner Field would have to manage without him for the rest of the day. He would not telephone to the mansion or mill, hardly knowing what to say, and not yet ready to talk to anyone. He needed to think.

Irene must be told. That had been Rosie's instruction. The boys could wait. Jim had gone to Irene's place of work. She would know what to do. For once he felt helpless, knocked off his perch. Irene's lunch hour had been and gone. He went to The Ship for pie, peas and a pint, and then walked about the town, waiting for Irene's finishing time.

He went back five minutes before her leaving time. One of her friends told him she had been sent to the GPO with a parcel. By the time Sykes reached the Post Office, there was no sign of Irene.

Sykes was not sorry. He had tried. Missing Irene gave him longer to think. What he must do was tell all three of his children at the same time. That was the fair and right thing to do. He called on Miss Merton and thanked her for being so good in taking telephone calls and passing on messages. 'I called at the hospital,' he said. 'If you hear from Irene or the boys, just say that Rosie is comfortable.'

Miss Merton gave him an odd look. She asked no questions but insisted he eat a small steak and kidney pie and bide awhile. He fell asleep, which was not like him, and when he woke he knew he must be getting back to Saltaire.

He would drive back to the South Lodge, go to bed and stare at the ceiling. That would be it. He could not expect sleep to come.

The gates to the grounds of Milner Field were open and pushed back to the wall. Lanterns hung from the gates. Two shadowy figures were moving. As he drove closer, Sykes saw by the light of his headlights two elderly men, with spades. They were digging. Neither man appeared to be making much progress. One stopped and held on to the gate to steady himself.

Sykes drove just beyond the gates and then brought the car to a stop. Now he saw that one man was Uncle Nick, old, white-haired. The other, tall and thin, wore entirely unsuitable clothes for digging. He had on a long black coat, a homburg hat and gloves. Sykes thought he looked like an undertaker.

Sykes got out of the car. 'Evening, gentlemen. Is everything all right?' Too late, he realised that his policeman's voice had spoken. The men looked at each other and took a step back. The man in the long black coat and homburg placed his spade by the gate, as if to say, *Nothing to do with me, I just suddenly found this spade in my hand, gov.*

'Everything is perfectly all right,' said the gentleman, in a soothing voice that took Sykes by surprise.

'I'll give you a hand,' Sykes said.

'Thank you, but we are perfectly capable. In fact, we are just about to go.'

'No, we're not,' said Nick. 'And this chap's all right.'

'It's confidential,' said the undertaker, clearly wanting Sykes to drive on.

'But it's urgent,' said Nick. 'We have to find—'

'Daffodil bulbs,' said the undertaker. 'I shall shortly be burying a lady in Hirst Wood Cemetery who wishes especially to have something from this patch of ground.'

'Which patch?' asked Sykes. 'Won't one side of the gates be as good as the other?'

'It would if a person could remember which side,' said the undertaker.

'The right-hand side,' said Nick, 'as on the right hand of God.'

'But coming in through the gates or going out? That is the question as to which side,' said the undertaker.

Sykes took the spade from him. 'Let me. I could do with a stretch. How deep are we going?'

'To the gravel,' said Nick, pointing, and in line with the third rail of the gate.

The undertaker stepped in. 'No need, sir. We shall manage.'

Sykes ignored him. 'Did the person who did the original digging come from inside the grounds or from the outside?'

'The outside,' said Nick.

'Then this must be the right-hand side and you must be almost there. Set down the lantern. When we reach the gravel, I will stop and you can tell me what to do next.'

This was the kind of madness Sykes could cope with. It gave him something else to think about.

Reaching the gravel did not take long.

At that point, Nick attempted to lower himself onto his hands and knees but became stuck. When he tried to move, one leg gave way and the other went into cramp, causing him to cry out. The homburg-hat companion shushed him.

Sykes took a piece of carpet from his car. He knelt on the ground. While he went to work, the elderly men held the lantern, neither willing to relinquish it, berating each other when it wobbled.

'I've got something,' said Sykes. 'Small, an old bag, leather, rotting.'

'That is it, as described to me,' said the undertaker. 'Thank you. You may leave us now.'

'What is it?' asked Sykes.

Nick cleared his throat. 'My old schoolteacher passed away. She entrusted me with uncovering a memento from her girlhood, which has been buried here for many years. It is now to be buried with her, thanks to the kind offices of this gentleman.'

The undertaker cleared his throat in a meaningful way,

300

as if to tell Nick he had said too much and must keep his mouth shut.

'What sort of memento?' Sykes took the lantern from the undertaker. He opened the bag, while holding it tightly so that it did not disintegrate. The tiny human bones would at any time have given him a shudder. In the long silence that followed, he felt Nick and the undertaker's eyes on him. Sykes was not a man given to fancy, yet oddly he also imagined someone else might be watching. The old schoolteacher.

After a long silence, the undertaker said, 'I am in your hands, sir. We are in your hands, and so is the reputation of a good lady and her stillborn child.'

Sykes suddenly understood, though he could not have put his thoughts into words.

'Let me,' he said, placing what he had uncovered onto the piece of carpet. 'You can't take the teacher's memento like this. It would not be respectful. I will bring the precious item to you tomorrow, in a proper way.'

They hesitated.

A white lie was called for. Sykes said, 'I am entrusted to ensure that all at Milner Field is in order before big changes occur. Part of my task is to draw a line under what went before. This delicate task of yours comes within my confidential remit. Your task becomes mine.'

Sykes was pleased with his speech. It made up for the largely wordless day when he could not straighten his thoughts.

The two men were silent for a moment.

The undertaker unbuttoned his overcoat. He reached thumb and finger into the top pocket of his suit jacket, took out a business card, and handed it to Sykes. 'I shall be at my premises from oh eight hundred hours tomorrow.'

Sykes nodded solemnly.

Nick climbed into the Morris Cowley saloon with an urgency that suggested he feared being left behind. The undertaker wished Sykes good evening. They drove away.

Sykes closed the gates. He drove round to the Lodge and parked.

A policeman appeared from nowhere. 'Good evening, sir.'

'Good evening, Officer.'

'May I ask your business?'

'I'm staying here,' Sykes said. 'Jim Sykes, guest of Mr Whitaker.' He took the key from his pocket.

The officer took out his notebook. 'Do you spell Sykes with an I or a Y?'

'Y.'

'Thank you, sir. Did you see anything suspicious on your way in?'

Sykes thought for a moment. 'I passed two elderly gentlemen in a car, not suspicious but unusual.'

This satisfied the officer. 'If you don't mind, sir, I'll take a look around the property before you enter.'

Sykes stepped back, and waited.

'What's going on?' he asked when the constable returned.

'We're on the lookout for a person of interest. Please keep your door locked. If you hear any disturbance telephone the police.'

'There are two ladies in the Tower,' Sykes said.

'Yes, sir, Mrs Shackleton and Mrs Sugden are under protection.'

Sykes went inside. Everything was coming to a head, and without him. He was conscious of holding the small, soil-covered package that in the darkness the police officer had not noticed.

The place felt uncannily empty and so sulkily silent that it seemed to him the walls of this house knew far more than he ever would.

He switched on the light, spread a newspaper on the table, and placed the precious parcel at its centre. Damp soil and a scattering of gravel surrounded it. Sykes decided he ought to light a fire. Although he knew what he would uncover, he was not entirely prepared for the reality of small bones, all present and correct. Why did I offer to do this? he asked himself.

He washed his hands, and would wash them again soon.

A search of the Lodge revealed abandoned items that would be of use. At the back of a cupboard, he found an old game in a wooden box. The playing cards were almost worn away. The box would answer as a coffin. Sykes could make out the name of the game, 'Blue Birds'. The board represented a honeycomb designed to house bees, its edges decorated with faded painted flowers.

He needed something silk or satin, but made do with a worn velvet cushion cover which had its good parts. Mr Creswell must be a handyman. In one of the outhouses there were tools and varnishes.

Sykes worked until dawn, creating a thing of perfection which he set in the centre of the table and would have covered with a pillowcase but the varnish had not dried. He had a fleeting memory of the morning of Irene's eighth birthday, when he had made her a doll's house and had covered that with a sheet. He could still hear her excited shrieks, and see the happiness in her eyes.

He bid the tiny bones a peaceful sleep, and wished he knew the little creature's name.

After that he went upstairs to the bed he had left unmade. Now he could allow himself to look at the ceiling, and then to close his eyes and go over the events of this strange day and night, beginning yesterday morning with his summons to St James's Hospital.

No information given, he was simply told to come to the hospital and report to the porter's desk. Not knowing what to worry about broadened the scope of dire possibilities.

The situation was made worse when the porter rang for a ward sister to come and talk to him. It was the person who had worked with Mrs Shackleton during her days in the VAD, and who had wangled a visitor pass for him last Sunday. She gave him a cheerful smile, which did not seem to fit with the worst of news, and ordered him to follow her to the stairs.

He followed her along a series of corridors until he heard a sound that was familiar but unexpected. A baby cried.

He thought his guide had taken him in the wrong direction. She said, 'We have moved Mrs Sykes into this small ward so that you can have some privacy.' The ward contained two beds, one of them empty. Rosie was sitting up in the bed on the left. She was holding someone's baby. Why give Rosie a baby to hold? Was the hospital short of nurses?

The sister said, 'You have a fine baby girl, Mr Sykes. Mother and baby are well.'

He could see that they were well. Rosie was beaming, the baby let out some sort of noise, the sort of noise he had forgotten.

'Sit down, Jim,' said Rosie. 'You're making the place look untidy.'

He sat down and reached for Rosie's hand.

'You have ten minutes.' The sister closed the door behind her.

When she had gone, Rosie said, 'What do you think?'

'I'm flabbergasted.'

'I feel such an idiot, three kids and I never knew this was coming. Are you pleased?'

'Pleased? I'm bowled over.'

'Give us a kiss, then.'

A nurse brought him a cup of hot sweet tea, for shock, and told them they had five more minutes. During that five minutes Rosie gave him a list of directions, top of which was to tell Irene, and give her a shopping list.

'How shall I tell her?' Sykes asked.

'One of the nurses is South African. She tells me that in Afrikaans, such a baby as ours is called Die Laatlam, the late lamb. Tell Irene we have a late lamb.'

FORTY-THREE

I lay in my bedroom at Milner Field, the window slightly open for air. From outside came that same eerie sound, like the cry of a baby, that had wakened me the night before. The fox again. What was the matter with the fox? Our own foxes, whose territory included Batswing Wood, were mostly silent, sophisticated urbanites who would go about their business, crossing the street at midnight without disturbing their human neighbours.

I reached for my torch and looked at the clock. Little hand on three, big hand on twelve, that terrible hour when it is always best to go on sleeping. What was it this time – fox, owl, badger? Could they not find somewhere else to vent their witching-hour anxieties?

Suddenly there were heavy footsteps outside, a slow *tramp, tramp*, coming closer. The fox, the owl and the badger didn't wear boots. Nor could this be Mr Creswell unable to sleep: Mrs Creswell had ushered him home.

I leapt out of bed, torch in hand and went to the window. I saw the clear dark shape of a constable, on patrol, and the tiny red dot of a lit cigarette. Police officers ought to have quiet shoes. If Aldous Garner was lurking behind a tree or round a corner, he would have time to run for the coach road and make his way to the nearest tram stop.

The footsteps faded. I took a sip of water and got back into bed, pulling the covers up over my ears and eyes, wondering whether PC Harrison would have heard his colleague and told him to walk on the grass.

The clatter came later, in that moment when sleep is just on its way and the door to dreamland lifts its latch. There was a scraping sound that seemed to be in the room. Then silence. It must be PC Harrison, attempting a silent patrol of the house in his stockinged feet and making floorboards creak. Now I was wide awake.

I listened for him to do his attempted tiptoe back downstairs. Silence. Once more I heard that scraping sound, from above this time. Had an owl or a bat found its way in?

Sliding from the bed, I put on my robe, picked up the flashlight, stepped onto the landing and trod up the stairs.

I opened the door to the top room. It took a moment for my eyes to adjust to the gloom, and the shape before me, swaying. I gasped as I shone the flashlight on a body with a noose around his neck. This body was alive, it had a face that belonged to Aldous Garner. He was smeared with dirt and covered with cobwebs. He glared hatred at me as the noose tightened. The sound had come from the chair as he had put it into place and climbed on. Now, he kicked it away. I picked up the chair and moved to put it under his dangling legs, holding him up as I did so and screaming for Mrs Sugden and PC Harrison.

He kicked out at me, but I grabbed his legs with both arms and screamed again.

Mrs Sugden had heard me. She was on the landing calling, 'Help!' Seconds later she appeared, a ghostly figure in her long white nightgown. From downstairs came the sound of a police whistle. Mrs Sugden and I joined forces over the leg-grabbing and lifting Garner until PC Harrison appeared.

Being tall has its advantages, but the hook on the ceiling was too high even for Constable Harrison to reach. Mrs Sugden and I held on to Garner, raising him as best we could, holding his legs while he kicked out and tried to tear at our hair. Harrison stood on the stool, grappling with Garner, and after what seemed an age, the rope fell free. Mrs Sugden drew back the curtains.

By then the patrol bobby had come in from the cold. Between them, he and Harrison brought Garner down, struggling to hold him.

My arms ached so hard I felt something would snap. PC Harrison's handcuffs dropped to the floor. He was fending off Garner's flailing arms. It took the two constables to hold him. I picked up the handcuffs. Mrs Sugden and I each grabbed a wrist and I cuffed Garner's hands behind his back as the constables held him.

The two men manoeuvred Garner down two flights of stairs. He was making horrible choking sounds. The fight had gone out of him, and yet Garner stayed upright. As the two officers marched him downstairs, I followed. Had we reached Sunday, I would have watched as he came out of church and known whether he had the gait described by Charlie Benson. Garner allowed himself to be dumped on the sofa, fighting for breath. He had stopped kicking but the police officers took off his shoes.

I took a look. One shoe was down at heel.

Charlie Benson was vindicated.

The patrol bobby went to the door and blew his whistle. PC Harrison, still watching his prisoner, picked up the telephone. I heard him ask for Inspector Mitchell. After a moment, he said, 'We have Garner, sir, in the Tower. Mrs Shackleton and Mrs Sugden are here.'

Mrs Sugden filled a cup with water and brought it across. I stood close by, just in case, but our prisoner had gone quiet. I held him by the hair as Mrs Sugden put the cup to his lips.

When I let go of Garner's hair, my hands were greasy and matted in cobwebs, his skin and clothing grey with dust. He was covered in decades of muck from the rafters and from crawling under the roof space, giving away his method of arriving from one end of the mansion to the other. I wanted to wash my hands and to be outside, among screaming foxes and screeching owls, to be out in the fresh air, away from him and the smell of despair and what I supposed was the Brylcreem David caught a whiff of as he went down to the reservoir.

Garner had been estate manager long enough to know every nook and cranny of the mansion, the trapdoors and the passageways. Everything here was built to last, everything therefore must be reachable, repairable.

'Why?' I asked. 'Why didn't you just go when your time here was up, move on, start again?'

'Where and with what? Ronnie Creswell took everything from me. It was my idea to take on management of the village houses at arm's length. That was to be a position for me, when the mansion was sold. But Whitaker had to bring in the golden boy. I should have got to the younger brother first. Mark could have warned me about the dud nag but he didn't. Any of them at the racecourse could have warned me. Mark and Ronnie spied on me instead,' he snarled. 'Undone by a grease monkey, a stable boy and a woman I would have gone on loving.'

'Why kill Gwyneth?'

'She was the one who talked to Mark about me, and he talked to everyone else. All she wanted was a lift back here. I didn't know until I brought her back that she wouldn't stand by me. I did everything for that woman. We went halves on the proceeds of the silver. When I said that we'd put our resources together to start again, she said her money was in the bank and stopping there. She'd never been fool enough to give money to a man and she wouldn't start now.'

Mrs Sugden loomed over him. 'If it was up to me, I'd drop you down the well and put the lid back on. You would have killed a child, left her to die. Because she saw you? Because she would have told a tale?'

He had no answer to that.

Inspector Mitchell arrived after Garner was led away. The inspector was concerned about us. Did we want to leave, or to have a police presence?

I felt a little shaky, but would not let it show. We assured him we would stay, and that we now felt safe. We avoided the place on the sofa that had accommodated Garner.

'We'd alerted Doncaster police,' Inspector Mitchell said. 'They were on the lookout for him. He was in a rented cottage near Doncaster racecourse.'

'We guessed as much,' I said.

'He and Gwyneth had been ordered to vacate the place. He still had some of his luggage there. He had a trunk of personal items along with some stolen goods.'

'Anything to link Garner to Ronnie's murder?' I asked.

The inspector nodded. 'Two pairs of knuckledusters, homemade, wrapped in Garner's neatly folded socks. One set of knuckledusters is a match for the wounds on Ronnie's face.'

I closed my eyes, but that only made the horrible image more bloody. 'Why didn't Garner throw his knuckledusters in the river?' I asked.

'I'm guessing at pride in his own work. It seems that he did at one time think of himself as a practical man, on his way to being skilled. He'd kept the items boys make in their metalwork class – ashtrays, caddy spoon, a copper cup, a tin-can rose.'

'What was his real name?' I asked, thinking of the boy who did metalwork, a boy with plans that didn't include false identity, cheating, thieving and murder.

'We'll find out, eventually. But by then Aldous Garner may be on intimate terms with a rope. Next time, the job won't be botched, or interrupted. He's on his way to Armley Prison now.'

Mrs Sugden and I exchanged looks. She knew my views and that I don't believe an eye for an eye will be of much help in the world's long run.

'How soon will all this be in the public domain?' I asked.

'Investigations are continuing.'

Mrs Sugden has a streak of cynicism. When Inspector Mitchell had gone, she said, 'It won't be public before the auction. Salts and Whitaker are too important.'

FORTY-FOUR

I knew Sykes had come back to Milner Field late last night. His car had been outside the Lodge first thing, when I went for a walk, to shake off the cobwebs and the stench of Aldous Garner.

Mrs Sugden and the cleaners were making an early start and putting in two full days to do their best for Milner Field mansion. The gardeners were all hard at work.

Sykes's car was gone from outside the Lodge by just after breakfast, when I made my way to see Mrs Creswell in the three-storey house on Victoria Road with the high window.

She must be tired of people asking after Nancy, but since we would be leaving soon I wanted to know how things stood.

We went upstairs. There were two suitcases on the floor and a small trunk in the corner.

I had bought a colouring book and crayons in the post office and gave them to Mrs Creswell to pass on to Nancy.

'The doctor says she was lucky,' Mrs Creswell reported. 'She fell on the flowers that Nick has been throwing down there these sixty years or more. The underground spring found another way to go but there is still a sliver of water that means to stay put and that may have helped my Nancy to have a soft landing. She has a broken arm and ankle, cuts and bruises, but it's a miracle that the damage wasn't worse, the doctor says—'

She took out her hanky. I feared bad news might follow good, but I was wrong. 'The doctor says she is a lucky girl. That monster Garner dropped her feet first into the well. She knew to bend her knees and somehow managed to land in one piece. It makes me wonder if the spirit of the shepherdess watched over her.'

'Perhaps she did.'

'A constable came to take her statement this morning. I was allowed to sit with her. She was very brave. It would be nice if people could see her, but it's best that she rests, and you know what hospitals are like with their rules. They seem to think children recover more quickly if they're kept quiet and left alone. I'd nurse her better twice as fast.'

I glanced at the suitcases and the trunk. It looked as if Mrs Creswell had her work cut out.

'Such a lot to do,' said she. 'I'm glad Nancy will miss this upheaval. There'd be no space for nursing her better here.'

She had not stated the obvious, and so I did. 'You are moving.'

'Yes. My husband has another job and so do I.'

'I'm glad. That's lucky, for the times we're in.'

'Mr and Mrs Whitaker had a hand in it, making the suggestion, giving the glowing reference Ronald deserves. He will be starting work with the Bradford Parks Department. I'm to be housekeeper for an elderly well-to-do couple in Nab Wood. They like children so are happy about Nancy. Ronald will keep up their garden. We've accommodation on the premises and it will be a short tram ride into Bradford. I'm hoping Nancy will get into the grammar school.'

I took my leave, wishing Mrs Creswell well, knowing that I would not see her again until Ronnie's funeral.

FORTY-FIVE

It is strange the way disparate events follow on from each other and ever afterwards feel connected. The third Friday of August was the day of Ronnie Creswell's funeral at Hirst Wood Cemetery. The mill closed for the day.

Sykes and I travelled to Hirst Wood together. For someone who had become father to a sudden and surprise baby, I thought he may have stayed at home. Sykes assured me that non-attendance never occurred to him. He and I stood close by Mr and Mrs Whitaker and Pamela, as did Mr Whitaker's secretary, Mrs Harrison. There was a police contingent, including Inspector Mitchell, a CID officer and PC Beale.

Mrs Sugden has very particular views on funeral attendance. Sykes and I must attend but she would regard herself as a hanger-on, there for the repast.

Alongside the Creswell family stood the Fairburns, Dorrie Fairburn between Ronnie's brothers. Uncle Nick held Nancy's hand. Nancy, wearing her bandages with pride, looked across at Pamela and might have waved. Pamela gave her a sad smile. They had made their connection. PC Tom Harrison was not with the police contingent, nor with his mother. He stood with the Creswell and Fairburn families, behind Dorrie.

As the funeral drew to a close, people made space for the family to leave. Those of us standing a little way back moved towards the path. Mr Creswell paused. He looked directly at me and said, 'Come back with us?'

'Yes.' I answered for both of us since we had driven there together. 'Did you catch that?' I asked Sykes. 'Mr Creswell wants us to go back to Saltaire, for the breakfast.'

'That's very good of him,' Sykes said.

'You're all right to stay on a little longer?'

'I'll be glad to. I've been left in charge of rearranging our bedroom to accommodate a cot. I won't tell you what else is on my list.'

Sykes drove us back to Saltaire. He parked on Victoria Road, outside the silent mill.

I thought back to what Pamela had told me about Ronnie and his father. They sit in the hut together and talk, she had said.

The funeral breakfast was in the mill dining room, a high-ceilinged room with a domed window above. At a table near the door there were a couple of spaces. Nancy must have been looking out for us. She came to speak to me. 'We're going to be moving away soon.'

'Your mother told me. Are you pleased?'

'I think so. It's not so far away. I'll go to a different school.'

'You'll make new friends.'

'But I'll come back to see Freddie and he'll come to see me. It's only a tram ride. Uncle Nick isn't coming with us. He's been accepted in the alms house.'

'Is he happy about that?'

'Yes. There'll be no steps to climb, and he has friends there. Mam thought they wouldn't want him because he doesn't see well, doesn't hear well and he's not the easiest person in the world. But he is the only person who was here before the mill and before the village, living in his hut with his grandmother on Milner Field grounds.'

'That makes him special.'

'I knew that but other people didn't.'

At the other end of the room, breakfast was being served. 'Don't miss your breakfast,' I said.

'Dad wants to talk to you. In the room beyond the kitchen, there's a quiet space. When you see him move from the table, follow him.'

With that she was gone.

Sykes had heard. 'He'll want to say goodbye.'

'That's probably it.'

'I'll wait for you in the car.'

When Mr Creswell left the table, after much hand-shaking and accepting of condolences, I followed his instructions.

He had set out two chairs. Being the kind of man who said little or nothing, he was also a man who came straight to the point. 'Mrs Shackleton, we who came back from what they're calling the Great War don't always tell the tale. I couldn't if I'd wanted to because when I came back I couldn't speak. I was of medical interest for a short time. I expected never to speak, but one day, my voice came back, when Ronnie asked me summat. He said, "Where's my clogs?" I said, "Cleaned and on the windowsill." I could talk again.'

'Like a miracle,' I said.

'Ronnie wanted to know things. I told him nothing that would scare his wits. I told him names of people and places.

317

I told him the name of our medical officer and how good he was. Captain Gerald Shackleton, from Leeds. According to Ronnie's information, he was your husband. You was a nurse, alongside the daughter of a mill that's not two miles from here.'

My mouth went dry. 'Yes.'

'Well, I can tell you how much Captain Shackleton loved to get your letters. He'd go to his tent straight off to read your letter as soon as one came. He was that happy.'

I felt an odd pain behind my eyes, and my body seemed not to be here, as if I'd floated off from it and in a minute the chair would be gone and so would I.

Mr Creswell went on talking. He had decided what to say, and he would say it.

'We all thought a lot of your husband. He were a good man and a good doctor. That's what our Ronnie said I must tell you. I said you would already know. Ronnie said, "But you were there, Dad. No one else will tell his wife about how pleased he was to get her letters." He'd got a bit like that, after taking up with Pamela, more interested in people and in life.'

Ronnie had addressed his letter to Mrs Gerald Shackleton. I had braced myself for an old comrade's story, and then forgot about it. Now I was unprepared.

Mr Creswell produced a big, clean hanky and gave it to me, saying, 'I shouldn't have told you here. I should have written.'

'It's better that you told me. Thank you.'

'Well, now you know. There was a big explosion. It was sudden. He'd read your letter. Had it in his pocket.'

We shook hands. 'Thank you, Mr Creswell, and especially for talking to me today of all days.'

'I had to do it for Ronnie. I didn't know he'd asked you to

come. You see, I think that's why he wrote to you. He would have sprung the surprise on me. I want you to think well of our Ronnie.'

'Oh, I do. I'm grateful to Ronnie, and to you.'

So Mark had not told his dad what he knew to be Ronnie's reason for writing to me. I hoped that Mark would not forever blame himself for passing on what he knew about Aldous Garner.

We went back into the main hall where Mr Creswell joined his family. They made ready to leave.

Uncle Nick followed me out onto the street, clearing his throat. 'You'll be very interested to hear what happened at the well.'

I already knew what happened at the well. I didn't want to hear it again, but my resistance was low. I blew my nose, which Nick took as a sign to continue. I thought he was going to tell me about rescuing Nancy, but it was something else.

'David Fairburn had himself lowered into the well. He is the leader of the mill's fire brigade. He does not believe there is a curse, but he prefers that them that buy the mansion, and villagers, and workers at Milner Field deserve a fair chance at life and happiness.'

Nick had my reluctant interest. Having someone staring me in the eyes meant that I must hold myself together. Nick did not need encouragement. He said, 'David brought up the bones, the remaining bones of the shepherdess. He took them to a vicar to bless.'

'Then I hope the shepherdess will rest in peace.'

'She will. She was buried with my old schoolteacher, Miss Mason. She who told us the shepherdess's story.'

'I should think your old teacher would have approved.'

'You are right.' He frowned. 'I hope Miss Mason knows she has company. I think she must. Last night, in my dream, Miss Mason spoke to the shepherdess. She said, "The more the merrier."'

I thought of young Mark Creswell's comment about the undertaker. The world is going mad. Sometimes capitulation outranks resistance.

Sykes had been sitting in the car. Not that he is an impatient man, but he came back to find me, rescuing me from Nick, saying, 'I take it we're ready for the off, Mrs Shackleton?'

Nick then tapped the side of his nose. 'Thank you for the perfect, beautifully made small, lined . . .'

'Box,' said Sykes. 'It was my pleasure, Nick.'

We got into the car. 'What was that about?' I asked.

He started the car, and pretended not to have heard me.

That did not matter. I had thoughts of my own. I had not expected to hear about Gerald. After seeing the photograph of Billy, I thought it might be about the death of the boy who shared Ronnie's likeness. And it was. More than that, it was a struggle for the soul of Saltaire. Who should take charge of managing the village houses, would it be Ronnie Creswell or Aldous Garner?

The plan was quietly dropped.

Sykes drove us to his home in Woodhouse so that I could see Rosie and the baby.

The downstairs room was crowded with infant paraphernalia.

There she was, the newest addition, a small bundle with eyes wide open, lying in a drawer. 'The cot's upstairs,' Rosie said. 'We can't be carting it up and down.'

'She prefers the drawer,' Sykes said. 'More people look at her when she's down here.'

'She's beautiful,' I said. And she was.

We sat down for cups of tea. Sykes poured. 'Enough of births, deaths and funerals. We've set a date for the christening.'

'We'd like you to be godmother,' said Rosie.

Suddenly it seemed possible that though deaths and funerals might never be forgotten, they could be overlaid with new events, fresh possibilities. 'What an honour. I would love to be godmother to young Miss Sykes.' I went to talk to the baby. 'If that's agreeable to you, Baby Sykes.' I thought she smiled, but it could have been wind.

'Have you thought of a name?' I asked.

'We have,' said Rosie. 'She's to be Catherine, named after you.'

The world, and I, felt suddenly so much better.

FORTY-SIX

Mr Whitaker settled our account promptly. He sent a letter of thanks and three suit lengths of excellent cloth. Mrs Sugden is still considering best use. I decided to go to Sykes's tailor, taking my own patterns so as to avoid extreme designs. Paris and London fashions come and go. A good piece of Yorkshire weave will last a lifetime.

Just before the auction of Milner Field, Pamela Whitaker telephoned. She had given up on the plan of returning to her teacher-training course, and would tell me what she was doing when we met. We agreed to meet for breakfast at the Midland Hotel, Forster Square, on the morning of the auction.

On that bright clear morning, I caught the train to Bradford. A little after nine o'clock, I walked through the Midland Hotel's marble hall. Pamela was waiting for me at the bottom of the stairs. She looked up-to-the-minute in a pale blue, calf-length V-neck dress with belted waist and turned-back cuffs. She gave a big smile. In the dining room, a waiter led us to a table in the corner.

We studied the menu. 'I don't know what to eat,' said Pamela. 'I need to sustain myself through the auction but not end up feeling sick with excitement during the bidding. There's been a lot of interest, even though news of recent events has trickled out.'

We agreed that scrambled eggs and toast would be a good choice, and cups of strong tea.

'Are you excited?' I asked, after we had ordered.

'I am, and I'll tell you why. I've formally joined the business. I had a small share, but now, thanks to my grandmother's legacy and a sprinkle of nepotism, I am on the board of directors.'

'That's such good news, Pamela. Congratulations!'

'It was always going to happen, and then my interest waned and I thought it wasn't for me. Now I know it is, and so does Dad. I'm determined to do this properly. I invested some of the funds left to me by Grandmother. If the worst comes to the worst and Milner Field doesn't sell, we'll keep going.'

'You'll be a ground-breaker!'

'I will, just as you are. That's why I want to talk to you. I have so many ideas and I know that the men on the board will find it hard to accept me.'

'Tell me, how far along are you, what have you been doing?'

Pamela told me that she had spent time with her dad's secretary, Mrs Harrison, and in each of the offices, finding out what was what. She had got to know the different departments and who was who among the staff. She and her dad had talked long into the night. He had taken her to Liverpool, to a wool auction. She had given him new ideas about what they might manufacture.

'We'll produce a cream and brown check and send samples

to customers with a pattern for a ladies' sports suit. We'll produce a reasonably priced plain light wool in colourful shades so that girls who go out to work in offices won't need to wear the colours of mice.'

'That all sounds wonderful. What is the difficulty?'

'Me. When I go in that boardroom, no one will take me seriously.'

'Yes, they will. Go in looking as if you mean business. Take your own advice. Don't go in wearing mouse colours. Be bold.'

'I wish I could be. One of the teachers at school called me a bold hussy, but I've forgotten how to do it.'

'You were training to be a teacher. Did you do any practical lessons, in a classroom?'

'Yes, and I made a hash of it.'

'Well, you won't this time. Speak plainly in words the men on the board will understand, as if you are speaking to the child at the back of the room who can't keep his eyes open. The men will interrupt you. Don't allow it. Be polite. Have phrases ready for all occasions. "If I may finish my point", that sort of thing. You are the chairman's daughter. You have clout.'

'You're right. I've grown up in that business.'

'Exactly!'

'I'm not allowed entry to the Wool Exchange, but that's a reprieve from being bored to death. Dad passes on whatever is useful.'

We finished breakfast. She looked at her watch. 'I'm meeting Mam and Dad at the auction rooms.'

I walked with Pamela to the Victoria Hotel on Bridge Street, where the auction would be held. Mr and Mrs Whitaker were waiting for her. I wished them luck.

I would be meeting Mrs Sugden. We would look in every excellent shop. She would choose a new coat. I would buy a christening gift for baby Catherine Sykes.

On the way to Busby's, I kept my fingers crossed for the successful sale of Milner Field.

POSTSCRIPT

Milner Field failed to sell when put up for auction in 1922. In 1930, history repeated itself. The gates were shut, the mansion abandoned. What remained of this grand but unlucky house was finally demolished in about 1957.

In 1987, Salts Mill was rescued by Jonathan Silver, who created a cultural hub within its walls, with art galleries, a book shop, a home shop, other retailers, cafés and restaurants. In addition, many small and medium-sized businesses are tenants of the Silver family in its vast spaces. The 1853 Gallery displays paintings by Bradford-born artist David Hockney.

As you walk around the building, breathe in deeply. You may catch the lingering scent of lanolin from the wool. Listen. You may catch the words of weavers and millwrights, words that were only ever lip-read, against the clatter of machinery.

ACKNOWLEDGEMENTS

Many thanks to Maggie Smith, Trustee of Saltaire World Heritage Association, a registered charity that houses the Saltaire Collection and manages buildings of significance in Saltaire; Colin Coates, Saltaire Researcher and Historian; Saltaire History Club; Flinty Maguire, Editor, Saltaire Village website (saltairevillage.info); Gina Birdsall, Customer Support Assistant, Keighley Library.

Hannah Wann and the team at Piatkus provided unfailing support, as did agents Judith Murdoch and Rebecca Winfield. Emma Beswetherick gave encouraging and insightful comments on the draft manuscript. Alison Tulett copy edited with great care. Any mistakes are mine.

Discover the first mystery in Frances Brody's Brackerley Prison series

1969. A job in the Prison Service is not for everyone. The training is hard, the cells are bleak and a thick skin is needed. But for Nell Lewis, helping prisoners is something she cares about deeply, and when she's promoted into a new post as governor of HMP Brackerley in Yorkshire, she's tasked with transforming the renowned run-down facility into a modern, open prison for women.

Just as Nell is settling into her new role, events take a dark turn when a man's body is discovered in the prison grounds. The mystery deepens still when one of their female inmates goes missing, ensuing a search across the country.

Can Nell resolve the sinister happenings at HMP Brackerley, before anyone else is put in danger?

A Murder Inside is available now